LAST LESSONS
OF SUMMER

Deborah Knott novels:

SLOW DOLLAR
UNCOMMON CLAY
STORM TRACK
HOME FIRES
KILLER MARKET
UP JUMPS THE DEVIL
SHOOTING AT LOONS
SOUTHERN DISCOMFORT
BOOTLEGGER'S DAUGHTER

Sigrid Harald novels:

FUGITIVE COLORS
PAST IMPERFECT
CORPUS CHRISTMAS
BABY DOLL GAMES
THE RIGHT JACK
DEATH IN BLUE FOLDERS
DEATH OF A BUTTERFLY
ONE COFFEE WITH

Non-series:

LAST LESSONS OF SUMMER
BLOODY KIN
SHOVELING SMOKE

MARGARET MARON

LAST LESSONS
OF SUMMER

Published by Warner Books

An AOL Time Warner Company

Mysterious Press books are published by Warner Books, Inc., 1271 Avenue of the Americas, New York, NY 10020.

Visit our Web site at www.twbookmark.com.

 An AOL Time Warner Company

The Mysterious Press name and logo are registered trademarks of Warner Books, Inc.

Printed in the United States of America

First Printing: August 2003
10 9 8 7 6 5 4 3 2 1

Library of Congress Cataloging-in-Publication Data

Maron, Margaret.
    Last lessons of summer / Margaret Maron.
      p. cm.
    ISBN 0-89296-780-3
     1. Family-owned business enterprises—Fiction. 2. Inheritance and succession—Fiction. 3. Women—North Carolina—Fiction. 4. Grandmothers—Death—Fiction. 5. Mothers—Death—Fiction. 6. North Carolina—Fiction. I. Title.

PS3563.A679L37 2003
813'.54—dc21
                                            2003045924

For the Long Island cousins—

Lisa Marie and Michael Paul Bonanni
Andrew James, Jacqueline Rose, and
Nicholas Joseph Quaranto
Kristy Nicole, Steven Anthony, and
Kimberly Margaret Quaranto

—with love from your Southern aunt

LAST LESSONS
OF SUMMER

Family Tree

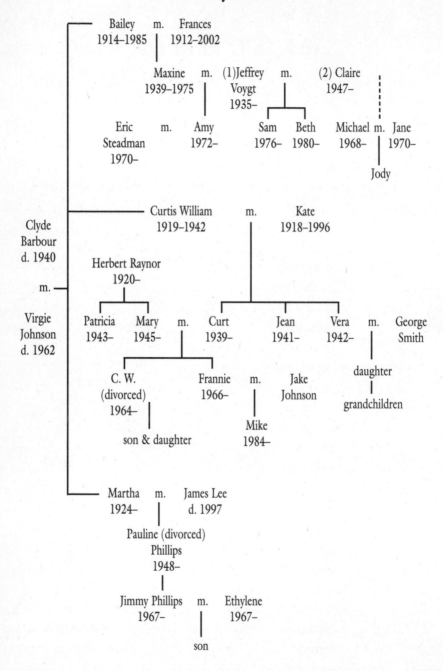

Bailey   m.   Frances
1914–1985   1912–2002

Maxine   m.   (1)Jeffrey   m.   (2) Claire
1939–1975   Voygt   1947–
1935–

Eric   m.   Amy   Sam   Beth   Michael   m.   Jane
Steadman   1972–   1976–   1980–   1968–   1970–
1970–

Jody

Clyde
Barbour
d. 1940

Curtis William   m.   Kate
1919–1942   1918–1996

Herbert Raynor
1920–

m.

Virgie
Johnson
d. 1962

Patricia   Mary   m.   Curt   Jean   Vera   m.   George
1943–   1945–   1939–   1941–   1942–   Smith

C. W.   Frannie   m.   Jake   daughter
(divorced)   1966–   Johnson
1964–   grandchildren

son & daughter   Mike
1984–

Martha   m.   James Lee
1924–   d. 1997

Pauline (divorced)
Phillips
1948–

Jimmy Phillips   m.   Ethylene
1967–   1967–

son

APRIL

All winter, the egg sac had hung unnoticed on the underside of the rose trellis. No bigger in size and weight than a ping-pong ball, it even looked a bit like one that had been carried outdoors by a dog, then abandoned there in rain and leaf mold till it was crumpled and stained and covered with delicate tendrils of dead vines. Suspended by strands of strong brown silk from a thorny cane that had already pushed out tender new leaves, the sac blended in with the grays and browns of the neglected rambler.

Inside the sac, awareness began with lengthening daylight, then warmth, then the drive to be *out*.

Smaller than the heads of common pins, the spiderlings had worked their way through the protein-rich fuzz that had insulated them from winter's worst, to make tiny holes in the tough outer silk. Now they tumbled out into the spring sunlight. Hundreds of pale white bodies, intricately articulated bodies almost translucent in their newness, soaked up the sun's heat; and the absorbed energy, combined with instinct, drove them upwards—up closer to the source of that bright heat, away from the dark and crowded confines of the egg sac, away from siblings already turning cannibalistic now that the nourishment inside each tiny egg was depleted.

When they reached the top of the trellis that arched over the side door of the big shabby house, they lifted their minute spinnerets up to the sky and sent out wispy filaments of silk invisible to the average human eye.

No human eye watched their passage, though. A forensics duo beneath the trellis were focused on the tool marks around the door lock where the intruder had entered.

"Old house like this, you gotta wonder why they didn't just smash that big window there and step inside," one tech said to his co-worker as he photographed and measured.

"Yeah," she answered. "Silence the dog quicker . . . assuming it was a barker."

The dog, a black Lab, its muzzle gray with age, lay in a pool of drying blood several feet down the hallway.

"It had to be barking," the first tech said with certainty. "Why else did she get up and come downstairs? Kill the dog quick and the poor old thing might've slept right through the burglary."

The body of the dog's elderly mistress still sprawled facedown on the bare wood at the foot of the stairs. It, too, had been photographed, measured, and meticulously examined and now it awaited transportation to the state morgue over in Chapel Hill while the forensics duo extended their search for evidence, widening the perimeter around both bodies.

Absorbed in their work, no one looked up.

The newly abandoned egg sac swung emptily among the rose canes as the soft spring breeze caught the spiderlings' gossamer threads and sent them flying through bright April sunshine, dispersing them upon the overgrown bushes and over the patrol cars parked around the unkempt grounds.

CHAPTER
1
(July)

Honey blonde hair fell across Amy Steadman's small heart-shaped face and she tucked a strand behind her ear in an absentminded gesture while her other hand doodled on a scratch pad where kittens and puppies romped in a meadow strewn with stylized flowers. Here in lower Manhattan, the weekly staff meeting of Pink and Blue and Max Enterprises was finally over. A new line of PBM toothbrushes had been licensed for sale in France, minor changes to the redesigned crib sheets and blankets had been examined and approved, and samples of the first consignment of PBM Halloween costumes had finally arrived from China and had been modeled by a couple of tots from the ad agency. The session had run long, but now only family lingered around the long conference table littered with tea and coffee mugs. Amy had let her mind go so idle that she barely heard the chatter about the house Sam and his girlfriend had booked in the mountains of Mexico and whether one could really trust the glowing pictures one saw on the Internet.

At the far end of the table, her half-brother, four years

younger and ever the optimist, was once again ready to jump in feet first without checking whether he would land on water or concrete. "With the rent they're asking, the cook and gardener's wages have to be included." Sam turned his laptop around so the others could see the colorful pictures that filled the screen. "And take a look at that pool! It's damn near Olympic size."

Amy glanced at it, then went back to her doodling.

Her stepbrother Michael peered over the rim of his reading glasses in that patronizing manner he had adopted lately as his hair thinned and his waist thickened on his way to forty. Michael would never leap before looking. He and his wife Jane had booked their Alaska cruise months ago through their usual travel agent. "Didn't you hear how the Sefowiczes got taken for ten thou last winter on that Italian villa Missy found on the Web?"

Amy sketched a drop of dew ready to fall from a blade of grass into a growing puddle around a chubby puppy whose superior expression and faint eye circles made it look suspiciously like Michael.

"I don't see why we still have to go to the lake first," grumbled Beth, youngest of the Voygt family and the newest to join the company after scraping through with a nondescript B.A. from Binghamton last month. "It's not like we're kids anymore."

"Claire asks very little of you four," said Jeffrey. "It means a lot to her to have everyone there for that week. What you do with the rest of your vacation time is up to you, but you owe her a long weekend at the very least."

"And it's good for Jody to interact with his aunts and uncle," said Michael. "You'll be glad we've kept this family tradition when the rest of you start having children."

Beth rolled her eyes. "If it's such a great tradition, why are you and Jane dumping him on Mom and Dad while you go off to Alaska?"

"We're not dumping him," Michael said, offended. "Mom

offered to take him so we could get away by ourselves for a few days."

"Yeah, right."

Beth had been with PBM Enterprises less than a month and was technically still a raw trainee who did not merit a vacation of any kind, much less the annual long vacation she seemed to think was her birthright. Although each of the others had, in their time, served real apprenticeships, working through the hot steamy days of August in New York, with only a short break at the family's summer home in New Hampshire, until they earned management status, they had thrown up their collective hands and decided to treat it as one more graduation present rather than argue with Beth about it.

Besides, so the family reasoning went, if it got her away from that creepy jazz guitarist she had recently picked up down in NoHo . . . (When Eric tried to give brotherly advice, she had acidly told him, "So he doesn't have a rich grandmother. Not everybody has your luck, Ivana.")

Time enough to sit Beth down and teach her the facts of adult life and adult responsibilities after Labor Day, when summer was over and everyone was rested and refreshed.

"Spain, is it?" asked Michael.

"Or Mexico. Sam says I can come crash on them till I hear if my friends are going to stay in Majorca or head up to Amsterdam."

Michael was appalled. "You don't have your tickets yet? Do you know how much it's going to cost you?"

Beth shrugged. "I met a pilot last winter," she said vaguely.

"You could always come with us," said Eric Steadman, well knowing her reaction to such a suggestion. "Amy and I plan to walk another leg of the trail this year."

He had been watching Amy's pencil as it wandered almost aimlessly back and forth across the pad, crosshatching shadows here, defining a blade of grass there. In the five years he had known her, he had come to realize that his wife's doodles were a window into her unconscious. The tussling animals probably symbolized her siblings, who really did squabble like cats and dogs at times, but what of the small reptilian head to which her pencil kept returning, a head Eric had not even noticed until one casual pencil stroke revealed a pair of eyes there in a tuft of meadow grass? A lizard? A turtle? Or did she sense a snake in the grass lurking, half hidden, somewhere in or near the family?

"All you need are hiking boots and a backpack," he told his sister-in-law.

"Not in this lifetime," said Beth.

Eric grinned at Amy, but her eyes were now on her father, who continued to thumb through a manila folder jammed with papers that needed his attention today. Above the vacation chatter all she had heard was "—and you've received an offer on the property."

"Property?" she asked. "What property?"

"In Carolina. Your grandmother's place." Tall and dapper in a beautifully tailored dark suit that enhanced his thick white hair, Jeffrey Voygt pulled from the folder several sheets of paper stapled together. "Her doddering old attorney's under the impression that you're still a minor, so he sent the papers to me. Damn fine offer, too. Nine-fifty."

That caught everyone's attention.

"Nine hundred and fifty *thousand?*" Michael, who possessed an accountant's instinctive knowledge of market values, looked from Jeffrey to Amy in disbelief. "For that dump? Out in the country?"

Born and bred on Manhattan's Upper East Side, Michael seemed to carry a bubble of New York around him wherever he went, insulation from the world's less favored places, be it China, California, or, in this case, a run-down farm in eastern North Carolina.

Her grandmother's funeral this past spring was only the second or third time he had even seen the place since he was eight and his mother had married her father, but nothing had changed his first opinion. Amy herself was barely four when her father took them all down to introduce his new family, and they had not actually stayed in the house then, yet she still remembered Michael's disdain for the admittedly somber old farmhouse and the nondescript acres on which it sat. "No wonder your mom offed herself," he had said—words incomprehensible then and therefore burned into her memory forever.

Did he remember? she wondered now, wondered but would never ask because asking would open the door to his own questions, and all her life she had shied away from those questions.

At least Michael had managed to keep his disdain in hand during the funeral. But then Michael did everything correctly these days. Married to a high-minded woman and the father of a ten-year-old himself, he had been punctilious in his show of respect for the woman responsible for the creation of PBM, the woman whose imagination and talent gave them not only their daily bread but the fine wines they drank with it.

"Who in hell is crazy enough to want it?" he asked. "It'll cost a quarter million to whip that house and grounds into shape."

"They're not buying a house," Jeffrey Voygt said dryly as he handed Beth the papers to pass down to Amy at the other end of the table. "They're buying a commercial location. The house will probably be bulldozed. The state's building a new interchange there on I-40 and the farm is a prime site for a new shopping mall."

"Hold out for a million then, Amy," Sam advised her with a grin.

"A million? Oh, wow!" Beth skimmed the short cover letter enviously before handing it on.

Amy knew that her sister's recent interest in money—who had it, who did not—grew out of the fact that she had never given money much thought before now. She had never needed to. It was always there and as taken for granted as water from a tap or electricity from a switch, until June, when their father turned off the main valve and pulled the plug. She was still sulky because he had required her to start work immediately after graduation instead of letting her party around Spain for the summer with several close friends. Never mind that she had partied away so many of her college nights that it had taken her an extra year to graduate. Some of those friends were coming into family trust funds, and Beth's three siblings had heard enough bitching this past month to know that having to get up every morning and slog down to this job five days a week made Beth feel like a Third World water carrier.

She slid the papers on down the polished table top and there was deliberate malice in her voice. "Real awesome, Amy."

That old razor was still so sharp that Amy saw Sam's normally cheerful face darken with disapproval, heard his "Oh, for Christ's sake, Beth!" before she fully comprehended how deeply she had been cut.

"What?" asked Beth. Her wide blue eyes were as guileless as the blue sky beyond the window overlooking lower Manhattan.

Sam muttered something beneath his breath and went back to his laptop while Michael hastily tried to distract Amy by suggesting possible ways to tie the new mall in with PBM Enterprises. "Maybe we could get them to use Pink and Blue as a theme in the food courts, Amy? As a condition of the sale? You could even make a case that some of the story lines were developed there. After all, that's where Bailey Barbour was born and died. And Frances lived there for so long, she was practically a native, too, right? Even Max—"

"No," said Amy.

Curtness from her was so unusual that it stopped him in midsentence. Automatically, Amy touched his arm in mute apology and softened her words. All her life, even before her grandmother's death, she had been careful not to set herself above her siblings, to act as if they were all equals.

"It's not for sale, Michael. Not now, anyhow. At least I hope it's not." She appealed to her father, standing at the end of the table. "We don't have to make a decision right now, do we, Dad?"

"Not 'we,' Amy. You," Jeffrey Voygt said. "It's personal real estate, not company property, so the decision is yours. I wouldn't wait too long, though. You look over the offer and we'll talk later if you want."

"Fine." Amy stuck the lawyer's papers in her notepad, gathered up pencils and coffee mug, and left them.

The instant the door closed behind her, Eric rounded on Michael. "Of all the thoughtless, inconsiderate—"

Sam chimed in right behind him. "Yeah, Michael. *That's where Bailey Barbour was born and died,*'" he mimicked. "You jerk! That's also where Max died and where Frances was murdered just three months ago, remember?"

"That's not what upset her," Michael said defensively. "It was Beth."

"*Me?* What did I do?"

"That's enough," said Jeffrey in a voice that reminded them who still held the reins at PBM. "Michael, I'd like those projections by tomorrow morning. Eric, doesn't your conference call start in three minutes? Beth—"

"Yeah, yeah, I know," she said with exaggerated weariness. "Back to the salt mines."

The singsong chant echoed down the years: *"Awesome— awesome— A-meeee."*

Amy closed the door of her office, but she could not shut out the hurt that threatened to dig up all the guilt she had kept submerged for so long. It had been years since she had heard those taunting words that set her immeasurably apart from the others, yet they rang in her memory as clearly as the day Michael first called her that, the day he abruptly realized what it meant that Frances Barbour was Amy's grandmother but not his.

Not his and not Sam's either.

It had been one of those command appearances whenever

Frances came north: Sunday morning brunch at Tavern on the Green because Amy loved the crystal chandeliers and Mrs. Barbour loved indulging Amy on her increasingly rare visits to the city. All of the family were required to attend, even though Claire was in her first trimester with Beth and fighting morning sickness. Amy had been almost eight so she vividly remembered the tension around the table that morning, despite her stepmother's attempt to keep the conversation pleasant for the children. Grandmother was annoyed about the quality of plush in the new Pink and Blue models. Dad quoted figures and sources and costs per unit. Grandmother brushed his arguments aside.

"Cost doesn't matter," she had said autocratically. "Quality does."

She had then looked directly at the small towheaded girl seated next to her. "Remember that, Amy. You will have an awesome responsibility to the children who love Pink and Blue."

Amy did not understand the significance of her words, but Michael, soon to be thirteen, picked up on it immediately.

Until that morning, Jeffrey Voygt had been the most powerful person in his world, the man who had erased the worry lines that pinched his mother's face after his own father died, a kindly enough man, but a man used to giving orders and having them carried out. Watching as his stepfather acceded to the old woman's demands and promised to change the plush, Michael understood that Mrs. Barbour was even more powerful and that, in the normal course of events, Amy would inherit that power.

"Pink and Blue will be all yours," he said when the three children were alone. "All that *awesome* responsibility," he mimicked. "Awesome, awesome A-mee! Awesome, awesome A-mee!"

Sam had picked it up, too, as kid brothers will when they sense how much a certain name can cut even when they do not know why. When she finally went weeping to Claire, the only mother she had ever known, her stepmother made the boys stop teasing her.

"But you can't blame them for being a little bit jealous," she had told Amy. "It's only natural, sweetie. You're your grandmother's closest relative, and when she dies, why your father might actually wind up working for you someday."

Even as she said it, Claire's eyes widened and Amy realized that this was something new to her stepmother, too.

After that, it was as though something had shifted in their spacious West Side apartment. Claire was just as kind, just as fair, just as loving; nevertheless, from that day forward, Amy had felt an almost imperceptible distancing, a you/us chasm that never quite widened enough to say, Yes, here it is, but no less real for remaining unacknowledged—something else never to be talked about in that household.

And now those hateful words had fallen smoothly from Beth's lips, as if it were a phrase so familiar, it had slipped out unnoticed. Was that what Michael and Sam still called her between themselves? What they had taught Beth, who wasn't even born when it started?

She wished she could just go back in there and ask them. Was it fear of their answers or a fear that she might learn more than she wanted to know?

Amy set her notes on the drawing table and swiveled her stool around to stare blindly out of her office window, a window that overlooked West 23rd Street here in Manhattan's Toy District. A familiar heavy dullness had settled in her chest, as if the weight of all the unasked questions she had been carrying around her whole lifetime were gradually smothering her. She took several deep breaths in an effort to lighten the pressure, then made herself turn back to the project that awaited her attention—the sixtieth-anniversary deluxe edition of the original *Pink and Blue and Max,* the foundation upon which PBM Enterprises had been built.

Not that anyone had considered those two stuffed animals a foundation for anything when they first appeared.

No, the originals had been created by one of Frances Barbour's dearest friends and lovingly bestowed at a baby shower given at the magazine office where Frances worked at the time.

Or so went the family lore. According to that same tradition, Frances's eyes had moistened at the sight of her friend's thoughtfulness, but it was only after the infant Max took them to heart that they became imbued with life.

2

(1938)

*A*nd *what in God's name are these?" Frances Barbour asks help-lessly when she opens the box wrapped in sheets of brightly colored comic strips from Sunday's* Journal-American *and peers inside.*

None of the growing heap of wrapping paper that litters the floor around her drawing table is in traditional cutesy-poo baby shower pastels. No pale pinks or blues, no neutral greens and yellows. This is, after all, the art department of *Dunlap's,* "The Modern Woman's Monthly," a magazine that only last month ran an article on clever ways to stretch one's pennies as the Christmas season approaches and the Depression drags on with no end in sight: "Use comic pages for children's gifts! Iron your brown paper bags for a masculine wrap! Waxed paper for a frosty gleam! Wallpaper remnants! Butcher's paper! Stamp! Stencil!"

Because the shower is for *Dunlap's* most sophisticated illus-trator, the presents have been wrapped both as a satiric com-ment on the article and as a jibe at Frances, who never counts pennies. "We may be broke, but we've never been poor," she says, stopping off to buy a bottle of wine on the way home, bragging about the hothouse flowers Bailey still brings her after four years of marriage.

Their supper may be beans on toast, but there will be flowers on the rickety table of their Greenwich Village apartment and the beans and toast will be accompanied by decent wine and highflown discussions of art and literature because Frances plans to paint seriously one day and Bailey's poems are starting to be published occasionally in some of the small literary magazines.

Unfortunately, literary magazines pay in copies, not cash, so the hyacinths for their souls derive mostly from Frances's salary, not from his sporadic assignments as a freelance copy editor. His wages are menial, but the work leaves him loads of free time for his own writing, which, both of them agree, is the important thing.

The mere thought of a baby in their third-floor walk-up is absurd. All the same, after declaring for years that she would never fall into the mommy pit, Frances has come up unexpectedly preggers, to the amusement of her chums and malicious delight of some of the junior assistants, who look sympathetic and say it's a darn shame to her face, but who giggle in the ladies' room together as they freshen their lipstick, straighten the seams of their stockings, and admire in the mirror the sleek fit of their sweaters and sheath skirts. They agree that it's fortunate that darling Frances can work at home now that she's starting to show so obviously and really, my dears, if she didn't want the thing, why hadn't someone told her how to get rid of it before it was too late?

"Don't think you can teach your grandmother how to suck eggs," one of the more knowing assistants says with a slyly arched eyebrow. "This isn't the first rabbit she's killed."

"Really?" They crowd around with avid curiosity, but the knowing one drops her voice till she is almost whispering. "I heard that this time, her husband realized she had a little bun in the oven before she could turn off the gas. He's from the South, you know, and every Southern man wants a son to carry on the old family name."

"I've seen him," sighs one of the girls. "A real dreamboat."

"Give me a tugboat any day," says the pragmatist among them. "I'd rather have something that works and will look after *me,* rather than the other way around."

"Yeah," says another. "Frances is the only grown-up in that marriage. How's she going to handle another baby?"

"And what if it's a girl?" asks the quietest of the group.

"It wouldn't dare!" the others agree.

"But what the hell are they?" Frances asks again, lifting up a squishy stuffed toy in each hand.

Champagne has flowed rather freely this afternoon and now adds to the hilarity of each gift.

Animals these clearly are, for each possesses four legs, perky ears, a tail, and button eyes. One is a bright navy blue, the other an even brighter flamingo pink. But beyond that?

"Hey, a little more respect here," protests the needlework editor, who is notoriously bad with scissors and thread herself, but seems to know intuitively what patterns and projects will please *Dunlap's* readership. "Every baby needs something to cuddle, and since there's no way to know whether it's a boy or a girl, I made your kid one of each."

Frances laughs and holds out her glass for more champagne. She knows she should be more diplomatic, but she is on the edge of tipsiness and these lumpy stuffed animals are a screamingly funny contrast to the modern bottle sterilizer, the latest scientific treatise on infancy, and the three dozen precisely folded cotton diapers that make her suddenly and uncomfortably aware that a flesh-and-blood baby really is coming.

"Cuddle?" More likely he'll wind up on a psychiatrist's couch forty years from now, telling the headshrinker how he was scared in his cradle by a pair of pink and blue monsters."

"Better that than how his mummy twisted his little psyche," says

the needlework editor, too good-natured to take real offense at Frances's occasional bluntness. Instead, she lights fresh cigarettes for them both and hands her colleague the next gift, a tasteful Tiffany rattle and teething ring from the wife of Dunlap's editor-in-chief.

CHAPTER
3

Jeffrey Voygt tapped on Amy's door and opened it without waiting for a response.

"You okay?"

"I'm fine, Dad."

"You shouldn't let them get to you like that."

His voice was mild, but she flushed like a child being reprimanded. "I don't. Here, want to see how the new sketches are going?"

"And don't change the subject. If you plan to run this company after I retire, you're going to have to stand up to worse than a little teasing from your brothers and sister."

"But I don't plan to run the company, remember? That's why I married Eric."

Having very little sense of humor himself, Jeffrey was never quite sure when this odd first child of his was joking and when she was dead serious.

"You haven't transferred any of Frances's stock to his name, have you?"

Amy shook her head and her hair brushed the collar of her blue silk shirt. Her straight hair was still fair, only a shade or two darker than the silver blonde of her childhood, and she kept it simply styled. Most of the time it was parted in the middle and, like now, tucked behind her ears.

"Not yet," she said, "but why shouldn't I? He's my husband."

"And you quite naturally think your marriage is going to last forever. I understand that. Nevertheless—"

"Did you?"

It was not like her to interrupt, and he momentarily lost her meaning. "Did I what?"

"Think your marriage to my mother was going to last forever?"

"Well, of course I did."

"You never cheated on her the way you've cheated on Claire?" Her tone did not accuse. It was merely curious.

"Really, Amy! What's gotten into you today?"

She flushed again. "Sorry. It's just that everything feels so muddled now. Ever since I began working on this project, I've thought of her a lot—about the way Pink and Blue and Max started. Then when Grandmother died like that? There's so much I'll never know now. I planned to go down and spend a week with her and finally ask all the questions you won't answer. Now . . ."

She shrugged and turned back to the sketches on the drawing table in front of her.

"That's not fair, Amy. When have I not answered your questions?"

Technically, that was true. He did indeed answer, but his answers never went beyond her specific questions and he never expanded or elaborated. He merely waited with kindly, exaggerated patience and a faint air of pain that she could be so insensitive, as if knowing she would soon grow too uncomfortable to persist. Eventually she quit asking altogether and just listened for the clues that he inadvertently dropped into casual conversations with her grandmother over the years. She had learned to be still, to sit quietly, to wait for a revealing remark that she could add to her private store of information.

"My little cat who walks alone," Grandmother called her, cupping the girl's small chin in her hand. And "Thank God for a child that doesn't chatter," she once said to one of Amy's great-aunts.

"I don't know," the aunt had protested, and Amy knew that she thought Grandmother's comment was a backhanded slap at her own daughter who talked nonstop. "How else can you know what's on a child's mind?"

"Why on earth would I want to know that?"

There was such astonishment in Grandmother's voice that Great-aunt Martha had laughed and shaken her head. "For someone who writes children's books, you really don't like children very much, do you, Frances?"

"In the aggregate? No," Grandmother had said. "And I don't write the books, Martha. Bailey writes them. I'm merely his illustrator."

"Did you love her?" Amy asked her father now.

"Certainly." Never mind that it was now so long ago that it was hard to remember exactly what his feelings for Maxine Barbour had been when she agreed to marry him.

"What was she like?"

"Much like you, actually." He looked at her as if laying a template of memory over her small face, her narrow chin, her wide brow. "You're prettier than she was. But you've seen the family photographs. You know that you got your mouth and nose from me and your hair and eyes from her."

Water eyes, Frances had called them the first time she painted Amy's portrait—a light indeterminate color that changed from pale blue to light green to silver gray depending on the color of her clothes.

"Tell me about the first time you met. What was she wearing? What did she say?"

Jeffrey smiled. "Now how am I supposed to remember that?"

Then, surprised, he said, "Actually, I do remember. It was late March. Negotiations with your grandparents were going nowhere and she came into their office wearing a green sweater . . ."

CHAPTER

4

(1959)

*O*ur daughter, Maxine," Bailey Barbour says in that slow drawl
that still contains a hint of his native South.

Jeffrey Voygt stands and offers his hand. "So you're the Max, Miss
Barbour? I was bit too old for them by the time the books became
popular, but my little sister loved them and we always assumed
Max was a boy."

"Most people do," she answers shyly, not quite meeting his eyes.

Today, her own eyes are sea green above her emerald outfit.
The sweater is loose, but he automatically notices that the
breasts are sweetly rounded and that the skirt defines slender
hips and shapely legs. Too bad about that honker, though, he
thinks to himself with the pitying condescension of a male ego
bolstered by good looks that many young women find irresistible. Were it not for her nose, a nose as prominently beaked
as her father's, she would be quite pretty. Because of that nose,
though, he is only conventionally polite, murmuring that it was
not until he got interested in marketing toys that could tie into

a popular series that he had learned about the real Max and had taken a closer look at the Pink and Blue and Max illustrations.

"That didn't help you, did it?" she says. "They never show Max's face."

She is right about that. The picture books about a child and that child's two stuffed animals are aimed at tots four years old and younger. While Pink and Blue are drawn with delightfully animated faces, Max is a pair of legs in the foreground, or, if seen full-figure, the back is always turned or head averted. Hair and clothes are usually an indicator, but Bailey Barbour has just handed Voygt this year's newest, hot-off-the-presses addition to the series, and once again the young child has short unruly curls and wears nondescript shorts and shirt. As with all the books, this one ends with the three of them safely back from their adventures and sound asleep in bed, the two animals inanimate stuffed toys again and the Max character in footed pajamas and only a nose (an ordinary snub nose, Jeffrey Voygt notes) visible above the soft white pillow.

"That's because of our first editor," Frances Barbour explains. "It was her idea for me to keep the rendering of Max neutral. Conventional wisdom says that while girls will enjoy books about boys, boys don't want books about girls."

"And realistically, girls wouldn't go off on these little adventures," adds Barbour.

"Oh, I don't know," Voygt says gallantly. "I'll bet Miss Barbour would have."

The girl flushes, too shy to rise to his banter.

"Maxie's adventures were always in her imagination," says her mother. "Are you aware that it was the way she talked to her stuffed animals when she was a toddler that inspired my husband's first letters?"

"Really?" Voygt has done his research and he has read several articles that described the origin of these successful picture books, but he is a clever young man and diplomatic enough to encourage what is clearly a story that the Barbours enjoy retelling.

"It was 1942, my last leave before I shipped out," says Mr. Barbour, leaning back in the padded chair behind the big desk. "I suddenly realized that I could be killed and that my little daughter would have nothing to remember me by."

"My husband didn't have to go war then," Mrs. Barbour says proudly. "They weren't yet drafting married men with children, but he volunteered."

"Frances was still working for *Dunlap's* so it was Maxie and me in the apartment all day. I was trying to put together a collection of my poems before I left." He gives a self-deprecating chuckle. "I used to think I was going to be Robert Frost, you know."

"You were better than Frost," his wife says loyally. "If the war hadn't got in the way—"

"The saddest words of tongue and pen, my dear," he reminds her. "That's all water under the bridge now. No going back. Anyhow, Voygt, all the time I was working, I could hear Maxie talking to her stuffed animals. She made up voices for them. In fact, that's where 'What do you think, Pink?' and 'What'll we do, Blue?' came from."

"Really?" says Jeffrey Voygt. These two questions are the familiar touchstone of all the books, questions the child always asks the little animals when things are at their darkest.

"Yep. For a minute there, I thought my little girl had inherited my talent—"

"Along with your nose," Mrs. Barbour teases.

"—but that was the only time she ever made rhymes."

Maxine Barbour flushes again and looks away and for the first time, Jeff feels a touch of sympathy for her. It is probably difficult to be the only child of two such talented and attractive parents. On Barbour, the nose adds character and keeps his handsome face from being too pretty, and the mother is still a stunner who moves with a grace and confidence the daughter lacks.

"When Bailey was shipped overseas, he sent back letters that were really bedtime stories for Max," says Frances Barbour, taking up the familiar narrative. "I would set his picture on her bedside table while I read them out loud so that she wouldn't forget him, and then later I started illustrating the margins of those letters. One of my friends had just gone to work for a children's publisher, and when I showed her one of Bailey's awfully cute stories, she insisted taking it to the top editor."

"And the rest is history," Barbour says expansively. "The books sell over fifty thousand copies a year, in five languages. We're not Dr. Seuss, but—"

"But with more aggressive marketing, you could be," says Voygt. "Children who grew up on *Pink and Blue and Max* will soon be buying houses and starting families, if they haven't already. They need to be reminded how much they loved the books and how much they could enjoy reading them to their own kids. Look at what Walt Disney's done with Mickey Mouse, Mr. Barbour. His toys are everywhere. I'm sure Pink and Blue stuffed animals could sell to every grandparent who ever bought one of those books for a child. And stuffed toys are only the beginning. There are dozens of possible franchises."

"I don't know," Barbour says, shaking his head. "You make a good case, Voygt, but writing the books keeps us busy enough. I don't believe we'd be wise to take on anything as complicated as what you're proposing. If Max really were a boy—? But she isn't. Besides, we have quite enough for our modest wants."

His complacent gesture takes in the large home where they sit. A comfortable four-story brownstone in the West Twenties has replaced their Greenwich Village walk-up, and the furnishings here might have been ordered from a luxury furniture store. Large windows at one end of the floor-through space provide a clear north light for Mrs. Barbour's drawing table and neatly shelved art supplies. This end holds overstuffed leather chairs and couch. A modern electric typewriter sits upon Mr. Barbour's wide mahogany desk for his personal use. In the ante-room outside, they can hear the steady clack of a second electric typewriter as the Barbours' part-time secretary answers letters from their readers.

"No. It's out of the question," says Barbour. "Just doing the tax returns and keeping up with our royalty statements is diffi-cult enough for Frances and me, right, dear?"

"With the extra money you'd be earning, you could hire a firm of accountants to do that for you. It doesn't have to add to your workload at all," Voygt assures them. "That would be my job. For you, it would be all profit with no risk."

Barbour continues to shake his head.

"What exactly has Mr. Voygt proposed?" Maxine Barbour asks, looking from one parent to the other.

Before he can reply, Frances Barbour says, "Maxie, dear, why don't you let Mr. Voygt explain it to you over lunch while your father and I discuss this between ourselves? If that's agreeable to you, Mr. Voygt?"

"Certainly. Miss Barbour?"

She nods shyly.

Bailey Barbour looks from his daughter to young Voygt and then back to his wife.

"An excellent idea," he says.

CHAPTER
5

"And you fell in love over lunch?" asked Amy.

"That's when I knew I wanted to marry her," said her father.

With her habit of listening between the lines, Amy considered his choice of words. Did he realize the two were not at all the same?

"Were you happy together?"

"I thought we were." This personal probing of emotions was usually where he would cut her questions short, but today, as if to prove to them both that he always answered her fully, he made himself continue. "She understood and approved of where I wanted to take the company."

"She was only twenty and you were what?"

"Twenty-five." He smiled. "I was hardly robbing the cradle, Amy. In those days, a young woman expected to marry as soon as she finished school, and your mother had been out of school for almost a year."

"Yes, I remember Grandmother saying she'd graduated early. That means she was intelligent, doesn't it?"

"Intelligent enough," he conceded, "and certainly conscientious enough to take summer classes from the time she was sixteen instead of wasting her time the way Beth did. But she was very shy and immature in other ways. Nothing like you young women today who take your degrees and do something with them."

"Coming into the family business is hardly doing something with my degree in art," said Amy.

"Don't put yourself down. You have your grandmother's artistic talent and you've made significant contributions to the line."

"Did Maxie contribute?"

"It was different then. Besides, she'd studied natural sciences, something totally useless to the company. She ran the house and was an excellent hostess. She never seemed to lack for things to do, and I was all over the map in those early years. I had to outsource the production of the toys and license the sidelines, make sure the standards were being kept, line up distributors, lease warehouses—it never stopped. Then after Bailey's first stroke, she helped with his nursing. It was a busy, stressful time for both of us. I worked sixty hours a week."

"No wonder there were no children," she murmured.

"It wasn't for lack of trying," he told her with the boyish grin that could make him seem more open and approachable. "She wanted children desperately and we'd begun to talk of adoption."

"Really?" Amy's attention sharpened. "I didn't know that."

"No reason you should. But then she came with me to inspect the Taiwan production process. We stopped off in Hawaii for a brief vacation on our way out and she was having morning sickness by the time we got home."

"Hawaii? I was conceived in Hawaii?"

"She thought so. At the Royal Hawaii Hotel. We'd never drunk Mai-Tais before and that was where they were invented." A brief smile crossed his lips, as if he remembered something amusing. Then he shrugged. "I always thought it was Taipei myself. Whichever, it wasn't an easy pregnancy. She had to stay off her feet the last six weeks and even then you were born early. But she was the happiest I'd ever seen her. Even Frances had to admit you were perfect and she wasn't easy to please."

Amy turned this new information in her mind. She had done the math on her own years ago and had come to the conclusion that her conception was either an accident or an afterthought. To learn that she had been both wanted and welcomed was unexpected.

"Yet, three years later, she shot herself. Why, Dad?"

"I don't know, Amy. I still don't know."

"Three years. Thirty-seven months, to be precise, so it couldn't have been postpartum depression. Not after all that time."

"No," he agreed.

"I was there in Carolina with her," Amy whispered. "In the house. Yet I can't remember her at all. Or anything about her death. Did I know? What did I say when you came for me?"

"You were still a baby."

"I was three. I must have known something bad had happened."

"We didn't talk about it in front of you. We thought it best to help you forget as soon as possible."

"Is that why I didn't go back for almost five years?"

"Leave it alone, Amy. Don't go dredging up hurtful memories."

"Then I *did* know. If only I'd been a little older. Maybe I could have stopped her."

Her father shook his head. "If you want to blame anybody, blame me. I should have gone down with her, but there was some crisis then and I couldn't get away."

The stiffness was returning to his voice and Amy knew there would be no more personal reminiscences now, yet she had to try.

"There's always some crisis. What was it that time?"

He shrugged. "I can't remember."

"Grandmother said there was a woman," she blurted.

"She said that?" He was instantly defensive. "When?"

"Years ago. Back when you and Claire were so at odds that Michael and I were afraid you were going to get divorced. She said you'd had other women from the first day she met you— that there had been someone at the time Maxie killed herself. That maybe that's why she did it."

He stood up, and when he spoke, it was very deliberate and with controlled anger. "Frances was wicked to have put that into your head. Max and I had a strong marriage. If there *was* another woman at the time, she wasn't important. Those things were always casual. Whatever drove her to take Bailey's revolver and shoot herself, it wasn't over some passing affair I might have been having. I would never have left your mother, Amy, and she knew it. So did Frances. She shouldn't have told you that. You've blamed me all these years, haven't you?"

"No, not really. Because Grandmother—" She hesitated.

"Yes?" His face was stern, but she persevered.

"Grandmother didn't really love Maxie, did she?"

"Why do you say that?"

"She never talked about her much. I mean, she would tell me how Pink and Blue got started and how they were Maxie's first toys, but whenever she mentioned Maxie as an adult, it was almost as an afterthought. As if she wasn't important. And she never painted Maxie's portrait."

"I'm not going to psychoanalyze your grandmother now that she's gone, but you and Bailey were probably the only two people she ever really loved."

"Not even her own daughter?"

"Frances was a strong-minded person, Amy. Blunt-spoken. She didn't suffer fools."

"My mother was a fool?"

"Of course not. Don't twist my words. But she never stood up to Frances and she was even less interested in the company than you are."

"I'm interested," Amy protested. "I just don't want to run it."

And now they were back to the battle of wills that had begun almost a year ago. After years of sharing power only with Frances, Jeffrey Voygt had belatedly realized that the two of them would not go on forever and that all along they should have been grooming Amy for the position she would inherit. Heretofore, she had seemed as compliant and biddable as the boys, but more and more often these days, he found himself glaring at her in baffled frustration.

"But why? You certainly could if you'd apply yourself. You're intelligent. You have a good eye. The others care about your opinion."

"Only because Grandmother owned controlling interest of the company," she said mutinously.

"Nonsense. Now I have every confidence in Eric, but—"

"You should have confidence. He's the one who put our video department solidly in the black," Amy reminded him. "And at least his eyes don't glaze over like mine every time you or Michael try to make us read a balance sheet. Besides, your retirement's years away."

"Not years, my dear. I'll soon be sixty-eight. I should already be lounging on a beach somewhere."

"You hate beaches."

"And you hate facing reality," he snapped. "You're thirty years old—almost as old as I was when your grandfather had his first stroke and I took over the presidency of this company—and it's time you started acting like it. Unless you want me to call Frankfurt and tell them we'll reconsider their offer?"

"No."

A German consortium had tendered an enormous offer for PBM back in the spring. Jeffrey, Eric, even Sam thought they should accept. Frances flatly rejected it. Sixty years after the fact, she still held a grudge. "They could have killed Bailey in the war. I won't let them have his work."

"Perhaps now is not the best time to talk about this," her father said, "but I do plan to start the transition after we get back in September and I want you to know what to expect. In addition to the original copyrights, to which the company still pays licensing fees, you now own your grandmother's shares of PBM Enterprises outright, so you are very well provided for. Do you agree?"

She nodded.

"That's why I've put my shares of the corporation into a trust for Michael, Sam, and Beth, and when I step down next year, I intend to let Michael and Sam vote the stock until Beth proves herself. Even though Michael's not my flesh and blood, he's been a son to me and a brother to you. He's worked hard for the company. It wouldn't be fair to exclude him."

Amy sat silently, looking at him with those wide, indefinitely colored eyes. Max's eyes. Max had looked at him like that the first time she'd found out about the other women.

"I hope you're not going to take this to mean that I care for them more than you," he said brusquely, feeling unaccountably guilty. "I'm merely trying to balance it out."

Her eyes did not waver. "It doesn't balance, though, does it?"

"It could. If you'd think of the next generation and keep it in the family."

"Eric *is* my family, Dad." Her gaze turned quizzical. "Why are you suddenly down on him? Is there something you aren't telling me?"

"Of course not. It's simply that—let me ask you this: do you have a will?"

"The O'Days drew one up right after Eric and I were married," she said, naming the attorneys who handled their personal needs.

"Did you specify who was to inherit your part of the company?"

"I didn't own any of the company then, remember?"

"So it was a simple will in which you each left everything to the other?"

"He's my husband," she said again.

"So that if you got hit by a cab tomorrow, your husband could control PBM."

"I never jaywalk," she said solemnly.

He rose. "If you aren't going to take this conversation seriously—"

"I do take this seriously," she said with unaccustomed heat. "You've just told me that I'm to have nothing from you when you die, and then you all but say that Eric married me for my money and that it's my duty to rewrite my will and leave everything to your future grandchildren in case he pushes me under a cab next week."

At this unwonted show of spirit, Jeffrey Voygt drew himself up to his full height. "Really, Amy!"

She immediately put out a placating hand.

"I'm sorry, Dad. I know you didn't really mean it like that."

Not displeased to think that he could still wither her in an instant, Voygt held the glare a moment longer, then softened his tone.

"I suspect you're tired. We're all ready for a vacation. Must you and Eric really go tramping through Appalachia? Wouldn't it be better to relax with Claire and me up at the lake?"

"Maybe," she admitted. "But Eric thinks the only real vacation is a complete change, and he does love roughing it in the woods."

"Then let him go off and do his thing and you come with us."

"I can't," she said. "He wants me with him."

"And what do you want?"

"I don't know," she said quietly, unwilling to voice the crosscurrents she felt building in her family and in her marriage. For the last few weeks, she had experienced a vague sense of uneasiness, as if something unpleasant were lurking at the edge of consciousness, something that could be held at bay if she could only keep from naming it. "I just want us all to be happy."

"So do I, my dear. So do I." Uncomfortable with displays of physical affection toward his children, Voygt gave her shoulder an awkward pat and turned to leave before she could clasp his hand. At the doorway, though, he paused and said, "Don't forget about the farm. You ought to tell the O'Days to contact Frances's attorney about the sale."

"You really think I should sell?"

"Absolutely. And the sooner the better. That was a generous offer, considering the current state of North Carolina's economy. You might get a lot less if you wait."

"But what about Grandmother's paintings? Her books and papers and furniture?"

"That's what moving and storage companies are for. I'm sure the attorney will know someone reliable. Or you could have him bring in an appraiser and consign it to an auction house. As I recall, some of the furniture was valuable."

"That's a good idea," said Eric when she brought it up over dinner a few nights later at their favorite Thai restaurant. "Sell everything. We certainly don't need any more furniture."

"But there's a wonderful chest at the head of the main stairs that would fit perfectly in our entry hall."

"Sweetheart, anything out of that house would look like hell with our stuff and you know it."

Although she was the one who'd studied art, Eric had pronounced tastes that ran toward modern glass and steel and ergonomically designed furniture upholstered in bright bold prints, all very comfortable and efficient. Not what Amy would have chosen on her own, but not worth arguing about if it made Eric happy.

Was he happy? she wondered, looking at him across the table. There were lines in his face that weren't there five years ago when they first met. She knew the work at PBM excited and absorbed him as much as it absorbed and interested her, but lately he seemed edgier, more impatient. And totally uninterested in refurbishing their apartment.

By the time Bailey Barbour inherited the family farmhouse down in Carolina, royalties from *Pink and Blue and Max* had allowed Frances to redo the house for a winter retreat. She had had the interior painted in mellow tones of cream and tan and, except for a few family pieces from Bailey's mother, she had filled the rooms with sturdy Arts and Crafts oak furniture. Across the front, the original clear glass windows were replaced with geometrically leaded panes that alternated blocks of frosted and beveled glass with colored strips that glowed like jewels.

After Bailey's first stroke, he had insisted on going home to die, and Frances, who could never deny him anything, gave the brownstone to their daughter and son-in-law and went south. By the time he finally did die, Frances no longer wanted to live in New York.

Eric and her siblings thought the house was gloomy, and certainly it was now shabby as well, but Amy had always liked the furniture and had secretly hoped to bring much of it back to New York for their own apartment.

"It's Roycroft and Stickley," she argued now. "A lot of those pieces are museum quality."

"Then donate them to a museum and get the tax credit," Eric said, ever practical. "I'll call the O'Days tomorrow and tell them to start the ball rolling."

For a moment, Amy felt as if a huge ball were rolling over her. "But what about Grandmother's papers? Her sketchbooks and manuscripts? And I'm sure she kept those first letters Grandfather wrote to my mother during the war. They never threw away anything. She always said that's what attics were for."

That gave him pause. The sixtieth-anniversary celebration of the original publication of *Pink and Blue and Max* had been his concept, and although it was still more than two years away, every facet of the early beginnings was being reexamined for its advertising potential.

"We'll tell the O'Days to have all the books and papers shipped to the Jersey warehouse and someone can go through them there."

"Not someone," she said. "Me. Some of those papers will be personal and I don't want a stranger pawing through them."

He started to object, and then reached across the table for her hand. "You think she's left an explanation for Max's suicide?"

"Not an explanation," she said, squeezing his hand in gratitude for his understanding, "but maybe things that outsiders shouldn't see."

"Good thinking. We certainly don't want *that* raked up during the celebration."

He freed his hand from hers and signaled the waiter for their check.

CHAPTER
6
(August)

Two weeks after Amy had given them the green light, Tom O'Day's wife and law partner called to tell her that the papers were ready for her signature.

"That was fast," Amy said, her heart irrationally sinking for reasons she couldn't begin to articulate.

"You were the last piece of the puzzle." The happiness of a successful deal bubbled in the attorney's voice. "It let us get them up another ten K."

"How was that?"

"Turns out that your land's sitting right in the middle of the parcel they want to develop. If you'd turned them down, they would have had to go to their fallback position and develop on the other side of the cloverleaf."

"That's bad?"

"You're not just whistlin' Dixie," Marie O'Day chortled. "That would put them so dangerously close to some environmentally sensitive wetlands that there would never be room for future expansion without paying off a bunch of politicians for an act of the legislature. I gather your cousins are ready to break out the champagne."

Cousins? For a moment her mind went blank. She had seen her grandfather's relatives so seldom over the last ten years that his sister was probably the only one she would recognize if they walked into the room. But yes, of course there were cousins, cousins who would have inherited shares of the original farm themselves: the children of Grandfather's sister and brother, cousins who must have tended the whole farm after that brother was killed on Guadalcanal in 1942.

Abruptly, she could hear her grandmother's voice.

"That's why your grandfather volunteered. After Curtis William was killed, he felt it would be unmanly not to go himself. Curtis William didn't have to go to war, though. He had three children. He was a farmer. His mother was a widow." Her voice grew bitter each time she told the story. *"But no. Curtis William had to go and be a hero and because of him, I spent three years in absolute terror, afraid to answer the phone, cringing every time the doorbell rang. I never really expected to see Bailey alive again."*

"So," said Marie O'Day. "You want to come by tomorrow morning and make it official?"

"Okay," she said. "Around nine?"

Before the attorney could respond, Eric appeared in Amy's doorway with a bottle of champagne and an enormous grin on his face. For one confused moment, she wondered if he had been in touch with her celebrating Southern kin, but then she saw her father and Michael right behind him with equally large smiles and a second bottle of champagne. Her own face lit up as she hastily got off the phone and jumped to her feet.

"Omigod! They're going to take it? *Really?* When?"

"They're going to add it to their Saturday morning lineup next summer, and if it tests well, they'll offer it to the rest of the stations next fall."

He swung her around in an exuberant hug, and as soon as he released her, Michael's own bear hug followed. Their excited voices brought secretaries and assistants out of their cubicles to see what the big deal was.

It was a very big deal indeed.

Thus far, the Pink and Blue and Max videos had attained only limited distribution. They were mainly shown in nursery schools, daycare centers, children's hospitals, and similar places that served the very young and needed fodder for their closed-circuit television systems. But if a major PBS station really did intend to broadcast the videos, it would take PBM to a whole different level.

"The last phone call just came," Eric crowed. "It's going to be a hell of a lot of work, but worth it. We'll need to move up the new production schedule, and that's going to be a bear."

The videos were Eric's area of expertise. When her father first hired him five years ago, their animation was of poor quality and the soundtracks were abysmal. Since then, he had exceeded Jeffrey Voygt's expectations: revamped the whole program, contracted with a group of savvy young animators who understood computer graphics, and brought the videos into the twenty-first century while retaining the gentle charm of the original books. By the time Eric came on board, Amy had already received her grandmother's approval to make subtle updates to the images of the stuffed animals and the child Max, and coordinating those changes with the videos had entailed long work sessions. Work soon became the excuse, not the reason, for other long sessions, which eventually led to their marriage two years later, something *not* in her father's expectations.

But all his misgivings seemed unimportant now and Jeffrey Voygt himself was uncorking the first bottle. He had always given credit where credit had been earned, and Eric had certainly earned his right to crow today. Plastic champagne flutes were hastily brought from the storeroom that held the company's office party supplies and the bottles went around for everyone to toast PBM's new venture.

The party went on for almost an hour, but when the last flute was drained and the other people had drifted away, Eric looked at Amy apologetically. "I'm afraid this knocks out our trail trip, sweetheart. There's no way I can take off now."

"That's okay. There's plenty to keep me busy here."

He shook his head. "You don't have to stay home just because of me. I'll be working ten or twelve hours a day and back and forth on the shuttle to Boston the rest of the time, so you might as well go on up to New Hampshire with the others Friday."

"You're sure?"

"Of course I'm sure."

He gave her a quick kiss and was heading out her door when Amy remembered the appointment with their attorneys and told him the results of the O'Days' negotiations.

"An extra ten thou? Cool." He grinned. "But chicken feed compared to what this PBS baby's going to earn us."

Impulsively, she said, "Maybe it's time to start thinking real baby?"

If her words jarred him for an instant, he quickly recovered. "If that's what you want, sweetheart, sure." His smile changed to an exaggerated leer. "Tonight?"

"I'll be the woman in the Saran Wrap," she said, leering back.

He warned her that one of the animators wanted to show him possible solutions to a couple of glitches that had come up, "so I may be a little late."

"I won't start without you," she promised.

Shortly before leaving the office, Amy spent a few minutes on the Internet. She knew she was being silly and sentimental, yet she still went to her favorite search engine and typed in the keywords. Then, printout in hand, she stopped by a liquor store near the apartment and read it off to the clerk. "Jamaican rum, and curaçao, please. And do you have something called orgeat syrup?"

He smiled as he rang up her bottles. "Making Mai-Tais, huh?"

She nodded happily.

Next door was a deli that was famous for its lobster salad. Three doors down was the vegetable stand, where she bought a couple of fresh limes for the Mai-Tais. Rock candy syrup she already had from making mint juleps for their Kentucky Derby party back in the spring, but as long as she was evoking Hawaii, she bought a large ripe pineapple, too.

At her building, the doorman hurried to take her bags and pass them on to the elevator operator. Their tenth-floor apartment, a wedding gift from her grandmother, was much bigger than they had needed, but Frances Barbour had waved aside both their gratitude and their misgivings.

"If there's a baby, you won't have to move. *And* you won't be bumping into each other every time you turn around the way Bailey and I did when your mother came."

O wise and prescient one, she thought, and grief shafted through her happiness at remembering anew how that difficult, bossy, indulgent old woman was gone forever, brutally struck down in her own home, never to see her great-grandchild.

She sighed and the elevator operator gave a sympathetic smile. "Tough day?"

"No. Actually, it was a good day. And getting better."

He carried her bags the few short steps to her doorway and waited till she had unlocked the door before handing them back.

Their current cleaner, a struggling actor, had been in that day, so everything was immaculate when she passed through to the kitchen, and she knew there would be fresh sheets on their bed.

Bed.

It was almost a machine for sleeping, with his and her radios, CD players, and white noise devices built into the sleek steel headboard and speakers just at pillow level on each side for individual listening, yet she looked at it as tenderly as if it were a canopied four-poster, already sentimental about the place where their first child would be conceived.

Abruptly she realized that, well, no, it would not be. Not

tonight, anyhow. Not when she had routinely swallowed a pill this morning.

She tried to recall what she had been told of how long it took to conceive after one went off the pill and drew a blank.

Ah, well, she told herself philosophically. If not this month, then next. In the meantime, tonight would inaugurate their intent.

She took a leisurely shower with sweet-scented oils, touched Eric's favorite perfume to her pulse spots, and put on the negligee he had given her for their anniversary. Black lace might be a cliché, but if that's what he liked her to wear for him, who was she to quibble? Their lovemaking had become routine lately and it felt good to feel sexy again, to have that delicious shiver of anticipation.

At seven o'clock, she laid two places at the table, put fresh candles into the crystal holders, and dimmed the lights. In the kitchen, she sliced the pineapple, arranged their salads on two plates, covered them with plastic wrap, and slid them into the refrigerator where they would be ready in an instant.

At eight, she went into the home office they shared and pulled out some work that needed doing.

At ten, she went to bed.

Alone.

Amy awoke in the gray dawn, long before sunrise.

No Eric.

Half alarmed, she grabbed up her usual cotton robe and went looking. The backpack he used as a briefcase lay in its usual spot on the brushed steel console in the entry hall. She crossed the living room to the guest suite beyond and eased open the door.

Her husband was sound asleep on the bed, his head under the pillow, one foot out from under the cover and hanging over the edge of the bed. It would probably be stiff when he stood on it, she thought.

His clothes lay on the floor where he'd dropped them, and

she automatically picked them up. They reeked of beer and tobacco smoke and there was a dark red smudge on the collar of
his shirt.

Talk about clichés, she thought. Any other wife would probably jump to conclusions and start to think there was another
woman. *She,* on the other hand, realized that the animators had
undoubtedly pressed him to celebrate with them, and since
there were at least three women on the alpha animation team,
this lipstick on his shirt represented nothing more than con-
gratulatory exuberance.

Didn't it?

Insidiously, the doubts crept in. She remembered her father's
unvoiced reservations about Eric.

Her father was a proven womanizer.

Takes one to know one, doesn't it?

Was this the source of the uneasiness she had been feeling
these past few weeks?

She took another look at the smudge. More purple than red,
a brunette's color. One of the animators had long dark hair and
deepset brown eyes. She would wear this shade of lipstick.

From earliest childhood, Amy had shied away from emotional
confrontations, and whenever she felt as impotent and indecisive
as she did at that moment, a set of familiar cartoon voices would
echo through her head like the beat of a primitive drum, quick-
ening her pulse, pushing her to actions she would never otherwise have taken:

"What do you think, Pink?"

"What'll we do, Blue?"

Never in a million years would the grown-up Amy consciously
admit to the influence of those two questions. If asked, she
would have said they were just there, background voices that
were almost indistinguishable amid the usual clutter of irrelevant
memories everyone carried around with them.

Nevertheless, she closed the bedroom door silently and went
back through the apartment to the master bedroom, pausing

along the way to dump the master's soiled clothes in the laundry hamper. From the house phone in the bedroom, she called downstairs and asked that her car be brought around.

Thirty minutes later, the doorman helped put her luggage in the trunk. At this still early hour, outbound traffic in the Holland Tunnel was light, and soon she was merging onto the Jersey Turnpike heading south.

CHAPTER
7

Somewhere south of the Delaware Memorial Bridge, Amy stopped for gas and coffee, knowing well that it was still too early for anyone to be at the office.

She got her father's voice mail on her cell phone and stretched her lips into a wide smile in the hope that mimicking cheerfulness would add a lilt to her voice. She did not want him asking Eric awkward questions.

"Dad? Hi! Isn't it a glorious morning?"

No, no, no! Too over the top. Tone it down, she told herself.

"Look, Dad, I decided on the spur of the moment to get a jump on my vacation. Since Eric's going to be tied up in production all month, I'm on my way to Grandmother's house." She winced at the childish storybook image her words conjured. "Sounds like Little Red Riding Hood, doesn't it? I was afraid that if I told you before I left, you'd talk me into coming up to the lake with the rest of you this weekend, and I really do want to go through the house myself, see what's worth keeping and what I should sell. If it goes well, maybe I can join you and Claire and Jody for a few days. If not, I'll see you when you get back."

Next she keyed in Eric's voice mail, and while she waited for the signal to speak, she thought how weird it was to plan on making a baby with someone one night and then be wondering the next morning if they had any future together. "Eric? Me. Since you're going to be so busy these next few weeks, I've decided to drive down and sort through Grandmother's things myself. Please don't call and definitely don't come. I need to sort myself out, too, okay? I'll call you in a few days."

Finally, she rang her attorneys' office, but instead of their answering machine, a live voice said crisply, "O'Day and O'Day. May I help you?"

"Mary Kay?"

"No, Ms. Kare is on maternity leave. This is Suzi Murakami. May I help you?"

"Amy Steadman here. Did she have the baby yet?"

The secretary's voice warmed. "Last night. A healthy little girl! Mother and daughter doing fine. Did you want to speak to Mr. O'Day or Mrs.? I'm afraid neither of them is in at the moment. Would you care to leave a message?"

"That's okay. I was supposed to come by this morning and sign something, but I won't be able to make it after all. Would you have one of them call me on my cell phone? They have the number."

"Certainly, Mrs. Steadman."

"Oh, and what hospital is Mary Kay in?" she asked before the secretary could hang up.

As soon as the connection was clear again, she called her favorite florist and arranged to have flowers sent to the new mother. She was genuinely happy for Mary Kay; nevertheless, the news made her unexpectedly sad. She almost felt as if she should be ordering flowers for the funeral of the baby she and Eric might never have now, and her eyes misted over.

"What would you like on the card?" asked the clerk.

Amy swallowed the lump in her throat. "How about 'Congratulations and best wishes'?"

"Certainly. And how would you like the card signed?"

She hesitated, then gave a mental shrug. It was too soon to start making symbolic gestures. "Just sign it 'Eric and Amy Steadman.'"

"Thank you, Mrs. Steadman. They'll go out this morning."

Her cell phone rang at ten after nine.

Eric. Just enough time to get to the office, check his voice mail, and discover that she had not gone into work early as he must have thought.

The screen flashed "Answer? Yes/No."

She pressed "No" and kept driving.

It immediately rang again. He tried twice more before leaving her a text message: SORRYSORRYSORRY—CALL ME!

The O'Days called at ten from a speaker phone, and they were not happy to hear that she was on her way to North Carolina.

"Don't tell us you've changed your mind about selling," Tom scolded.

"It's not that I've changed my mind, exactly; it's that I don't want to sell till I've had a chance to see the house again and make a decision about what to do with the contents."

She eased off on the gas to let a car on her right pass, then moved over to the slow lane and lowered the speed on her cruise control while she talked.

"How long do you think that'll take you?" Tom asked. "We can overnight the papers to you there and we'll stipulate that you don't have to vacate till when? A week? Ten days?"

"Longer than that," Amy protested. "Maybe till Labor Day."

Silence from the other end. Then Marie said, "Amy, sweetie? Is something else going on here?"

"N-no, of course not." She heard the indecision in her voice and said more firmly, "I don't know why everyone's in such a hurry. What difference does another month make, anyhow?"

"It keeps the broker cooling his heels," Tom said patiently. "If you let him think he's never going to get a firm commitment from you, he just might opt for other alternatives."

"I thought you said the developers don't want to go across the cloverleaf because of some wetlands."

"They may not *want* to," he agreed, "but you keep jerking them around and they could change their minds."

"And what about your cousins?" Marie asked. "The money may not mean much to you, but it's different for them. You're not being fair to them."

Amy sighed. "Okay. Send the papers down. I'll sign."

"We'll stipulate that you have till Labor Day to vacate the house," Tom promised. "And we'll even see that you have the option to move it if you want, okay?"

Amy played with that idea as she continued on down I-95. Moving a hundred-year-old house probably wasn't very practical, but it would mean she could keep all the furniture. Maybe she could take the money from the sale and buy a lot on a lake or river? Move the house there and use it for a winter retreat the way her grandparents had?

Of course, Eric would never approve.

But then Eric's approval might not matter by the end of summer.

At Petersburg, I-85 splits off from I-95 to take a more westerly course toward Atlanta. Heretofore, Amy had always flown into Raleigh-Durham International and rented a car, so she was not totally confident that she was taking the most direct route. She fumbled her way onto U.S. 1 as the sun slid down behind a bank of clouds on the western horizon, then got so disoriented trying to decipher the confusing signage posted on the beltlines around Raleigh that she made a complete circle of the city before finding a familiar exit that would take her to the old farmhouse southeast of town.

Formal guests had always parked on the circular drive at the front of the house, while locals, including the domestics her grandmother employed, usually pulled around to the back door and entered through the kitchen. Ever since acquiring a driver's license, Amy always continued on past the kitchen and parked her car around the corner at the side entrance because it was closest to the staircase that led to the bedroom she slept in whenever she visited.

With night coming on fast, old habits took over, although her heart did skip a beat when she drew up beside that door and saw the bright new metal plate around the doorknob, a plate that covered up the splintered wood where a killer had levered the door open.

Now that she was here alone in the gathering dusk, she was painfully aware that her grandmother's killer was still at large. Amy did not consider herself a brave person. She shrank from verbal fights, she was timorous of driving alone at night, and when camping with Eric, she always shook out her sleeping bag in case spiders or snakes had crawled in unnoticed. Now, with the drumbeat of those totemic words pounding wildly through her head—*"What do you think, Pink? What'll we do, Blue?"*—she tried to step from the car as if it were any other time.

As if Grandmother would be in the den watching the news.

As if Miss Pat would be in the kitchen fixing supper.

As if King would be waiting inside the door with cold nose and wagging tail.

Thick humid air flowed over her, hot and smothering, like a damp wool blanket. *Welcome to North Carolina in August.*

The muscles of her neck and shoulders ached from the tensions of the last hour. She flexed herself, extracted her bags from the trunk, and located the key to the new lock on her key ring.

Inside, the house was uncomfortably warm and smelled musty and unused. In her entire life, Amy had never been in this big house completely by herself, and now she was conscious of its size, its shadowed hallways, its secret places. It was one thing to boldly state her intent to be here, quite another to do it.

Alone.

She locked the door behind her, switched on a light, and steeled herself to take a careful look at the floor around the side staircase. She had been told that this was where Grandmother and King had died, and she expected to see bloodstains. Or if not bloodstains, then two large patches of bleached wood. Whoever had cleaned had done a meticulous job, though, and had scrubbed the whole floor right up to the doorway that led to the main entry. There was no way to tell precisely where the bodies had lain.

Relieved, she went hunting for the thermostat, and cool air soon flowed from the floor vents.

Like Robert Browning, who originated the phrase, and Mies van der Rohe, who popularized it, Grandmother had also believed that "Less is more" when it came to decorating the house Grandfather grew up in: Arts and Crafts chairs and settles of solid oak instead of overstuffed upholstered furniture, bare wood floors instead of wall-to-wall carpets, etched and beveled stained glass windows left curtainless instead of draped in heavy damask. Amy's footsteps echoed in her own ears as she passed back through the austere rooms and carried her bags up to her bedroom. The house had never felt so quiet.

Upstairs, she discovered another source of silence. The tall, eight-day grandfather clock that stood on the landing diagonally across from her bedroom door had stopped. She immediately dropped her bags and pulled on the heavy brass weights to start the pendulum swinging again, then reset the hands on the engraved brass face. Encouraged by the clock's steady tick-tock-tick, she pulled linens from a hall closet that still held the scent of lemon and lavender. By the time she had finished making her bed and putting fresh towels in the bathroom, she was more tired than hungry even though her only food had been a candy bar somewhere in Maryland.

The refrigerator was almost empty—nothing but pickles and condiments, three cans of diet cola, and a half-pound chunk of moldy cheddar in the back of the dairy drawer. But she found an unopened packet of crackers in the walk-in pantry, and once the mold was cut away there was enough good cheese underneath to take the edge off her hunger. She ate standing at the kitchen counter, tidied away the mess she had made, and yawned her way back upstairs. When she switched off all the lights, there was still an afterglow in the west—not even full dark yet.

A quick session with her toothbrush, then she hung her clothes over the back of a rocking chair, slipped on a short cotton gown, and was already half under by the time the grandfather clock on the hall landing began to strike the hour in familiar melodious tones.

It was the sound of summer, resting on the bed with a new book after lunch, waiting for sleep to come after a day of playing barefooted outside or after an evening of cutthroat Scrabble with Grandmother. The simple pleasures of those unstructured days always seemed so exotic compared to winters in the city, where she and her siblings spent their days in planned activities meant to enrich their minds or strengthen their physical skills. Here in Grandmother's house, she could let down her guard, speak without monitoring her words lest they be taken wrong, be indulged without anyone else feeling jealous.

With each stroke of the hour she felt herself sinking deeper into contentment, and was sound asleep before the clock had chimed the full eight.

She awoke in darkness, groggy and disoriented. Voices floated up the stairwell as from a radio someone had forgotten to switch off. A heavy thump shook the old house and she heard a woman's impatient voice. "Would you be careful? You're going to dent it."

Amy crept across the landing and cautiously peered through a front window. Light streamed from the open front door and she watched two men hoist a chest into the back of a large white

van. A pair of chairs, part of her grandmother's dining room furniture, stood on the paved drive, and when the men moved
aside she saw at least two more chairs already aboard. She tiptoed back to her room, found her cell phone, and dialed 911.

The dispatcher answered immediately. Amy whispered her
name and explained that her grandmother's house was being
robbed.

"Address?" asked the dispatcher.

Amy told him, he repeated it back, then said, "Now if you'll
just keep the line open, we'll make sure you stay safe until a
deputy gets there."

With the dispatcher's soothing voice in her ear, Amy stopped
shaking. "I could see the van from the landing. Should I try to
get the license number?"

"Ma'am, if they don't know you're in the house, I think it'd
be better for you to stay put."

"They're making an awful lot of noise down there. I don't
think they'll notice."

"Ma'am—"

"Shhh!" Amy hissed and opened the door.

The smell of cigarette smoke was so strong on the landing
that she instantly froze until she heard the woman say from
some distance, "Put out that cigarette. Right now! She never allowed smoking in the house."

"So what's she gonna do?" asked a boisterous male voice
from even further away. "Call the sheriff on us? She's dead. Remember?"

"I mean it!" the woman said imperiously.

"Okay, okay."

Amy tiptoed down to the railing, but this side staircase was
for utilitarian service and from directly above she could only see
a spill of light from the main entry hall where a grander staircase
rose to this floor at the center of the house. Shadows flickered
across the lower walls as the thieves moved back and forth. From

their voices, there seemed to be three of them, a woman and two men.

Emboldened, she went back to the front window, but the light was too dim to make out the numbers on the license plate. Nor could she read the printing on the side of the van from this angle, though there seemed to be a picture of a child holding something.

As she turned from the window, someone flicked on the lights directly below and she heard him start up the stairs.

"You wanted a dresser out of her bedroom, right?" he asked.

There was no way to get back to her own room and nowhere to hide on this uncluttered landing, no convenient drapes, no broom closet or empty cupboard, only the tall case clock. She cowered next to it, knowing she would be seen the instant anyone drew even with it.

She heard his footsteps mounting higher on the bare treads, felt the vibration as he reached the landing, heard his breath coming hard from the climb. She herself stopped breathing when he fumbled along the wall and bumped into the clock so that it swayed against her shoulder.

She heard him mutter, "Where's the damn switch?" Then the hall light overhead came on so abruptly that she was momentarily blinded.

"Will you get your butt back down here?" the woman called from below. "There's no room for nothing else on this load but the table. You and Jimmy'll have to take it apart to get it on, though. You got a screwdriver?"

"I thought them things was pegged," said the man, but to Amy's infinite relief, she heard him turn toward the stairwell.

"And shut off that light," snapped the woman.

The landing immediately went dark.

Amy's legs turned to water and she sank to the floor, unable to make herself leave the safety of the clock's bulk and cross the landing to her room.

Her cell phone glowed in the darkness. She held it tightly to her ear and whispered, "You still there?"

"Listen, ma'am," said the dispatcher. "Don't you do that anymore. We've got a patrol car—"

Static buzzed along the ether.

"You're breaking up," Amy said softly. "I can't hear you."

More static. Amy stared at the face of the cell phone and watched while the battery icon registered empty and the little screen faded to black. Too late to realize that she had not charged the phone in three days nor thought to plug it into the car's charger on the drive down.

The dispatcher had said a patrol car was on its way. On its way from where, though?

She huddled on the floor beside the clock and leaned her head against it until her pulse slowed to the clock's steady tick.

"Hey, Paulie!"

It was the voice of the same man and it sounded as if he were at the foot of the stairs again.

"What?" answered the woman.

"There's a car parked out here."

"What?"

Amy heard the outer door open, then mingled exclamations from the three below.

They knew she was here.

Terrified, she leaped to her feet and raced silently down the wide hallway, stubbing her bare toe on the corner of the old blanket chest that stood outside her grandmother's bedroom. Blanket chest? She lifted the lid and felt inside.

Empty!

The hall light blazed on and running footsteps pounded along the staircase.

(Think, Pink! Do, Blue!)

She slid into the chest and lowered the lid. It smelled of mildew and dust motes prickled her nose.

"Who's here?" the woman called from the end of the hall. "Anybody here?"

They must have opened the door to her room and switched on the light. She heard disjointed phrases: "—suitcase—shoes—should've checked, dammit!"

"—not in the bathroom."

Closet doors banged in the distance, then the woman's artificially friendly voice advanced along the hallway. "Come on out, honey. You don't need to be afraid. Nobody's gonna hurt you."

"Let's just go," said a lighter male voice.

The one they called Jimmy?

"Yeah," said the other man.

"No!" The woman sounded out of breath and was puffing loudly. The chest creaked when she sat down on it. "She's somewhere in this house and we need to find her before she—"

"What's going on here?" demanded a voice of authority.

"Oh, shit!" said one of the men.

"Don't shoot!" cried the other.

"Now, now. You don't need to be waving that gun around, honey." The chest creaked again as the woman stood up. "I believe I know your brother. Aren't you Steve Richards's little sister?"

"I'm Deputy Mayleen Richards. Sheriff's department. And you are?"

"Pauline Phillips. This is my son Jimmy and my—"

Amy was listening so intently that she forgot to keep pinching her nose against the dust prickles. It was not a very loud sneeze but it sufficed.

Someone instantly lifted the lid and she squinted at the sudden light.

Two men, an older heavyset woman, and a sturdy young woman in uniform with a gun in her hand stared down at her.

One of the men said, "Well, hey there, Cousin Amy. Welcome back."

CHAPTER
8

You're Mrs. Steadman?" asked the deputy. "Mrs. Amy Steadman?"

"Yes," said Amy with as much dignity as is possible when unfolding oneself from a dusty chest dressed only in a skimpy nightgown.

"My dispatcher said you reported a burglary in progress?"

"Yes," she said again.

"Burglary?" The older woman's tightly permed short gray curls bounced with indignation. "We weren't stealing anything."

"Just my grandmother's furniture," Amy said with more firmness than she felt ever since hearing the woman declare herself to be Pauline Phillips and after recognizing that familiar nose. "Weren't you my mother's cousin?"

"That's right, honey. Her cousin Paulie. Your granddaddy was my mama's brother. This here's my son Jimmy. And C.W. here—" She paused and tried to figure up the relationship on her fingers. "Well, he's my cousin Curt's boy, so I reckon y'all are cousins, too."

The men gave her awkward nods. Both were dark-haired six-footers, about ten years older than she, but, like his mother, Jimmy was carrying an extra twenty-five pounds that the other one—C.W.—could have used on his rawboned frame. Like the woman, both men also seemed to have inherited the Barbour nose.

"Sorry if we scared you," C.W. said. "We didn't know you were anywhere around. Should've figured somebody was here soon as we noticed the air-conditioning was on."

"You have the right to take this furniture?" Deputy Richards asked, getting back to business.

"Yes," said the woman.

"No," said Amy. "It belonged to my grandmother. I'm the current owner and I certainly did not give anybody permission."

"It never belonged to Aunt Frances." Pauline Phillips's pear-shaped body was encased in tight beige stretch pants that strained to cover her heavy thighs and calves and a loose white shirt that would have disguised the bulges of her waist and hips had she not stood with both hands on those hips to dispute Amy's claim. "We didn't touch a single piece belonging to her. What we're taking's what came down from my Grandma Virgie, things that were supposed to've gone to my mama and to Uncle Curtis William's children."

"What are you talking about?" asked Amy, painfully aware that the two men were eyeing her thin gown.

"They left the house to Uncle Bailey, but there wasn't anything in the will about leaving him the furniture. It was supposed to be divided up, and since my mama was the only girl, she should've got her pick. But Aunt Frances kept all the best pieces and wouldn't let the others have anything but her leavings. Mama was always so crazy about Uncle Bailey, she wouldn't fight him on it when Grandma died. Uncle Curtis William was already long dead by then, killed in the war, and Aunt Kate was too rabbitty to say 'Boo' to a grasshopper, much less to somebody strong-minded as Aunt Frances."

Amy's head was swimming trying to keep up, and the deputy

seemed equally confused. She holstered her gun. "How about we all go downstairs and get this sorted out?"

The others obediently turned and let her herd them along the hall to the end staircase.

"I'll be down as soon as I change," Amy said as they passed her open bedroom door.

She slipped inside and quickly shed the gown for the slacks and shirt she had worn on her drive down. While she dressed, she tried to remember what she knew of the people who still lived on this land.

The whole extended family would have been at her grandmother's funeral in May, but they were muddled in her memory with the many neighbors who had thronged the funeral home where all the services had been held. Too, there had been several newspaper and television reporters who came either because Frances and her late husband had written the Pink and Blue and Max books or because Frances had been murdered in a burglary gone sour. Indeed, the house was still being treated as a crime scene then, which meant that Amy and her immediate family had stayed at a nearby motel, further complicating the possibility of sorting out the various faces and reestablishing relationships that had never been strong to begin with.

Martha, her grandfather's sister and the mother of tonight's Pauline, had stood at her side throughout the visitation at the funeral home. Amy remembered her great-aunt's soft Southern voice in a running stream of thumbnail introductions: "And this is So-and-So, your cousin Such-and-Such's sister-in-law/ oldest child/ best friend/ minister. And this is Mr. and Mrs. Blank, who sat on the library's board of trustees with/ played bridge twice a month with/ was in a book club with/ on a cruise with your grandmother."

After the first twenty-five, Amy had quit trying to fix the names and faces in her memory. It was enough to take their hands and thank them for their expressions of sympathy. She had never really expected to see any of them again, yet here they were, laying claims on her inheritance, citing old wrongs as justification for breaking into the house in the middle of the night and—

At that moment, as if to mock her, the clock on the landing chimed the half-hour and she glanced at her watch automatically. Only nine-thirty?

She ran a comb through her hair, added lipstick for courage, then descended the stairs.

The others were gathered outside around the open end of the loaded van; and when Amy joined them, two men were just emerging from an unmarked patrol car. At least, she assumed that the car's permanent North Carolina license plate signified an official vehicle of some agency. Both men were white and both wore casual civilian clothes.

Deputy Richards introduced the taller man as her boss, Major Bryant.

"And I'm Agent Wilson," said the other, stepping forward to shake her hand. "Terry Wilson. State Bureau of Investigation."

"SBI?" yelped Jimmy. "Mama, what kind of trouble you got us in?"

"Now don't get all bent out of shape," Wilson said. "I'm not here officially. Major Bryant heard the call and we thought we'd swing by as long as we were in the neighborhood."

In the neighborhood? thought Amy. When it had been at least twenty minutes since she first dialed 911?

"I'm sorry," she said. "Did we meet before? After my grandmother died? I remember talking with Sheriff . . . Poole, was it?"

"Bowman Poole, yes, ma'am," said Wilson. "We were there, but most people don't notice us if Bo Poole's around."

That made her smile, because Agent Wilson would have made two of Sheriff Poole, who was small and trim in body, but had an outsize personality.

"Are you any nearer to finding who killed her?"

"We'd like to talk to you about that," Major Bryant said, "but first I need to know what's been happening here tonight?"

Before Deputy Richards could report, Pauline Phillips wiped perspiration from her plump face and immediately plunged into her story about furniture that belonged to her grandmother and how she was only taking back what the rest of the family had been unfairly deprived of for almost fifty years now, "ever since my grandmother, Virgie Barbour, died and Aunt Frances claimed it was all left to Uncle Bailey. Mama and Uncle Curtis William and Aunt Kate chipped in to help Grandma buy this dining room suit when the Parkers went busted and sold out and went to live in Norfolk the year before Grampa died and Uncle Bailey might've helped too but he and Aunt Frances sure as heck didn't give a penny more than anybody else 'cause they were still as poor back then as everybody else in the family so they certainly didn't have a right to keep it just because they got so rich later."

By the time Pauline paused to take a deep breath, Amy had taken a good look at what was loaded on the truck: twelve ladder-back chairs, a corner china cupboard, a sideboard, and three leaves from the partially dismantled table that was still in the entry hall, all in vernacular country oak. The simple design fit in well enough with her grandmother's Arts and Crafts decor, but even to her untrained eye, she could see that the furniture was nothing exceptional.

"You were going to take this to Aunt Martha's house?" she asked.

"Well, no, not exactly," the older woman hedged. "I mean, well, Mary and Ethylene and me? We've not decided yet who's going to get what."

"Mary and Ethylene?"

"Mary's my cousin Curt's wife. C.W.'s mama—"

Her thin cousin gave a sheepish shrug.

"—and Ethylene's my daughter-in-law. Jimmy's wife."

Jimmy appeared to be studying the fingernails of his chubby hand.

"Seems to me," said Major Bryant, "that this is something y'all's lawyers need to settle. Mrs. Steadman, we can cite your cousins here for breaking and entering and—"

"We never did any breaking," said C.W. "We used Aunt Martha's key."

Pauline Phillips glared at him.

The deputy held out his hand and she huffed a moment, then extracted a key from the pocket of her tight pants and dropped it in his palm. He immediately passed it on to Amy.

"Did Aunt Martha know?" she asked.

"I was going to tell her tomorrow." Pauline mopped her sweaty brow and glared at Bryant. "You going to arrest us or can we just put this stuff back inside and go on home?"

"Well . . ."

It took Amy a moment to realize that the officers were waiting to take their cue from her as to how seriously they should pursue this. The night air was almost as hot and sticky as when she arrived; and now that adrenaline no longer pumped through her veins, all she wanted was to end it and go sit down somewhere cool with something liquid.

She looked from one to the other. "Could we just let it go? I mean, I wish you had asked me first," she told her cousins, "but if these things mean that much to you and the others, then you should have it, only . . . perhaps you could wait and come back for the table tomorrow?"

"Now that's real generous of you," said C.W.

"There's a chest of Grandma's upstairs, too," said Pauline.

Jimmy rolled his eyes. *"Ma!"*

"Well, there is," she insisted. "But I reckon we can talk about that tomorrow."

While they finished loading the chairs, the officers checked to see that the rest of the doors and windows were securely locked, then Deputy Richards followed the van down the long drive to the highway.

"I think there's coffee in one of the canisters," Amy said, leading Agent Wilson and Major Bryant into her grandmother's formal front parlor, "but I don't know how fresh it is. I could make a pot if you'd like some?"

They assured her that would be unnecessary.

"Then I'm going to have a glass of wine. I don't suppose you're allowed to join me?"

"Where you reckon people get that idea?" Terry Wilson asked his colleague.

Dwight Bryant smiled. "Beats me. Television maybe?"

They trailed along after her to the butler's pantry and the wine rack.

"I'm afraid I don't know any of these labels," she told them.

"I always say, when in doubt, go with the red," said Wilson.

"Works for me," said Bryant.

While Amy pulled stemmed glasses from the cabinet and carried them to the kitchen sink to rinse off the dust, the SBI agent wielded the corkscrew. Throughout it all, the two men kept up a flow of banter between themselves that somehow did not exclude her. From their good-natured jibes at each other, she gathered that they were probably old friends of long standing, and by the time they were all seated around the kitchen table, she felt more at ease than she had expected. Both of them were big and solid. If the two were dogs, Bryant with his sandy brown hair and watchful brown eyes would be a sturdy German shepherd, and Wilson would be a basset hound, amiable and easygoing with those big sad eyes. Her fingers itched for a sketch pad.

"That was a nice thing you did," said Agent Wilson. "I don't know I could be that forgiving if somebody'd come busting in like that, scaring the bejeesus out of me. Don't blame you for hiding."

Amy flushed, realizing that Deputy Richards had probably given them all the details of how she'd been found cowering in that blanket chest.

"They're not bad people," said Major Bryant. "Never been in any trouble with the law, anyhow."

"They get along okay with Mrs. Barbour?" asked Wilson.

"So far as I know."

"Your grandmother never felt worried or threatened by any of her husband's people?" asked Bryant.

Amy had to smile at the idea of her grandmother being intimidated by anybody. "If anything, people felt worried or threatened by her."

The big deputy leaned forward in quickened interest. "Who?"

"Nobody in particular. I just meant that Grandmother was a woman who always did what she wanted without worrying about how it might affect anyone else. My grandfather was the only person she ever deferred to. She adored him. It was a real love match. Everybody else came way down the totem pole behind him. Like this thing with the furniture tonight. That's so her. If it fit the rest of her decor, she wouldn't lose a minute's sleep over its sentimental value to someone else."

"Yeah, I had an aunt like that," said Wilson. "If she thought somebody had their eye on something of hers, she'd hang on like a snapping turtle till it thundered, even if it was something she didn't really want. Just for the fun of it."

Amy frowned. "That wasn't Grandmother. She never went out of her way to spite someone. If she didn't like something, she wouldn't care who got it. From what Pauline said, Grandmother let the family take a lot of the old pieces when Grandfather inherited the house."

"It's just that if she *did* want something, she wouldn't care that someone else wanted it, too?"

"Exactly."

Bryant had been listening quietly. Now he said, "She couldn't put herself in someone else's shoes?"

"I know that makes her sound selfish and self-absorbed, but she wasn't a monster, Major Bryant."

"We heard she was holding back the sale of the land."

"She was an old woman. She didn't want to give up her home."

"She was also a wealthy old woman, Mrs. Steadman. She could have lived anywhere in the world. The rest of the family couldn't, though, could they?"

Amy drew herself up. "They were free to sell."

"The broker's option was contingent on getting this parcel, too. Least, that's what we were told. If she wouldn't sell, the broker wouldn't buy. But now she's dead and we hear that you've agreed to the sale."

Amy stared at him. "Are you saying Grandmother was killed because of this land deal? That one of my cousins—?"

Terry Wilson reached over and patted her arm. "Naw, now, what ol' Dwight here's trying to say is that in a homicide, we always look for reasons somebody might want the victim dead."

"But it was just a robbery, wasn't it?" A second, more horrible possibility occurred to her. "She wasn't—I mean, they didn't—"

"Molest her?" asked Wilson. "No, nothing like that, Miz Steadman. Just one quick blow to the back of her head. Might be she never even saw it coming."

Dwight Bryant leaned back and let his colleague calm her down. The woman had gone dead white, probably imaging her grandmother being sexually assaulted. Times like this, Terry was good to have along. The more agitated someone became, the folksier he could be, till he'd have witnesses, especially female witnesses, charmed into wanting to help them.

He'd seen Terry checking out her ring finger. Married and divorced three times and damned if he didn't stay optimistic, swearing it was just a matter of time till he found the right one.

Not this one, though. She might look small and vulnerable,

and she might have sounded a little wistful talking about her grandparents' love match—trouble there with her own marriage?—but money and power put her way out of Terry's league.

His own son had loved the Pink and Blue and Max books when he was younger, and while Cal now scorned them as being too babyish, some of the phrases were still part of their family in-jokes. "What do you think, Pink?" was right up there alongside "An elephant's faithful one hundred percent" and "Let the wild rumpus start!"

And books weren't all, either. One of his sisters had decorated her first baby's room with Pink and Blue and Max wallpaper, and family members had showered the kid with stuffed toys, a growth chart, night lights, and crib sheets, all with the same design.

It might not be Walt Disney's Magic Kingdom, but it was still a small empire that Bailey and Frances Barbour had started, and their granddaughter had inherited the bulk of it, according to the papers the Barbour attorney had filed at the courthouse. Hard to know just how much money was involved, because the company stock seemed to have been put in an irrevocable trust for her up in New York several years earlier, but one of the courthouse clerks had said that Mrs. Barbour's personal estate— "Her walking-around money," said the clerk—added up to over three million.

With a kid in college and alimony to the first wife, there was no way Terry Wilson could begin to compete for Amy Voygt Steadman on an SBI agent's salary.

When the dispatcher alerted him this evening, he and Terry had both been more surprised that Mrs. Steadman was at the Barbour house alone than that a presumably untenanted and soon to be bulldozed house was being burgled. During the interview at the time of Frances Barbour's death, she had been ringed by husband, father, brothers, and an attorney. Why was she here tonight all by herself?

"So, will your husband be joining you?" Terry asked guile-lessly.

Dwight suppressed a grin, but Mrs. Steadman didn't seem to notice.

"No." She twirled the wineglass in her fingers. "He's in the middle of something and can't—" She broke off abruptly. "No, he's not coming."

"You plan to stay here alone?"

"Only for a couple of weeks. The rumors you heard were true: the farm *is* going to be sold and I'm down to empty the house."

"All by yourself?"

Automatically, their eyes swept the big kitchen, a kitchen that had been added on when Frances Barbour remodeled the whole house for a winter retreat. The huge stove was restaurant size, copper-bottomed pans of every shape hung from overhead hooks, and the glass-fronted cupboards were filled with several sets of china. This room alone would take days to dismantle and pack up.

And while Mrs. Barbour didn't seem to have gone in for the figurines and framed snapshots and bric-a-brac that cluttered the homes of some old ladies, this was, nevertheless, a big house, fully furnished.

"I guess I wasn't thinking clearly," she admitted.

"Maybe your secretary or some of your maids are coming down?"

"Maids? Secretary?" She shook her head. "I'm afraid I don't have either. I mean, I have an assistant at the office, but just a cleaning person twice a week for the apartment." Her chin lifted. "I know what you must be thinking—what my cousins think—that we have half the money in the world. But it's not true. PBM is still a relatively small company, Agent Wilson. Family owned and family operated. Grandmother and my father controlled it. The rest of us live on our salaries. Despite what you may think, we've never been what you'd call rich."

Maybe not what *you'd* call rich, thought Dwight, keeping his face in neutral.

Terry lounged in his chair and lazily sipped his wine. "But now that she's gone, don't you own your grandmother's share?"

"Technically, yes, but my father still runs things for the time being."

She lifted the wine bottle and gestured to Dwight's glass. He covered it with his hand and shook his head.

"Agent Wilson?"

"Maybe just a little more."

Terry was famous for his hollow legs, and Dwight hadn't seen him totally wrecked in at least five years. All the same, best if one of them stayed alert.

Mrs. Steadman topped her own glass, then took a deep breath. "This whole conversation has a point, doesn't it?"

"Ma'am?"

"There's something you saw or something you've heard that makes you think she was deliberately killed, isn't there?"

"Well, yeah," Terry admitted. "Some chairs had been pushed over in the front parlor and a couple of drawers were pulled out and the contents dumped on the floor, but nothing was taken."

"The lamp," Dwight reminded him.

"Yeah, well . . ."

"No reason she shouldn't know."

"Know what?" she asked.

"There was blood on the lampshade," Dwight told her. "Mrs. Barbour's and the dog's, too."

"I don't understand."

"It means the parlor was messed up after they were dead," Terry explained. "That particular lamp wasn't in the way of somebody rifling the room, yet it looks like it might've been nudged over by the same blunt instrument they'd been hit with. Left a smear. He was trying to make us think she had discovered him in the middle of robbing her, when she was already dead out by the side door, thirty feet away. Same upstairs. The contents of her medicine cabinet had been dumped in the sink like he was looking for drugs, but Valium by the bedside was left untouched."

Dwight made his voice flat and vaguely accusing. "Big house like this, old lady here alone, how come she didn't have a burglar alarm?"

That stung her all right, and she flushed at the implied criticism.

"She used to have one, but it was always going off by accident so she canceled the contract. She hated having to remember to switch it off or switch it on every time she went in and out. She had King for protection and she wasn't nervous about being here alone. I wasn't worried either, although we did talk about having someone come in to sleep at night. She promised to wear a panic button, one of those electronic beepers so that she could call for help if she fell or got sick. Did she have it on when you found her?"

Terry nodded. "Too bad she didn't use it before she came downstairs. She must've been a brave lady."

"I talked to her the day before it happened. She was starting to get a little frail, but she'd just come back from getting the follow-up report on her annual physical and the doctor had told her she was good for another ten years."

Her voice trembled and her eyes suddenly brimmed with tears. "She should still be here!"

Terry pulled a clean handkerchief from his pocket and handed it to her with comforting wordless rumbles.

Dwight set his glass on the table. If Terry was going to keep playing the good cop, he reckoned it was time for him to ratchet up his bad cop routine while she had her guard down.

"Mrs. Steadman," he said, "we know you were in New York the night your grandmother was killed. But what about your husband?"

CHAPTER
9

But what about your husband?"

After those two lawmen finally left and she could go wearily back to bed, Amy had expected to lie awake staring at darkness.

"But what about your husband?"

In truth, she fell asleep almost instantly, as if her brain were determined to block out that question, a question that seemed to be looping endlessly though every circuit now that it was morning and she was wide awake again.

"But what about your husband?"

"He was in Washington," she had told them. "Interviewing an actress to voice Max. The woman who did the last few videos died in a car wreck and we needed someone fast. As soon as I heard about Grandmother that morning, I called him at his hotel. How could you possibly think—? I woke him up, for pete's sake!"

And then, like an idiot, when Major Bryant continued to look at her with that skeptical expression on his German shepherd face, she had blurted, "Eric did *not* marry me for Grandmother's money."

"People saying he did?"

"You are, aren't you? You, Dad, Beth."

"Who's Beth?"

"Half-sister," said Agent Wilson, which further rattled her to think that they had scrutinized her family so closely that they knew every intricacy. "Dwight here's not trying to say there's anything wrong with your husband or your marriage, Miz Steadman. But Miz Barbour's death does put a lot of people on easy street, so we look at everybody—you and your husband, your aunt and cousins now that the farm's gonna be sold, the broker who's already tied up a lot of his own money on this project, not to mention all the people in your grandmother's will."

"I'm the only one who benefits from that," she said tightly.

"Well, now, we heard she left money to a bunch of people."

"Just token amounts. Local charities, people who were working for her when she died her housekeeper, Patricia Raynor; the Johnson brothers that did the yard; the last cleaning woman, I forget her name—they each received two to fifteen thousand, depending on how long they'd worked here. Aunt Martha did get fifty, I believe. But you must have seen a copy of Grandmother's will. I'm the only one who received a significant amount."

The two men had looked at each other and something wordless seemed to pass between them.

"But what about your husband?"

Someone had smashed Grandmother over the head and control of PBM Enterprises was now legally in her hands.

"If you got hit by a cab tomorrow, your husband could control PBM."

The hall clock struck seven and she threw back the sheet. This was crazy. Okay, so Eric had grown up fairly poor. Not foodstamps, wolf-at-the-door poor, but his father was a mediocre insurance salesman and his mother had clerked in a department store until the four kids were through school. And yes, he did like the comfortable life they made together, the large West Side apartment, the trips abroad, control of his own development department. But he was bright and hardworking and in time would have achieved as much, if not more, on his own. He didn't have to marry someone he didn't love to get it.

He certainly didn't need to kill for it. And anyhow, he couldn't have. He was in Washington, for God's sake.

How stupidly dramatic could she get? Yes, she was still hurt and angry that he'd gone partying with the animators instead of coming home to make love, but did that justify letting those officers mess with her mind last night? How could she be so easily disloyal?

Enough already! Time to get started on what she'd come to do.

She padded across the polished wood floor to her morning bath and discovered another thing she would have to do: locate the water heater's thermostat, which someone seemed to have switched off. Instead of a hot shower, she had to settle for a cold sponging.

The bedroom had been hers since childhood and she kept a small selection of seasonal clothes here. Pulling on a pair of white shorts and a blue T-shirt, she headed down to the kitchen, where she brewed a pot of coffee using what she had found in a canister on the counter. It tasted stale but delivered the jolt of caffeine she needed to get her thoughts in order while she started a grocery list. Clearly she was going to need help, so she started another list:

Assistant
Appraiser
Moving/storage company
Miss Pat?

As her pencil doodled aimlessly, the question mark after Grandmother's cook and daily help was transformed into a spatula first, then a stylized daisy. She thought there was a family connection, but she could not quite remember what it was.

Patricia Raynor had to be pushing sixty by now. She and her parents had come as tenant farmers soon after Uncle Curtis William was killed in the Second World War. Patricia was a baby then and wasn't there—?

Oh, yes, that's where the family link came in. Her younger sister grew up to marry Curtis William's son Curt. Miss Pat had never married, though. Their mother died when the sisters were still in their teens and she continued to live on in the tenant house with their now elderly father.

The daisy on her notepad had morphed into a bouquet in a milk bucket and a honeybee hovering above it.

If Miss Pat hadn't taken another job, maybe she'd be willing to come back and help for a month? Amy tried to recall why Grandmother had spoken impatiently about the woman the last few times they'd talked. That she complained all the time? That meals had quit being interesting? That she'd slowed down a lot?

Well, none of those would bother *her* if the woman could pack up the kitchen and do a little light cleaning while she was here.

The honeybee became a snail with an intricately patterned shell, and Amy was adding eye stalks to the head when the front doorbell rang. Probably her cousins back for the rest of the dining room furniture.

But when she opened the door, it was to see SBI agent Wilson's pleasantly homely face. He was holding a small dog.

"I tried to call you first, but your phone's been disconnected."

"Not disconnected, just turned off for the duration. But thanks for reminding me. I'll call and get it turned back on. Who's your friend?"

"This here's Barkis, but I reckon he'd answer to Pink or Blue after a while if you give him a pork chop every time he comes."

Amy laughed and held out her hand to the dog. "Barkis? Because he's willing?"

"Willing to protect and a real good barker. I got to thinking about you out here alone, no burglar alarm. Figured you could use a good dog."

The terrier squirmed in Wilson's arms and tried to lick her hand.

Amy was both touched and dubious. "That's very nice of you, but I've never owned a dog before. I wouldn't know what to do with one."

"Aw, there's nothing to know. You just feed him every morning, keep his water bowl full, let him go outside to do his business twice a day, and give him an old rug or blanket to lay on beside your bed. He'll do the rest."

Amy continued to look doubtful.

"Yeah, I know," he said. "Most folks out here would say what you really need's a gun, but a dog's a lot easier to learn how to handle than a gun is."

He set the little animal down between them and handed her the leash. His tail had been cropped, but what was left wagged furiously as he jumped up on her bare legs. The agent gave a sharp "No" accompanied by a hand signal and the dog instantly quit jumping.

Amy pulled the heavy front door closed and stepped out onto the porch. It was wide and low, only two steps up from the ground, and was furnished with brown wicker rocking chairs and a big wicker swing. Today was going to be another scorcher, but here on the shaded porch, the morning air was still a sweet caress.

"How did you do that?" she asked, sinking down into the nearest rocker. She hadn't yet decided whether to accept the dog, but it wouldn't hurt to know how to control it in case she did.

"My sister," said Wilson. "She gives obedience classes."

He demonstrated the hand signal for "No," "Heel," and

"Stay," and she mimicked them while the terrier sat on its haunches and watched alertly.

" 'Course now, if you don't want him, I can always take him back to the pound."

"Pound?"

"That's where my sister got him. She makes the rounds every month, picks up the most likely ones, trains 'em, then sells 'em to customers who want a good dog and don't care about the pedigrees. She hasn't found a home for ol' Barkis yet."

"Yes, she has," Amy said, surprising herself at her sudden decision. "How much is she asking for him?"

Wilson held up his hands in protest. "No, no, that's okay."

"Don't be silly. I'm sure the pound didn't give her the dog for free."

"Tell you what. Why don't we wait and see if you want to take him back to New York with you?"

His suggestion brought her back to reality. What on earth would she do with a dog in a city apartment? Did Eric even like dogs? She'd never heard him express a desire for one or speak of owning one as a child. King had been too elderly to romp the few times Eric had flown down to the farm with her, and she couldn't remember that he'd ever followed them on their walks. She had come alone the last two or three visits, and King had done little more than sleep at Grandmother's feet, his big head resting on her foot. Old and incontinent, he occasionally forgot to ask to go out in time, and after cleaning up yet another one of his messes, Amy had tried to suggest that perhaps it was time to have the vet put him to a merciful sleep.

Grandmother had drawn herself up sharply. "You're as bad as Martha and Pat. Next you'll be saying it's time to have me put down."

Amy hated that poor old King had died violently, too, but who else would have taken the dog had it lived?

Barkis suddenly jumped to his feet, almost jerking the leash from her hand and barking sharply as an unfamiliar car came into view at the far curve of the long graveled drive.

Her own heart turned into a seesaw when she recognized the driver. Half of it sank in dismay, the other half rose up in the air with shy pleasure.

"Somebody you know?" asked Wilson.

"Yes," she said.

The terrier was going crazy until she remembered to give a firm "No" and the proper hand signal. He silenced, but a low growl deep in his chest let her know he wasn't happy about obeying. She gave the leash back to Wilson and walked down the steps to meet her husband.

The morning sun glistened on Eric's light brown hair as he sprang from the car, put his arms around her, and kissed her with a thoroughness she had almost forgotten, it had been so long. His kiss swept away all the doubts and hurts of the last twenty-four hours and her own lips melted into his.

"I know you said not to come," he said at last, "but I couldn't stand it, knowing what a jackass I'd been."

He buried his face in her hair. "It was so stupid of me, but the guys wanted to celebrate and the time just got away from me. I should never drink anything stronger than beer. Amy, I'm so, so sorry."

She pulled back, looked into his dark blue eyes, and caressed his cheek with her small hand. "It's all right, darling. I guess I overreacted."

With his arm still around her as they came up the steps and out of the sunlight onto the shaded porch, Eric noticed the man and the dog for the first time and looked to her for an explanation.

"Darling, this is Agent Terry Wilson of the State Bureau of Investigation, one of the officers investigating Grandmother's death. My husband, Eric Steadman."

The men shook hands and Eric smiled down at the dog, who

sniffed at his pantlegs and still seemed wary. "I thought lawmen used bloodhounds."

"Agent Wilson thought I needed a watchdog."

"But now that you're here, I guess that won't be necessary," said Wilson.

"He's not staying," said Amy.

Eric started to protest, but she shook her head. "You know you can't, darling. Not with Boston hanging over you. My husband's about to take our videos national," she explained to Wilson. Then, turning back to Eric, she said, "You're getting back on a plane tomorrow morning."

Eric looked at Terry Wilson and grinned. "Is your wife this bossy?"

"Well, my second one was," Wilson drawled. "The third one wasn't around long enough for me to notice."

Before Eric could respond to that, the terrier started to bark again.

This time it was a black pickup truck and the white van from the night before. When the van pulled up behind Eric's rental car, Amy saw that the picture on the side was that of a curly-haired girl who held a slice of bread. She didn't recognize the van driver, but C.W. drove the pickup and her cousin Pauline was with him.

"This here's Jake Johnson," said the woman. "C.W.'s brother-in-law? Frannie's husband? He let us borrow his bread truck last night 'cause they were saying it might rain and Jimmy couldn't find his tarp."

Jake Johnson was small and dark and painfully shy. He bobbed his head during the introductions and squatted down on his heels to pet Barkis, who wagged his stubby tail and allowed the man to scratch his ears.

"Oh, you got you a dog!" Pauline exclaimed, then added piously, "Now if you'd've had him with you last night, you would've known the minute we got here and not been so scared of us."

"An maybe if you'd knocked or rung the doorbell—" Wilson began, but Pauline had already moved on to Eric.

"You're Amy's husband, aren't you? You just get in? I'm her cousin Pauline Phillips. We met at Aunt Frances's funeral, but I don't expect you remember me what with so many others there?"

"Sorry," Eric said, "but I'll remember you now." He turned back to Amy. "What's this about last night?"

"Nothing, darling," Amy said hastily. "I'll tell you later. Right now, you'll be happy to know that they're here to take some of Grandmother's furniture off our hands."

"And I bet we're hindering y'all," said Pauline. "Anyhow, Jake needs to get on back to Garner, so why don't we go in and get started. And, Agent Wilson?"

"Ma'am?"

"You didn't write up nothing official about last night, did you?"

"No, ma'am."

"Good. I wouldn't want Jake to get in any trouble about using his delivery truck."

Eric watched bemused while Amy opened the double front doors. C.W. propped them wide, then he and his brother-in-law began carrying out dining room chairs.

Pauline busily lowered the tailgate on C.W.'s pickup and spread the bed of the truck with old blankets. "I figure this way, we wouldn't have to take the table apart."

Eric and Agent Wilson soon found themselves pressed into service. With Pauline directing and admonishing the whole way, the four men gingerly carried the long table out to the truck and laid it topside down with its legs sticking up in the air.

"Now what about Grandma's dresser up in Aunt Frances's room?" said Pauline.

"I'll speak to Aunt Martha about it," Amy said firmly. "I'll probably give it to her but I want to empty the drawers first."

"I can do that for you. You're gonna need some help anyhow and I'd be glad to lend a hand."

"That's all right. Actually, I was hoping that Miss Pat could come back for a few weeks."

"Pat? Oh, Lord, honey, didn't you hear? She had knee surgery the end of May. She's doing real good, mind you. Started walking without a cane just this week, but she couldn't come back here now. Even with the elevator, it's way too much walking and climbing. If you want me to, I'll ask around, see if I can't find somebody to come do a little cooking and cleaning for you and your husband."

The men were already back in their respective trucks with the motors running almost as fast as Pauline's mouth.

Amy was happy to wave good-bye without correcting her pushy cousin's mistaken impression. Just as well if word passed around the farm that she was no longer in the house alone.

"I reckon I'll go along, too," said Agent Wilson. During all the activity, he had transferred a sack of dry dog food from his car to the porch and Barkis was taking a strong interest in its smell. "My sister didn't feed him this morning so that he'll look to you as his food source."

"How much should I give him?"

"Just follow the directions on the bag. Once a day's enough, and try not to give him snacks from the table, okay? Nice meeting you, Mr. Steadman."

He handed each of them his card, told them to call if they thought of anything useful, then he, too, was gone.

Eric turned to Amy for another long kiss. "Feed your new dog and then let's go upstairs," he said huskily. "I'm a little hungry myself."

CHAPTER
10

The first time Amy returned to the farm after marrying Eric, she found that the single bed of her childhood had been replaced by one that was king-size with a Mission headboard built to order. When Amy shyly thanked her, Mrs. Barbour had smiled. "Frost said that good fences make good neighbors. I myself think good beds make good marriages. At least it worked for Bailey and me."

That strong and willful woman suddenly looked so bereft that Amy had impulsively jumped up and hugged her. Grandmother seldom encouraged physical demonstrations of affection, but she had returned her hug that morning.

"Enjoy every moment of it, my dear," she'd said. "It can disappear on you in the blink of an eye."

Now, lying in her husband's arms, Amy wondered if this were the first blink. She had fallen onto the bed in happy anticipation, fingers eager and busy with buttons and zippers.

And nothing happened.

Heretofore, even though the walls were thick and almost soundproof, knowing that Frances Barbour was next door had always had an inhibiting effect on Eric. But never this complete and utter failure. In four years of marriage, it had, of course, happened before. Usually after too much to drink or when he was on the edge of exhaustion.

"It doesn't matter," she whispered, holding him closely when it was clear that none of her wiles were going to work today. He was always so confident, so in charge, that she found these rare moments of embarrassed helplessness more touching than frustrating.

"I was awake half the night wondering if you'd even speak to me when I got here," he groaned. "And now this! I feel like such a—"

"Shhh," she murmured. "You're just tired. Why don't you take a quick nap while I run over to the grocery store?"

"Maybe I will," he said. "Wake me as soon as you get back, okay?"

It was almost noon when she and Barkis returned from the grocery store near one of the bedroom towns ringing Raleigh, and she had bought enough food to last a week. She found Eric rummaging through the pantry, where he had unearthed several bottles of decent wine, and there was a UPS envelope addressed to her lying on the kitchen counter.

He helped her bring in the bags and unload them on the counter near the refrigerator.

"Ah, peppers, onions, eggs, and cheese! Does this mean I'm cooking lunch?"

"From each according to his ability," she teased. "I'm a better shopper; you're a better cook."

If today followed the usual pattern, there would be no further mention of what had happened (or rather *hadn't* happened) earlier. Eric was himself again, confident and assured and ready to slay dragons for her, if necessary. He poured them each a glass of wine, and while they put away the groceries he questioned her about the night before.

She tried to make it sound like an amusing farce with herself as the butt of the joke, but he was not amused.

"What if it'd been the thief who killed your grandmother?"

"They don't think that was a burglary," she said, and told him what Agent Wilson and Major Bryant had told her, how they now believed that Grandmother had been killed deliberately, either because she wouldn't sell the farm or because someone wanted her money and was no longer willing to wait.

"But you're the only one she left much to," Eric protested.

"I know. They checked where I was the night she died. They even wanted to know where you were."

"Me?" He looked at her sharply. "What did you tell them?"

"The truth, of course. That you were in Washington and I called you there early that morning."

"Lucky thing you were at the symphony that night with your dad and Claire."

"Actually, what was lucky for me was that poor Sam got one of his bad migraines so that they were left with an extra ticket. If I'd been home alone, they'd probably be trying to check our credit card records, see if I bought a plane ticket I couldn't explain."

"I don't like this, sweetheart. I really don't. Come home with me. Let professionals clear out the house. It was bad enough when we thought Frances was killed accidentally. If there's a deliberate killer running around this farm—"

"Then he already has what he wanted, doesn't he? Don't worry, darling. I'll be careful and Barkis will keep me company."

After the groceries were put away, she perched on a stool with the UPS envelope while Eric chopped tomatoes, onions, and green peppers for one of his famous omelets. These last few months had been so busy that they either ordered in or else picked up salads from their corner deli. Now she savored this moment of domestic tranquillity, the smell of onions sizzling in olive oil, the way Eric tucked the tip of his tongue in the corner of his mouth whenever he concentrated on a task, whether it was editing a video or cooking.

He glanced at the envelope in her hands. "What do the O'Days want?"

"It's the sales agreement," she said, scanning the cover letter her attorneys had sent.

"Great! If the police think one of your relatives—"

"Or the broker," she reminded him.

"Or the broker," he agreed. "If somebody's ready to kill to push this deal through, then the quicker it's done, the safer you'll be."

"I have to sign in front of a notary, though."

"That shouldn't be a problem. I'll bet there's a bank near the grocery store." He dropped the diced peppers into the hot olive oil with the onions and stirred briskly. "We can run back over after lunch."

"Or we can wait till tomorrow. I'm sure we'll be needing other stuff."

Abruptly, she remembered that she'd insisted he fly back tomorrow instead of staying here with her. "I mean that *I'll* probably need to pick up a few more things. You're going back to New York."

"Bossy woman!" He held up one of the cherry tomatoes she'd bought at a roadside stand and she opened her mouth for it like a baby bird. At her feet, Barkis watched every movement.

The small red globule, no bigger than a grape, had ripened on a local vine until it was bursting with a tart sweetness unlike anything they could buy in New York.

"Oh, but what about your plane ticket?" she asked, reaching for another tomato. "Don't you have to call and change it?"

"No, it's for tomorrow morning."

For a moment, Amy felt as if she'd stepped down onto a step that wasn't there. "Oh?"

He shrugged. "That was in case you really were too angry to let me in the house."

"And you would have given up that quickly?"

"Of course not, sweetheart. I wasn't thinking clearly so when Lisl—"

"Lisl booked your tickets?"

Lisl Harris was Eric's scatter-headed assistant. Physically angular and uncoordinated, she seemed bright, well-meaning, and detail-oriented, yet she screwed up at least once a week. Lisl always made Amy remember Grandmother's assessment of a yardman she had decided to fire: "Works hard, but not smart." So far, Lisl's pluses outbalanced her minuses, but there were times when Eric exploded and Lisl would flee to the restroom in tears.

"You can't blame her this time. I certainly couldn't explain why I wanted to come down so unexpectedly, could I? Yet your dad and I are supposed to be in Boston tomorrow afternoon. When I asked her to get me a round-trip ticket, she automatically assumed I still planned to make that meeting and set it up so I could fly there directly from RDU. I'll cancel it though and help you arrange for storage and shipping if you'll come back with me the first of the week?"

He swiveled her stool around to give her a kiss and the cherry tomato slipped from her fingers to the floor, where it rolled toward the refrigerator. Barkis gave a happy yip and pounced on it immediately. Before she could stop laughing enough to tell the dog "No!", he had swallowed it down and was ready for another.

Then they both noticed that the skillet was smoking and Eric had to fumble through all the nearby drawers to find a pot holder so he could rescue the sauteed vegetables before they burned.

Somehow they never got back to the question of his return ticket.

After lunch, they walked through the house together, trying to assess the full extent of the job Amy was determined to take on.

Downstairs would be easy enough. Except for a portrait of

Amy at ten and some landscapes that her grandmother had painted after she moved down from the city, there were very few personal items. These were formal public rooms where Frances Barbour had entertained friends, granted interviews to the media, and conferred with her stockbroker, her attorneys, and various business associates before she turned effectual control of the company over to her son-in-law after Bailey died. Eric admitted that the Roycroft furniture worked nicely in this house, but other than a pair of table lamps with panels and shades handcrafted in leaded, opalescent glass that he grudgingly admitted would fit okay in their guestroom, Amy could not budge him.

"We'd have to scrap everything in our apartment and I like it the way it is. I thought you did, too."

"I did. I do. But this is different."

"You can say that again!"

"Tom and Marie said we ought to just move the house itself somewhere else."

He started to laugh, then realized she was not joking. "Sweetheart, you can't be serious?"

"Why not?" She seldom opposed him, but this had her wavering between rebellion and despair.

"It's just not practical." He looked down into her troubled eyes. "These old things really mean a lot to you, don't they?"

Amy nodded mutely.

"Tell you what. Why don't you pick out some of your favorite pieces, enough to furnish say, six or eight rooms? We'll put it in storage and then when we're ready to buy a summer place of our own, we can use it there—maybe somewhere along the Appalachian Trail where it's halfway cool in the summer and there's good climbing. Fair?"

"Fair," said Amy, pleased by his concession. She would miss North Carolina's winters, but not its hot and humid summers.

And anyhow, shouldn't marriage be a compromise? Grandmother always put Grandfather's wishes above her own, as

Claire deferred to Dad, but she and Eric were different—weren't they?—and if he was willing to bend, so could she.

Upstairs presented a different set of problems. Although the east wing was given over to guestrooms, the west wing and landing held the heart of the house. Amy's room was on the end. Next came her grandparents' master suite: their bedroom, separate baths, and walk-in closets that held a surprisingly spartan selection of Grandmother's clothes.

"Grandfather liked to see her in bright dresses, but after he died, I doubt if she ever bought another one. She stopped caring about clothes after he was gone."

A large portrait of Bailey Barbour hung on the wall opposite the bed. He was thirty-two when Frances painted it with such joy and thanksgiving. She once told Amy, "You can't possibly imagine how damn grateful I was to have him home from the war, safe and unscarred in any way."

The portrait was limned in radiance, from the fair hair that fell boyishly across his clear brow to the silver pen in his hand. It was as if he'd been writing in the notebook that lay open before him and had looked up just as someone dear to him entered the sun-drenched study. She had captured a writer's impatient body language at being interrupted in mid-thought, yet the smile that had begun to curve his lips and light his eyes made it clear that he would always forgive interruptions from this person.

"What a great portrait," said Eric.

"You never saw it before?"

"I was never even in this room. And the door was always closed when we walked past. Did she do a self-portrait? It would be nice to pair them for the anniversary promo, don't you think?"

He took another look and said, "Thank goodness you didn't inherit that nose."

Amy laughed. "The Barbour Beak. That's what Grandmother used to call it."

She herself was artist enough to know that the nose lent strength and masculinity to a face that might otherwise have been too weak and pretty. All the same, she was glad Dad's nose gene had proved stronger than Maxie's.

The inner wall of Grandmother's bedroom held a floor-to-ceiling set of glass-fronted bookcases, and each shelf was crammed. One section held first editions of all the Pink and Blue and Max books.

"These we definitely keep," said Eric.

Another section held first editions of their contemporaries.

"Look at this!" he exclaimed. "It's a signed first of Margaret Wise Brown's *Goodnight Moon*."

"Someone gave it to my mother when she was a child," Amy murmured.

"But it's in perfect condition. Almost as if it was never opened or—oh my God! A first of Dr. Seuss's *Horton Hatches the Egg*. With the dustjacket. And look how he inscribed it to Frances and Bailey with a sketch of Horton! Do you know how rare these books are?"

"This is what I've been trying to tell you," Amy said. "There's too much here to let just anyone sort through it. You never looked at the inventory sheets Grandmother's attorney sent the O'Days, but the appraiser he brought in to value the contents of the house for tax purposes lumped all these under the heading 'miscellaneous children's books' and said they were worth about seven hundred dollars."

"*Mike Mulligan and His Steam Shovel*," Eric moaned, pulling more books from the shelves. "*Make Way for Ducklings. Charlotte's Web*. All signed, too."

She dragged him away from the books, through a connecting door that led to a smaller room, one that once upon a time had held a hospital bed and other paraphernalia for the therapy and care of her grandfather after his second stroke. Those things were gone now, and except for a desk and some filing cabinets the room was almost bare. As was the nurse's room across the hall.

"I used to be so scared of Grandfather," said Amy as they passed through. "By the time they let me come back to the farm after Maxie died, he was completely bedridden and pretty much out of it. He always knew Grandmother, but sometimes he'd think I was my mother or his baby sister Martha. The third stroke left him unable to speak clearly and he'd tell me, 'G'wan now, Mashie. Da-da's worring.'"

"Mashie?" asked Eric. "Worrying?"

"Maxie. And not worrying. *Working.* Grandfather once planned to be a serious poet, not a children's writer, and they say Maxie was always breaking his concentration when she was little."

Wide pocket doors at the far side of the sick room opened into a large open landing that ran from the top of the formal staircase to an exterior wall that was all glass, broken by French doors. Across the landing, the wall had been removed to create the space that Frances had used as her studio. When the doors slid back into their pockets, the invalid could see and be seen while she painted.

The bright and airy landing itself was furnished like a lounge, with deep Mission chairs, a low coffee table, and comfortable settles.

The French doors led to an upper terrace lined with brick planters. Normally, the planters would be spilling over with bright summer annuals. Today, only sturdy weeds flourished in the hard dry dirt. If Grandmother had planted flowers before she died, they had long since died as well, and grasshoppers skittered away as Amy and Eric approached.

The wrought-iron patio furniture had begun to flake and chip after a summer in the relentless sun. There was an awning that could be cranked out for shade, but just as no one had watered the flowers here, no one had thought to look after the tables and chairs. An empty hummingbird feeder swung from a hook on the awning supports.

A thermometer on the wall registered ninety-eight degrees. No breeze stirred the surrounding trees, and heat radiated back from the tiled floor. A tractor could be heard in the distance, along with the swoosh of heavy trucks on the interstate highway beyond the far trees, but the heat had stilled even the birds. There would be no flash of red cardinals or bright yellow goldfinches, no burst of song from the mockingbirds, until the sun moved farther down the sky.

The heat didn't bother Amy, and she would have lingered on the terrace to look out over the unkempt grounds to the open fields where tobacco and cotton still grew, but Eric was already moving back toward the French doors and the air-conditioned coolness that had made the South so liveable for non-natives.

After Grandfather's first light stroke, a shaft of stone and glass had bumped out the exterior wall beside the upper terrace, and a small glass-and-steel elevator had been installed from the sun-room below to the large airy attic above so that he and his walker, and later his wheelchair, could access the whole house. To Amy, the glass capsule had been a space ship, a magic carpet, or an enchanted bubble that floated between sky and earth; and when she tired of make-believe, she had her own set of art supplies and a place to work alongside Grandmother, who patiently taught her the basics of color and perspective.

The north-facing glass wall flooded the studio with neutral light, and Frances had continued to work here even after there were no new Pink and Blue and Max books to illustrate. There were easels, a broad drawing table, banks of large flat drawers filled with sheets of drawing paper, racks of canvases, and cabinets full of colored pencils, watercolors, brushes, tubes of oil paint, and acrylics as well.

Eric was familiar with the studio. Indeed, Frances had done a quick pen-and-ink sketch of the two of them in this very room when they were down last Christmas. Amy found it pinned to the easel along with several color snapshots of their faces, and her eyes brimmed with sudden tears.

"Look, darling. She started a portrait of us."

The canvas had been primed, a *terre verte* ground laid down, and the ghostly lines of their faces had been sketched in charcoal.

Eric put his arm around her and gave her shoulder a consoling squeeze. "Too bad she didn't have time to finish it. Why don't you bring it home with you and finish it yourself?"

Amy shook her head. "I'm not a real artist."

"Yes you are. If you'd let yourself be."

"Wishing could make it so?"

"Not wishing," he said gently. "Believing."

They rode the elevator up to the attic, another part of the house that was new to Eric, and mind-boggling in its scope. While the rooms below were orderly and uncluttered, with papers properly filed, books shelved alphabetically by author, and cupboards logically organized, here were confusion and chaos and stacks of boxes that looked as if they'd been hauled up by the movers when Frances and Bailey gave up the New York brownstone and never once opened in all these years. There were boxes marked "Authors Copies" with the specific Pink and Blue title scrawled across the top. Boxes of foreign editions. Boxes with early versions of the plush toys. Boxes marked "Papers / 1930–1935" and "Business corresp. 1948–52."

Piled near the front of the attic were toys Amy had played with as a child: a plastic tub full of blocks, a dollhouse shrouded in plastic, a tangle of dress-up clothes, jigsaw puzzles spilling from their boxes, board games and yard games of every description.

"Wow!" said Eric, brushing the dust from a sturdy yellow road-grader. "You had Tonka toys?"

"And John Deere scale models, too," said Amy. She rooted around until she found the bright green tractor that had been her favorite the summer she was ten. "Grandmother may have had old-fashioned ideas about marriage, but she was something of a feminist when it came to buying me toys."

But Eric seemed to have stopped listening and she saw that he stood dreamy-eyed, with a metal toy in his hands, lost in an old memory. Then he sighed and started to put it back in the box.

"What?" she asked softly.

He gave a rueful shrug. "When I was a little kid, I wanted this road-grader so bad that it was the only thing I asked Santa for that Christmas. With four kids to buy for, it was a real stretch for my parents, but there it was, under the tree when we got up that morning. I couldn't believe it was really mine at first. I played with it the whole Christmas vacation, then the first day we went back to school, Bill, who must have been around four then, sneaked it outside and forgot to bring it back in. He left it in the driveway and Mom backed the car over it. Flattened it like a pancake *and* punctured the tire as well."

"Oh, Eric! You must have been furious with Bill."

"Actually, no. I can't explain it. It was like it was such a neat toy that it was *too* neat. Like something so completely out of reach that it was never meant to be mine. Does that make any sense?"

He so seldom talked of the disparities between their child-hoods that Amy was touched.

"It was the stuff that dreams were made of?"

"Yeah, something like that."

Again he started to set the road-grader back in the box, but Amy stood on tiptoes to kiss him tenderly on the cheek.

"You can have mine," she said.

Eric laughed, but the toy was tucked under his arm when they turned back to the elevator.

He took a final look around the cavernous attic, at the hundreds of decisions waiting for Amy to make, and shook his head. "Okay, sweetheart. You win. Just promise you'll be careful and try to get home before spring, okay?"

CHAPTER

11

They made love more successfully that night.

At least it was successful in the technical sense. Apprehension made them both tentative and Amy was so fearful of hurting Eric's pride again that she faked an early climax, which he was too relieved to notice. While it left her unsatisfied, it did result in a tender and harmonious morning, and she counted that a good trade-off.

As soon as he left to catch his plane, she picked up her recharged cell phone and began working through her list. First came the phone company, which promised a restoration of services by noon. Next was Grandmother's attorney. She made an appointment to bring the sales papers in on Monday morning as her own attorneys had advised, and the receptionist assured her that there was a notary on their staff.

After that, she walked her fingers through the Yellow Pages and asked several antiques dealers to recommend the best appraiser in Raleigh. Not surprisingly, none of them named the one Grandmother's attorney had used when settling the estate; and after a Jacob Grayson was enthusiastically mentioned four times in a row, she phoned him and he agreed to come out Monday afternoon.

"Moving/storage" was next on her list, but she decided to wait and see who Mr. Grayson would suggest.

That left two items: an assistant to help with the sorting and someone to replace Miss Pat on a temporary basis.

In midmorning, she went out to the kitchen for a glass of milk and was startled when Barkis suddenly rushed over to the outer door and began barking loudly. She hadn't heard a car or truck drive up to the house, but she trusted the dog's hearing better than her own and peered out the window in time to see a plump white-haired woman climb out of an electric golf cart parked near the door. She must have driven silently through the fields that adjoined the grounds.

Amy quieted Barkis and threw open the door in welcome.

"Aunt Martha! I was planning to come see you after lunch."

"And now I've saved you the trip. What a nice dog. Hey there, little guy." Her grandfather's younger sister held out a plate wrapped in tin foil and offered her wrinkled old cheek for the obligatory kiss. "Welcome back, honey."

The sugar cookies were still warm from the oven and her great-aunt was quite happy to sit down at the kitchen table and join her for a glass of cold milk. Barkis sat politely on the floor between them, ready to lick up any stray crumbs that should fall his way.

"Paulie told me what she did. Honey, I'm so sorry she scared you like that. Fifty-four years old and there are times like now when I still want to put her across my knee. She wasn't even born when my brothers and I chipped in and bought Mama and Daddy that dining room suit for their twenty-fifth wedding anniversary, but it's been a sandspur in her tail ever since she was a teenager. I wasn't but fourteen myself when the Parkers lost their farm and their furniture got put up for auction, but I used all my tobacco money to pay my share and couldn't buy a new winter coat that year and I guess I must have bragged about doing without once too often when Paulie was growing up. 'Course now, I only did it to try and teach her she didn't need new clothes every time she turned around, but she took it to mean I was owed, so that when Mama died and Frances and Bailey kept the table and all, she's just been waiting for the day she could grab it."

Her cousin Pauline might not have learned the lesson Aunt Martha intended, but she must have absorbed nonstop speech through her mother's milk.

Her aunt broke off a piece of cookie and dunked it in her glass. "I sure didn't raise her to be like that, honey."

Amy heard the shame in her voice.

"It's okay," she said.

"No, it isn't. Frances always wanted what she wanted but she would have given it to me back then except that Bailey wanted it, too, and I'd already got Mama and Daddy's bedroom furniture, her bread tray that she used to make biscuits every day of her married life, and just about anything else I really wanted, and Kate took things, too, things that Curt and his sisters still have in their own houses. The dining room was kind of special to all of us, though, it being their anniversary present, but I couldn't ever say no to Bailey and he was right when he said that none of the rest of us had a house big enough for a table like that. And he and Frances did always have the whole family over for big dinners before he had his stroke so it wasn't like we never got to eat off of it."

"Pauline said that a dresser in Grandmother's bedroom belonged to your mother, too."

"Did she?"

"I'd like to give it to you if you want it."

"Oh, honey, you don't have to do that. Paulie's already helped herself to more than you should have to give up."

"Not at all," Amy said, looking for a tactful way around Aunt Martha's continuing embarrassment. "You'd be doing me a favor. I'm only going to have to find a buyer if you don't. Come on up and let's take a look around in case there's something here that Pauline didn't remember."

When they stepped out of the elevator and onto the landing, Aunt Martha looked sadly at the chairs and coffee table in front of the windows that overlooked the terrace.

"We had tea up here at least twice a week. I'm not speaking out of school, honey, when I tell you that not everybody loved Frances. But I did. She stretched my mind. She was smart, she was from New York, she'd made a lot of money herself instead of having it handed to her, and she read and thought about things besides who had on a new dress at church or who said what on the last Oprah show. And maybe her tongue was a little too sharp at times, but she could've talked ugly as she wanted and I'd still have loved her for the way she took care of Bailey all those years. So awful her getting killed like that. She'd just come back from the doctor and called me and said he'd told her she was good for at least another ten years. I know we all have to go sometime, but I sure do miss her and I guess you do, too."

"Yes," said Amy, her eyes misting.

The old woman looked at her shrewdly. "You don't talk much but you feel things, don't you, honey? I never thought about it before, but you're a lot like Maxine."

"Am I? I don't remember her at all."

"She was real sweet and real quiet."

"Aunt Martha, has there been any talk that maybe Grandmother's death was deliberate?"

"For drugs, yes. Must be like having the devil in your head. So sad."

"No, I meant for personal reasons?"

"Because they were mad at her?"

"Or because she didn't want to sell her part of the farm?"

She was shocked. "Oh, no, honey. Now I know D.C. might've said some strong things about Frances, but—"

"Who's D.C.?"

"D.C. Brown. He's the one took an option on the place. He used to joke about setting the house on fire sometime when she was out, but that was just talk. Besides, I'd been working on Frances about it and I do believe she was starting to come around. No, honey, you just put D.C. right out of your mind. It's one of those dope dealers and they'll catch him one of these days, don't you worry. Now about that dresser. Is it still in Frances's room?"

It didn't seem to occur to Aunt Martha that someone closer to her might also want Grandmother dead, and Amy decided to let it drop for now.

They moved through the lightly furnished room that had once held Grandfather's hospital bed. Upon entering Grandmother's bedroom, Aunt Martha stopped short and her wrinkled face became suffused with love as her eyes drank in the portrait of her brother.

"Oh my goodness! I'd almost forgotten about this picture. There he is, big as life and just as handsome. You don't remember him when he was still able to get around on his own, do you, honey?"

"No, by the time they let me come back, he'd had another stroke and was pretty much bedridden."

"I'll just have to bring you over some of our movies," said Aunt Martha.

"Movies?"

"Bailey gave James a movie camera one Christmas after those Pink and Blue books started selling so good, and right before he died, James had all the movies put on videotape so we could watch them on the television, and there's a lot of Bailey on them. I believe there's even one of you when you were a baby and Maxie brought you down. He was smart, Bailey was. The only one of us to do something besides farm all his life till Curtis William's girls went off to college. Mama was so sure he was going to be a famous poet someday the way he went up to New

York City and started writing for a living and getting his poems in those funny-sounding magazines and such like. And she was real proud of him when he came home from the war and he and Frances thought up those books and made all that money, which maybe it was better than being a poet because I never heard of poets making much money, did you?"

Dazed, Amy could only shake her head.

"He was so sweet, Bailey was. You know, when he came back from the war and they didn't have hardly any money at all except what Frances was making, Mama went up to take care of Maxine so he could write without her underfoot every minute and he never forgot that. Made Mama's last years real comfortable and every time I came over when he was down, I'd get back home and find a fifty-dollar bill in my pocket or stuck in my purse and he'd just laugh and say he didn't do it. I'd watch him like a chicken hawk watching a biddy, but he was so quick and clever-handed I could never catch him out. We did have some happy times after he and Frances fixed up the house and started coming down for a month at the time. I'd've never believed this was the same old house we grew up in. We thought it was so big back then. The folks Daddy bought it from had eight or ten young'uns, and we just rattled around in it but by the time Bailey got through with it, it was even bigger and of course they did do a lot of entertaining—all sorts of people from New York came down, and now here you are back and I reckon the house is going to get knocked down and everything else we knew's going to be gone before we know it."

"Are you sad about that?" Amy asked.

"Oh, heavens no! James and I had us a house down in Beaufort—rental property right on the waterfront, that we always planned to retire to so he could fish every day if he wanted to." Her smile dimmed and she went silent for a moment. "Well, that didn't happen, did it?"

"No," said Amy, reaching out to squeeze Aunt Martha's

hand. She had come down for Uncle James's funeral five years ago. A catastrophic heart attack.

("He was dead before he hit the floor," Grandmother had said dryly. "At least she didn't have to watch him die by inches like we did with Bailey.")

"Paulie and I are going to move down there soon as the money for the land comes through. Practical nurses can work anywhere, you know, not that she'll really need to work. Reckon that's why she came over and took the table. With the leaves out, it'll fit in the Beaufort house."

"What about the others?"

"Well, Paulie's Jimmy wants to get into yard care with C.W. and we'll probably help them get started. Curt's two sisters are living in Raleigh—Jean's still teaching at State and Vera works at the Arboretum—so he and Mary'll buy a house near them. Maybe buy C.W. a house there, too. C.W. never cared a lick about farming. That's another reason Curt was willing for us to sell out. He's about ready to retire and get in some good fishing time himself."

She took a final wistful look at the portrait. "I suppose you'll be wanting to keep that?"

"Yes, but I could have a copy made if you'd like."

"It'd sure mean a lot to me," Aunt Martha said.

Upon seeing the dresser again, Martha confirmed that it had indeed been her mother's. As was the blanket chest in which Amy had hidden.

"If you're certain you don't want them—?"

"I'm certain," Amy said firmly.

They agreed to a time for Pauline and Jimmy to come get the two pieces and headed back downstairs.

"What about Jean and Vera?" Amy asked. She barely knew Maxie's cousins, but she had a vague idea that the three girls had played together as children and had remained fairly close until Maxie's death.

"I'll ask them." Aunt Martha hesitated, then said, "You asked if we were sorry to be leaving here?"

"Yes?"

"Well, there's one thing that *is* worrying us."

"What's that?"

"Herbert Raynor. Pat and Mary's daddy? He's eighty-three and got nothing but Social Security now. And Pat's in the same boat, only she can't draw it for another six years, and yes, Frances did leave her a little money, but she had to have surgery on that bad knee of hers and she didn't have insurance, so that's probably taken most of it."

"No medical insurance?" Amy was horrified.

"Honey, you've got to be working for a big company or the state to get benefits these days and Pat's never worked off. She stayed right here on the farm, kept house for Herbert, worked like a man. She used to help out when Frances and Bailey would give those big house parties and have a half a dozen people staying with them for a week or more till Bailey got to where he couldn't do that anymore and the couple they had living here up and quit just when Frances needed them the most. These last few years, Pat's cooked and looked after Frances, and Frances paid her better'n what she'd get cooking in a restaurant, paid all her Social Security, too, but it wasn't enough for insurance. But Pat'll be all right. Curt and Mary are hoping to get one of those mother-daughter houses with a little apartment on the side for Pat. And once they get a place for Herbert, she can get herself a job.

"And that's the problem. Herbert's old and worn out and his mind's near 'bout gone so he needs to go into a nursing home, but not one of those throw-away places because Mary and Pat won't hear of that and besides it wouldn't be fair, because if it hadn't been for him, the farm might've been lost after Curtis William got killed in the war. Bailey was at the war, too, and then off in New York and James couldn't tend it all by himself. Wouldn't be any land to sell maybe if Herbert Raynor hadn't come and worked like a mule. Curt and the girls say for us to decide and they'll kick in whatever we agree to, if that's all right with you?"

"Certainly," said Amy. "How much were you thinking?"

"There now!" Aunt Martha beamed. "You're surely Bailey's granddaughter. I told the others I just knew you'd do the right thing without blinking twice. Soon as Pat and Mary find a good place, they'll let us know how much it'll take to get Herbert in and what the yearly fees will be. I have to say I don't think he'll go another five years."

With long-standing familiarity, she transferred the cookies she'd brought from her plate to one in the cupboard, then walked toward the door. "I know you have tons of stuff to do, but don't you work too hard and don't you be a stranger. Lord, feel how hot it is! Enough to knock you down, isn't it?"

"Aunt Martha, wait!"

She paused in the open doorway. "Yes, honey?"

"You said there's a video of me as a baby. Does that mean my mother, too?"

"Maxine? Why surely." The old woman seemed puzzled by her eagerness. "Didn't you ever see any of the movies? Your daddy had a camera, too. I remember that first Christmas y'all came down, between James and Jeffrey, it was just like Hollywood—'Lights! Camera! Action!' every time we turned around. You want me to see if I can root them out for you?"

"Oh, yes! Please!"

By now, Aunt Martha was back in her cart. As she leaned forward to turn the key, she said, "Much as you've got to do here, I bet you might could get Mary to come over and help you. She got laid off last winter and I'm sure she could use the work till the land money comes through. If you go see Pat, you might best ask her to ask Mary. Mary can be a little proud about stuff like that. Don't you just love my golf cart? The boys got it for me for Christmas. Better'n a horse, isn't it?"

As she neared the fig bush, she paused and called back to Amy. "You going to use these figs?"

"No, do you want them?"

"I don't, but Curt loves them better than candy."

"He's welcome to them," Amy said.

"I'll tell him you said so. He's too shy to ask you himself and he'd never pick a one without permission, but he kept the bush pruned for Frances and she always let him take as many as he could put up."

Still talking, Aunt Martha drove on past the bush, straight across the back lawn, and headed toward her home on the other side of an open field of corn that shimmered with heat from the relentless August sun.

Amy retreated to the air-conditioned coolness of the house and her amused smile faded as she thought of Aunt Martha's words. Dad had owned a movie camera? Had taken movies of her and her mother down here? And if in Carolina, then surely in New York as well. Where were they and why had she never seen them?

By the time Sam and Beth came along, he had one of those bulky camcorders, which, through the years, kept shrinking until his current model could be easily held in one hand. There were videos of all of them as children—diving into the gifts piled high beneath the Christmas tree, blowing out birthday candles, at swim meets or first day of college, vacation trips.

Every tape was neatly labeled and shelved in chronological order, yet there was nothing from before her mother's suicide.

Why?

CHAPTER
12

If Aunt Martha spent words like a drunken millionaire strewing money in the streets, Patricia Raynor budgeted her speech today as if every word were a withdrawal from a miser's bank account. Grandmother's housekeeper had never been loquacious, and coming so soon after Aunt Martha, who had certainly been chattier than usual, the contrast was even more striking.

On the other hand, thought Amy, it could be that her visit was making Miss Pat self-conscious. Today was the first time she had ever stepped inside this shabby little sharecropper's house on the edge of the farm. And shabby it was: paint peeling on the outside, walls in sore need of freshening on the inside, and while the scatter rugs here in the living room were bright and new, the carpet they scattered across was old and stained. Through the open doorway she could see into the tidy kitchen, where the floor tiles around the sink, stove, and kitchen table had worn right down to the concrete slab they were glued to.

Miss Pat saw her noticing. "No sense fixing up something they're gonna knock down. Least that's what Curt's said the last six years."

Six years ago would have been when rumors first started about ·

the I-40 interchange, but to let the house go like this when his father-in-law still lived here?

"Ain't like Pa's still able to help farm," she said, as if she sensed Amy's criticism of Curt and, by extension, her own sister.

It was a subtle reminder that most farmers these days hired migrant workers and that this rent-free tenant house no longer sheltered an able-bodied man.

Herbert Raynor sat in a recliner in front of the television less than five feet away. He might as well have been in California for all the notice he'd taken of her arrival. He had once been big and handsome; now he was gaunt and stooped with arthritis and he had stared at her blankly when she spoke.

And that was something else she had forgotten, Amy realized, flushing with a self-consciousness of her own. Country people came to the back door, only strangers knocked at the front. If she'd followed Aunt Martha's earlier example, she might now be seated cozily at the scrubbed oak table in the kitchen instead of being treated like company here in the living room.

Miss Pat had brought her a glass of iced tea without asking if it was wanted. She was still tall and unstooped and her softly waved dark hair had only the barest sprinkle of gray, but her face was as leathery as an old baseball glove from all those early years of farm work out in the sun. "I was Pa's boy," she used to tell Amy, proud of her prowess with tractors and their gear, the way she could plow a row straighter than Curt or put a flatbed loaded with sweet potatoes right where it was wanted in the curing shed with fewer backings and haulings than any of the men, the way she could help at hog-killings without going squeamish, or chop a copperhead snake in two when other women shied away.

"Heard you was here," she said.

"Guess you heard about me hiding in the blanket chest, too?" Amy asked ruefully.

A small smile twitched Pat Raynor's lips.

Amy remembered Grandmother complaining once how every little thing she did traveled around the other households on the farm almost before she finished doing whatever it was. Evidently the family grapevine still flourished.

She took a long swallow of the iced tea and its cold sweetness was a welcome treat.

"I've missed your tea," she said. "I don't know what they do differently in New York, but no matter how much sugar I put in, it never tastes this mellow."

"That's 'cause you might as well drink it without sugar than try to sweeten it after it cools down," said the older woman, thawing slightly.

"Is that the secret? Sugar it while it's still hot?"

"That and the water. I imagine they put right much chlorine in it up yonder?"

"You're probably right," Amy said. "You get used to it, but it certainly doesn't taste like the farm's well water."

She had to raise her voice as a burst of raucous laughter blared from the television.

Pat rose and went over to take the remote from her father's hand. She lowered the volume a couple of notches, then put the remote back in his gnarled fingers, all without a word from either of them.

"You seem to be walking all right, Miss Pat. I heard you had a knee operation back in June?"

It was bait few people could resist.

"Why don't we go out to the kitchen where it's quieter? And you don't need to call me anything but Pat now that Miss Frances is gone."

In the next half-hour while Amy picked at a thick wedge of fresh coconut cake, she heard more about what happens in knee surgery than she'd ever hoped to. Miss Pat—Pat, she reminded herself—pulled up her pantleg and displayed the angry red scar that ran vertically from the top of her shin to an inch or so above her knee.

"What they do is cut off the ends of your bones and give you a new metal joint. It's got prongs that they pound right down into the marrow. That's why it still hurts me some at night."

Amy tsked and murmured commiseration throughout the narrative, and it did sound like a painful procedure with a long recovery that required Mary to move in with her for six weeks to take care of her and their father both. "I know you're hoping the other knee never needs it."

"If it needed fixing bad as the first one did, I'd go to the hospital tomorrow," Pat Raynor said sturdily. "I already walk a hundred times easier than I used to. Just to get to the mailbox and back? You can't know how that hurt. Kept swelling up like a balloon, too."

"What was the problem? Arthritis?"

"The surgeon said it was just bone grinding on bone. No cartilage left. Even with the elevator, doing that big house got to be too much. I finally told Miss Frances I'd have to quit but she said she was too old to get used to somebody else's cooking. Said if I'd stay on and fix breakfast and supper for her and do what I could, she'd pay somebody else to do the rest. Mary got laid off about then, so we got her to do the laundry and stuff the regular cleaning woman didn't do. Gave me the same wages as always, too." She shook her head. "I hate it so bad she had to die the way she did."

"You were the one who found her, weren't you?" Amy asked.

Pat nodded. "Mary and me."

Like the story of her knee surgery, finding Frances Barbour's body was evidently something Patricia Raynor had described so many times since the event that she did not have to hesitate and gather her thoughts.

"It was Mary's morning to do the wash so she came by and picked me up. We went in the kitchen door—oh, and while I'm thinking about it—" She got up and took a key from the windowsill. "Here's the key to the back door."

Resuming her narrative, she said, "King was usually there at the door, waiting to go out if he hadn't already done his business on the floor somewhere and wanting to eat, but I didn't pay that much mind because the stairs were getting to be too hard for him, too, and sometimes he'd just wait and come down the elevator with Miss Frances. I went ahead and put the coffee on and mixed up the eggs and milk for French toast, got the bacon started— breakfast was Miss Frances's favorite meal. She'd eat like a bird the rest of the day, but she really did like her breakfast."

"I know," Amy sighed.

"You sure you want to hear this?"

"Yes."

"We drank a cup of coffee, then Mary went up to get the bed-sheets and saw the bedroom door open and Miss Frances not there. Then she saw all that mess in the bathroom and came running down to me and we went looking. Reckon you heard where we found her."

"Yes," said Amy. "It must have been a dreadful shock to you."

Pat nodded grimly.

"Especially since the doctor had just given her a good report on her physical."

"That's what Mary said Miss Martha told her at the funeral. Said she was strong to go another ten years."

"Speaking of Mary," said Amy, seizing the opening, "I know you can't do it, but Aunt Martha said maybe Mary could come over and help me while I'm going through Grandmother's things. Do you think she would? I'd pay her the same as Grandmother did."

"I could ask her," Pat allowed.

When Amy got back to the house, Barkis greeted her as if she'd been gone for years. She checked her messages—Dad had called to voice his displeasure and Claire's disappointment that she wouldn't be coming to New Hampshire as planned, and Eric reported that they'd made it to Boston and were now off to their meeting—then she opened the kitchen door and followed the terrier outside.

Someone had mowed the grass recently, but the perennial flower borders were weedy and grass had edged into beds that were usually bright with summer annuals. Someone had also covered the fig bush at the rear of the yard with bird netting. She lifted one corner and picked a handful of the ripe brown figs to eat as she continued her tour of inspection. Off to one side stood a fifteen-foot-tall Breath of Spring bush. Its long branches drooped to the ground, and she pushed them apart to peer inside. This was where she'd played as a child. It was like being inside a leafy green teepee. She could see out, but no one could see her.

Rounding the bush, she spooked a rabbit. Barkis was after him in a flash and she didn't try to call him back. Let him get the exercise, she thought, wishing it were ten degrees cooler so that she could run with the two of them herself. Just run away and forget about everything waiting for her inside.

Eventually Barkis gave up on the rabbit and came back panting with heat and thirst.

Back in the kitchen, she ran fresh water for them both before heading upstairs, fully resolved to work hard the rest of the day.

Barkis had a different agenda. He yawned widely, then went over to one of the floor vents and lay down with his nose in the cool air.

Immediately off the landing, Grandmother had used one corner of Grandfather's old room as an office, and it was as well ordered as the rest of the house. An electric typewriter sat squarely in the center of the desk. Grandmother refused to have anything to do with computers and she was unswayed by Amy's arguments that e-mail would give instant communication.

"That's why we have telephones," she said. "Anything else can go in a letter."

Letters? A four-drawer file cabinet stood on either side of the desk with a bulletin board on the wall between them. One drawer held the warranties and instruction booklets for everything from the VCR in her bedroom to the sprinkler system for the lawn; a second was devoted to local property tax records, receipts for various house and car repairs, and a miscellany of art supply catalogs and exhibition notices. The other six held a large and varied correspondence

Trying not to let herself get sidetracked by instruction booklets for old kitchen appliances she barely recognized, Amy emptied the first two drawers into a plastic garbage bag and tied it shut. One bag down, only another hundred to go, she thought pessimistically.

The letters gave her serious pause, especially when she found a thick file of notes and letters she had sent Grandmother over the years. Here was a copy of her own birth announcement, then those first shaky attempts at writing, through adolescence when she dotted her I's with little circles. Grandmother had saved every letter from summer camp, every postcard from Europe, all the birthday cards, all the dot-matrix letters from college, right up to the wedding invitation and Christmas cards signed "Love, Amy and Eric."

Virtuously resisting the impulse to dawdle over childhood memories, she put the file in the drawer she'd just emptied and almost immediately came to one labeled "Maxine."

A huge flock of butterflies suddenly erupted in her stomach. (*Oh, Pink! What do you think?*) She'd never seen her mother's handwriting, and now here was a whole sheaf of cards and letters written in a handwriting as elegant as the copperplate one sees in old illustrations. Tempted as she was to sit right down at the desk and read every single one of them, she dutifully put the folder in the drawer with her own letters.

But what to do with all these others? Grandmother usually typed her letters, and it appeared that she'd kept carbons of most of them. The correspondence wasn't just with personal friends, either. Amy recognized the names of early editors and a dozen famous children's authors, some of whom were still living. How could she throw all these away? Yet what would she do with them in New York? And these were just six drawers. There was an attic full of boxes waiting over her head.

Her eyes lifted in despair to the bulletin board above the desk. More paper to sort, she thought drearily: postcards from traveling friends, a snapshot of herself, scraps of paper with phone numbers, a calendar, a small chart that showed the phases of the moon, a sketch of the new cover for *Pink and Blue and Max and the Green Tunnel,* a cartoon clipped from the *New Yorker,* and a letter bearing the seal of a university library in the Midwest. Across the bottom, Grandmother had scrawled "Why not," followed by three question marks for emphasis.

Why not what? she wondered and leaned forward to read the letter.

Afterwards, Amy would say half-jokingly that Grandmother must have been drumming ghostly fingers on the desktop waiting for her to finally look up.

She reached for the phone, was gratified to hear the newly restored dial tone, and carefully dialed the number Grandmother had circled. There was no reason to believe that any academic would be in his office. Not on a Friday afternoon. Not in August. Not—

"Basil Mills," said a voice on the other end of the line.

"Dr. Mills? This is Amy Steadman. I'm holding a letter that you wrote my grandmother back in January to ask if she would consider donating her papers to the university's collection of Twentieth Century Children's Authors."

"Would your grandmother have been Frances Barbour?" he asked cautiously.

"Yes."

"Then please let me offer my sympathies for her untimely death."

"Thank you. But the reason I've called is to ask if you're still interested in her papers."

"The papers of the illustrator and co-author of *Pink and Blue and Max?*" She heard the suppressed excitement in his voice. "We're *very* interested."

Caution reentered his tone. "Are you offering us a chance to bid on them?"

"Not exactly. I was thinking—isn't there something called a permanent loan?"

"There is indeed, Mrs. Steadman."

"And what about restrictions? Some of her letters are from living people. There's probably nothing embarrassing in them, but all the same . . ."

"I understand," he said.

"It's just that there's so much here, I don't know where to start."

Happily, Dr. Mills had been down this road many times before, and Amy listened in growing relief as he explained that his staff would sort, catalog, and archive all the material and that Amy could then come out at her leisure and decide what would be open to the public now and what would have time restrictions.

"Of course, with the way our funding's been cut, Mrs. Steadman, it may take a couple of years, but unless you're in a hurry—?"

"I'm not, Dr. Mills. Not especially. But there really is an awful lot of paper and I couldn't possibly ship it all to you without writing a check to help with the cataloguing costs."

"We never say no to money," he said cheerfully.

He promised to send her shipping labels and said he would start clearing a space in the archives now. By the time she hung up, they were on an Amy and Basil basis and she felt as if she'd made a friend for life. She also felt as if that life was suddenly so much more uncomplicated.

Tomorrow, she'd go into Garner, find an office supply store, and buy shipping boxes and strapping tape.

And having taken care of six drawers of letters in less than twenty minutes, she felt perfectly justified in carrying her mother's file over to the comfortable chair next to the plate glass window overlooking the upper terrace where the light was better.

An hour and a half later, Barkis still drowsed beside the air-conditioning vent and Amy's own eyelids were beginning to droop. She had begun the letters in eager anticipation; she was finishing in bewildered boredom.

The letters were articulate. They described in great detail the places Maxie was seeing, the activities she was pursuing, the people she was meeting, whether it was summer camp as a young girl or trips to visit grandparents—Bailey's mother here in Carolina, Frances's mother and sister out in Ohio—or summer study groups in Europe. But there was absolutely nothing of the girl herself in the letters nor of the woman she became between the first letters and the last. It was all action and almost no reaction; interesting enough as a factual journal of her mother's life, immensely disappointing in illuminating what her mother felt about that life. Of course, it might be that everything personal was said on the telephone. Many of the letters began with "Good talking to you last week/ last night/ this morning."

And there were references to letters that Frances, and more rarely Bailey, had written to her, but no carbons of those letters survived to let Amy piece together the whole relationship.

In the last half-dozen letters, Maxie wrote of her baby daughter. Of me, thought Amy, eagerly reading the comments about her size and weight, of the ounces gained, the first tooth, how much she'd grown. There was maternal love in every phrase.

And yet . . . overall . . . there was still that sense of emotional withholding.

Only once did she catch a flash of something. Evidently Grandmother has wondered about her imaginative play because Maxie wrote,

You ask if she talks to herself or to her toys? Of course she does. Every child does. But I will not repeat the things Amy says nor turn them into anecdotes for your morning amusement. Even though she's not quite three, I respect her privacy and hope that I never violate her trust.

Amy looked at the date at the top of the letter. Less than three months before Maxie shot herself in this house. *And hope that I never violate her trust?* Nice words, Mommy, but where was your concern for my trust when you picked up that revolver?

CHAPTER

13

With the sun casting long shadows across the far edge of the terrace, Amy stared blindly past its tiled expanse to the fields beyond, as the old puzzle gnawed at her heart. How could the Maxie of those straightforward, unimaginative, and unemotional letters become so emotional as to take her own life when she had a little girl to care for and love? A child she'd wanted, according to Dad, and by the evidence of these letters.

Grandmother suggested that she was depressed over Dad's infidelities, yet in none of the letters was there a single negative comment about Dad. Nothing positive either, now that she thought about it. All references to him were as factual as the rest of Maxie's comments: "Jeffrey traded in my Volvo wagon for a Mercedes sedan." Or "Jeffrey and I had dinner at a French/ German/ Italian restaurant. We saw a movie/ went to a play/ heard a concert afterwards." Or "Jeffrey went to bed early; I stayed up to watch *The Late Show*."

Dad said that they had an unspoken agreement that his affairs would be no threat to their marriage. Amy couldn't imagine staying in such a marriage herself in this day and age, but thirty years ago? When Maxie had no desire for a career of her own?

When she was content to be the efficient little wife for a husband who could take care of her family's business so much more capably than she?

"You could run this company if you'd apply yourself."

Amy felt her face go hot in a sudden jolt of recognition that she instantly denied. She wasn't like Maxie at all, she told herself. This was different. Deciding not to take over after Dad retired was her own choice, a choice Maxie had never been given.

And yet . . . if Eric weren't her husband, would she still be saying she didn't want to do it? Would she step aside for Michael or Sam?

She sighed and was gathering up the sheets of stationery to put them back in the folder when something moved on the periphery of her vision. She turned in the chair to see what it was and instinctively recoiled. There, just inches away from her face, was a huge spider. The span of those long thin legs looked to be a good two or three inches across, and she jumped up to find a newspaper or something with which to swat it before she realized it was on the other side of the glass.

It hung upside down in the precise center of a circular web that had to be almost two feet in diameter and stretched from the near rim of the planter box just outside the window to the window itself. A narrow white band of Z's ran down the center of the web.

Repelled and fascinated at the same time, she pushed the heavy chair back so that she could get a closer look. Most spiders she encountered on camping or hiking trips with Eric seemed timid, fleeing as soon as she came close. This one held its ground, unafraid of her nearness, and she was glad for the glass between them. She wondered if it was poisonous. And what if it got into the house? The thought of something that big and leggy crawling around her bedroom while she slept was enough to make her skin crawl.

And yet its colors were strangely beautiful, a velvety black interspersed with bands of bright yellow and clear white. She fetched a strong magnifying glass from Grandmother's desk, but even though she was only a few inches away from those legs and that body, the spider remained oblivious until she accidentally bumped the window where one edge of the web attached. Then it swung around toward the noise.

She drew back. Window or no, she did not want that creature trying to get to her.

The spider waited a moment, then repositioned itself as before.

At that instant, a blue jay swooped down onto the terrace and Barkis rushed over with shrill yips. Startled, the jay flew off, but the spider hadn't seemed to notice even though the terrier's barks were much louder than the clink of the magnifying glass against the window.

Curious, she gave the window a cautious rap with her ring just below the spider.

No reaction. How odd. If it didn't respond to sound, then why had it gone on alert before? Unless—?

She gave a sharp rap in the first spot, where the web was attached to the window.

The spider reacted immediately.

And this time, Amy noticed that the front legs touched a ray of silk that ran directly to the spot she had rapped. Vibrations?

She rapped again. The spider took another tentative step up that particular ray and gave a tug with those front legs. Then, as if realizing the vibration wasn't a natural signal of any sort, it eventually settled back in the center and continued to wait, motionless.

Interesting, Amy thought, and wished that something would bumble into the web so she could watch what would happen.

Of course, this wasn't getting any work done. Spinach before ice cream, she reminded herself and hauled down more boxes from the attic. These were filled with bank statements, canceled checks, and checkbook stubs that went back more than sixty years. Flipping through several at random, she was amazed to see how tiny Greenwich Village rents were in the thirties, how minuscule the utilities. Even so, it took almost every cent of Grandmother's monthly salary to cover just their basic expenses. Sometimes, there was less than a dollar left in the checking account before the next deposit, and more than once she found a statement with a red "Overdrawn" printed across the bottom.

The account was in both names, but deposits from Grandfather's work were sporadic and much smaller.

Out of curiosity, she rummaged for the checkbook that dated back to her mother's birth and was bemused to see that they had paid the obstetrician thirty-five dollars.

Knowing it was morbid, but unable to resist, she found the checkbook for the period surrounding her mother's death. Maxie's ashes had been interred at a cemetery on the edge of Raleigh, and yes, here were stubs for payments to the appropriate funerary establishments.

As she flipped through the surrounding stubs, she saw that a rather hefty check had been written to the live-in couple who had worked for her grandparents. It was dated the day after Maxie's death and was notated "Severance."

That was odd. Amy had always had the impression that the Hahnemanns had just up and quit on Grandmother at the time of her greatest need. She carefully went back through earlier stubs and confirmed that this check must have represented three months' salary.

Now why would Grandmother pay a generous severance to someone who resigned without notice? Yet another question that would probably never be answered.

Trying to get a feel for the circumstances, Amy continued looking. A rather large check to Dad was stubbed "Nanny for Amy." She'd had a nanny before he married Claire?

Something else to add to the growing list of things she couldn't remember.

Three weeks after Maxie's death, Grandmother had hired the first of Grandfather's live-in nurses. There were also checks to a series of domestics, none of whom seemed to have lasted very long. Then, a full six weeks after they decamped, the Hahnemanns had received a second check from Grandmother, again the equivalent of three months' salary.

Bewildered, she quickly skimmed through the stubs for the next two years. She found sporadic checks to Patricia Raynor, who didn't come to work full-time for Grandmother until six or seven years later, but nothing else to the Hahnemanns.

There was only one logical conclusion: either Grandmother had willingly paid them to leave so that they couldn't talk about what they had seen or heard that bloody day, or else they had blackmailed her for their silence.

One more thing she would never know.

Sighing, she stood to go bring more boxes from the attic and gave a casual glance to the spider.

Oh, damn! So much for spinach before ice cream. While she'd worked so conscientiously, the ice cream had, figuratively speaking and mixing her metaphors, gone and melted.

The spider still hung upside down as before, only now it was feeding on something clasped firmly in its front legs, something wrapped head to foot so that she could not make out what it was.

And she had missed the whole thing.

She repositioned her chair so that any movement on the other side of the glass would catch her eye, but as she sorted through another box, the only thing that happened was that the spider finished its meal, ate all the silk off what was now revealed to be a small moth, and let the empty remains fall to the terrace floor.

As twilight entered the house, Amy fixed herself a salad and ate while watching the evening news in the den. Afterwards, she stacked her few dishes in the sink and stepped out into the warm night air with Barkis. A glance at her watch told her that Eric's meeting must have been long over, yet he hadn't called. Or else—?

Annoyed at herself, she remembered setting her cell phone down in the attic this afternoon. Where it still sat.

On the kitchen phone, she punched in the string of numbers that accessed her voice mail and heard Eric's exasperated voice. "Are you okay? Why don't you answer your phone? I've been trying to get you for the last two hours. Call me!"

Immediately, she dialed his cell phone.

He answered on the first ring. "Amy? You all right?"

"Sorry, darling," she said and explained about her absent-mindedness.

"You had me going crazy, you out there alone, no way for me to call you. The operator said that number's still unlisted."

"Isn't it on your Rolodex back in the office?"

"Yeah, but the office was closed by the time Lisl remembered. I was about to call that SBI agent and ask him to drive out and check on you."

"Lisl's there?"

"Um, yeah, we needed her to take notes."

Was it her imagination or had his voice suddenly become more cautious?

"Hang on. Let me key up my Palm pilot and enter that number right now before we forget."

While she waited, she heard music and laughter and voices in the background.

That was the trouble with cell phones, she thought. When telephones were hardwired to walls, the number you dialed had a fixed address, and when someone answered, you knew where that person was. Of course, wireless was easier in some respects. More convenient. One number was all you needed to locate your mate. You didn't have to go through secretaries or hotel clerks or, okay, secretaries. Especially not through dark-haired secretaries bright enough to act scatterbrained and too gawky to arouse a wife's suspicions.

"Okay," said Eric. "Area code 919, and then?"

She read off the number on the phone in her hand, then asked, "Where are you? Sounds like a party going on."

"Just the usual thank-God-it's-Friday in a Boston Irish pub," he said. "I was waiting for you to call before we went on to dinner."

"Sorry," she said for yet the second time. "How was the meeting?"

"Very productive. Your dad had to leave early. Some crisis with Claire, but the liaison guys strike us both as people easy to work with. In fact, their point man's invited me to go rock climbing with his club this weekend."

"Are you going?" To please him, she gamely hiked and camped and braved spiders, snakes, and bears, but rock climbing terrified her. She couldn't do it herself and she couldn't bring herself to watch him either.

"Don't worry, sweetheart. These guys have a lot of experience. It'll be safe. Honest."

"Is Lisl a rock climber, too?"

"Lisl? I doubt it. Clumsy as she is, can you see her on a rock face? Anyhow, she's heading back to New York first thing in the morning. This is just going to be a guy thing. You'd hate it."

"I bet," said Amy.

They talked a few more minutes. Before he hung up, he reminded her that his phone would be turned off most of the weekend since rock climbers can't risk losing their concentration.

"I'll call you when I can, though," he promised.

Don't call us, we'll call you? she wondered.

No sooner had she put the phone back on its wall hook than it rang. Thinking it might be Eric with something he'd forgotten to say, she was momentarily disoriented by Agent Terry Wilson's easy drawl.

"Just thought I'd call and see how you and Barkis are getting along."

"We're fine," she said. "He's right here at my feet. Doesn't want to let me out of his sight, in fact."

"Smart dog," he said, his voice as warm as hot fudge sauce. "You make Mr. Steadman get on a plane this morning like you were saying?"

"Oh yes. In fact I just talked to him up in Boston."

"I was also wondering if you learned anything today we ought to know about?"

"About Grandmother's death?" She thought about her conversations with Aunt Martha and Pat Raynor and the letters her mother had written. "No."

"Nobody planning to move to Beverly Hills on the money y'all are getting for the farm?"

"Not really. Aunt Martha plans to share hers with her daughter and grandson. And Uncle Curtis William's children sound like they're going to do the same."

"Y'all are getting what? A million apiece for each of the three families?"

"Less for them because they signed an option a year or so ago. I think it's more like six or seven hundred thousand for each of the two families. And I know that sounds like a lot, but when you split it that many ways—"

"Yeah, seven hundred thousand just doesn't go as far as it used to, does it?"

"You're making fun of me," she said.

He laughed, a rich, rolling chuckle that made her smile, too. "Naw. It's just that when you've seen guys killed over a three-dollar bottle of fortified wine, that much money sounds like winning the Virginia lottery."

Amy thought about Aunt Martha's intent to move to the coast, of Curt's desire to trade in his tractor for a bass boat, of C.W. and Jimmy's modest plans for a lawn care service.

"I don't know my cousins well enough to say who needed or wanted money in a hurry, but I just can't believe anybody was holding a stopwatch, waiting for Grandmother to die."

"You're probably right," he said agreeably, "but you be care-ful out there and if you hear anything you think I ought to know about, you'll call me, right?"

"Right," she said. Then, before he could hang up, she said impulsively, "Agent Wilson?"

"Ma'am?"

"Did you know that my mother shot herself in this house when I was three?"

"Well, yes," he admitted slowly. "I did hear some talk about that."

"Would there have been any sort of official investigation?"

"Of a suicide with a firearm? Oh, yes, ma'am. The sheriff's department would have taken a close look and there would have been a coroner's inquest, the whole nine yards."

"Are they public records? Could I read them?"

This time his answer came less promptly. "Mind telling me why, Miz Steadman?"

"It's just that no one's ever known exactly why my mother put a bullet through her head and I've spent my whole life won-dering why."

"I can understand how you feel, but, ma'am, the reports aren't going to tell you that."

"Not even if someone—one of my grandparents, or maybe even me—made a statement to whoever was investigating? And what about the couple that worked for them at the time?" She told him of the check stubs she'd found that would seem to in-dicate a payoff for something.

Again a pause. "Tell you what. I'll speak to Major Bryant. See if the case file's still there in the courthouse, okay?"

"Thank you," Amy said.

"Probably won't be till Monday," he warned.

"That's okay," she said. "I've waited twenty-seven years. I can wait two more days."

*   *   *

Twilight had faded to darkness, but there was still plenty of time to sort through more cartons. The phone calls had left her on edge, though. She hated feeling jealous and suspicious of Lisl and Eric, hated the pictures her imagination painted of Lisl in his arms, covering his face with kisses, her deep red lipstick smudging his collar. On the other hand, his tone had definitely been evasive when her name came up, and he had changed the subject as quickly as possible.

Was he sleeping with her? *What do you think, Pink?*

And if he was? *What'll we do, Blue?*

But if they really were having an affair, why would he even tell her that Lisl was in Boston? There's no way she would ever have known unless Dad happened to say something about her. Very unlikely.

Or did he think Michael might add up the evidence? Michael was almost anally detail-oriented, and as a vice president and comptroller of the company, he theoretically okayed all their expense accounts. Was this Eric's way of throwing down a smokescreen in case Michael noticed and called him on it?

Or was mentioning Lisl a Freudian slip of his guilty tongue?

Was this what Maxie had felt with Dad before she knew for sure? He said his affairs hadn't made a difference in their marriage, and maybe knowing was better than this corrosive uncertainty.

But if she did know, what then? She couldn't be Maxie. She couldn't—*wouldn't!*—stay in a loveless marriage. Except that their marriage *wasn't* loveless—not when Eric's hungry kisses still left her breathless and wanting more, not when he still confided in her as he had only yesterday in the attic. How could she possibly just walk away from him when she still cared for him so deeply?

Arguments and counter-arguments circled through her head and there seemed no way to stop them. Certainly going through more boxes wouldn't do it. Her eyes lit on the list of numbers posted on the wall beside the phone. Aunt Martha!

As if reaching for a lifeline, she dialed her great-aunt's number, and when the woman answered, Amy asked if she could run by and borrow the videos she'd mentioned.

"Oh, honey, I haven't had a chance to go through them yet."

"That's okay, I can do that. They're labeled, aren't they?"

"Well, yes, but—" Silence hummed along the line.

"Aunt Martha?"

There was a long sigh. "After I left you, I got to thinking that maybe I shouldn't have said anything about those old movies. If Jeffrey never showed you the ones he made, then maybe it's because he wanted you to just remember the happy times, not go hurting yourself with things over and done with."

"But that's just it, Aunt Martha. I don't remember any of those happy times. I don't remember my mother at all. Or Grandfather, either," she added craftily, knowing how much her aunt doted on his memory. "So if it's convenient, I'll come over now and—"

"Well, actually, it's not. I hate to sound ugly, but we're just sitting down to supper and I'm really too tired to mess with it tonight. How about tomorrow? You can come over here and we'll watch them together. Home movie cameras didn't have any sound back then, so I'll have to tell you what's happening. You get yourself a good night's sleep and we'll all be fresh tomorrow, have us a real matinee. Maybe I'll even microwave some popcorn, all right?"

"All right," she said meekly.

"Now you make sure all the doors are locked before you go to bed and I'll see you tomorrow. Sleep tight, honey."

"You, too, Aunt Martha." Amy hung up the phone, feeling unaccountably disappointed, yet what could she do? Go over and snatch the tapes off Aunt Martha's shelves?

Barkis sat at her feet, his head cocked and a quizzical expression on his face as if he were ready to aid and abet.

She laughed. "That's all we'd need. Bet Pauline keeps a loaded shotgun behind the kitchen door."

Nevertheless, she went around the house checking on her own doors and was disconcerted to realize she hadn't locked the side door behind her when she came back from Pat's. Anyone could have walked right into the house.

Had walked right into the house?

It was a big place. She and Barkis had been back and forth to the attic several times. No way could the dog have heard a door softly opening down here. She looked around the big rooms, at the many closed doors that could conceal who knew what.

Feeling like a timorous idiot, she went back to the kitchen for a sharp knife, then gingerly opened each downstairs closet and invited the little terrier to have a look inside. Tail wagging, he happily obliged, and she sent a mental wave of gratitude to Terry Wilson for bringing her the dog.

She switched off the downstairs lights and they continued the inspection tour through all the rooms upstairs even though she was almost certain that Barkis would have alerted her to any stranger up here. Retrieving her cell phone from the attic, she brought another box down with her, then abruptly decided the hell with it. Let it wait till morning.

She was tired, she was dirty from the dusty boxes, and she was emotionally drained from her calls to Eric and Aunt Martha and her uneasy search of the house. What she wanted now was a long hot soak in the tub and something to deaden her brain.

There was nothing on television, though, so after her bath she plucked a nature guide from one of the bookshelves and carried it to bed with her. Barkis jumped up beside her and settled himself into the curve of her legs. It didn't take her long to discover that her spider was an orb weaver, a Black-and-Yellow Argiope, to be precise. She read enough to learn that all orb weavers have very poor eyesight before her own eyes became too sleepy to continue.

As she reached for the light switch, her cell phone rang. The number displayed on the screen had an unfamiliar area code.

"Hello?"

There was loud static and a droning buzz, then a rapid string of words too garbled for her to tell if the speaker was male or female. She waited to see if it would clear up.

Abruptly the connection was lost.

She tried to remember where 804 was. Virginia? Who did she know in Virginia who would be calling at this hour?

She lay back on the pillow to see if whoever it was would try again. When the phone remained silent, she finally switched off the light and fell asleep.

Out in the hall, the grandfather clock struck ten. Barkis heard it, Amy did not.

Nor did she hear a car come to a silent stop a little past midnight. Deep in troubled dreams in which she inched herself over loose rocks in frantic search for a lost magnifying glass, she slept obliviously until Barkis leaped off the bed and began living up to his name.

CHAPTER
14

In her dream, the rocks became strings of videotape that caught at her legs and ankles while raucous noises blared from a speaker overhead and—

She woke with her heart pounding, her legs entangled in the bedcovers, and Barkis in full throat at the bedroom door.

She switched on the light, grabbed up the cell phone, and signaled for him to be quiet. He grumbled, but he obeyed. Amy eased the door open a crack to listen for sounds of an intruder and the terrier zipped past her bare legs, along the hall to the landing and the main staircase. She hurried after him, switching on lights as she went, and he raced down the wide oak steps, across the entry hall, and pulled up short at the front door, where he began to bark again.

Which meant that whatever he'd heard was outside the locked door and windows.

Adrenaline coursing through her veins, Amy turned on the outside lights and peered through one of the clear slits in the stained and frosted window. Outside on the circular drive sat an old white Volvo sedan, which suddenly explained the garbled Virginia phone call she'd received and probably the crisis with

Claire that had sent Dad home from Boston early, leaving Lisl alone there with Eric.

She opened the door and Barkis was instantly over to the car, growling ferociously.

"*Beth?*"

The window rolled down half an inch.

"Does he bite?" her sister called.

Amy spoke to the terrier and Beth cautiously opened the door and put a blue-thonged foot onto the gravel drive. "God, my shoulder hurts! I feel like I've been driving for a week. Do you know how hard this place is to find? Where's your bathroom?"

"Beth—"

"Or, if you'll hold on to that damn dog, I can just go squat over there in those bushes."

"In here," Amy said and pointed her to a lavatory off the entry hall. "What are you doing here? I thought you were on your way to New Hampshire with the others."

Beyond the half-closed door, Beth said cheerfully, "Nope. New Hampshire's for family members who work for PBM Enterprises. I don't."

"Since when?"

"Since about ten o'clock last night."

The toilet flushed and Beth emerged from the lavatory drying her hands on the seat of her jeans. "Don't you have any guest towels?"

"I wasn't expecting guests."

"Does that mean no food or drink either? I'm starving."

"Does Dad know you're here?"

"No, and it's none of his fucking business. I'm not a child anymore to be told what I can or can't do or when or where or why."

Standing there in the middle of the shadowy entry hall in her cropped top and low-cut jeans, a festive straw bag slung over one shoulder, a gold ring twinkling in her navel, her long brown hair in tangles around her shoulders, Beth looked about sixteen and hardly old enough to be making such declarations of independence. She had been an adorable baby, but the age difference between them had precluded any true closeness. By the time Amy went off to college, Beth had grown into a pouty and difficult preteen, and their roles in the family were set. Amy was to be the compliant and dependable daughter while Beth became the beautiful spoiled princess who expected the world to curtsey and bring her golden apples on a silver tray.

"Ever since he started talking about retirement, he's been impossible. Like the company's going to go down the slop chute if I don't pull my fucking weight. I don't know why I ever let him bully me into working there in the first place."

"The starting salary perhaps?" Amy asked, leading the way to the kitchen.

"Yeah, well, okay, so I got paid a little more than I would've someplace else, but money's not everything and it's not like I'm ever going to have a say in the way things are run."

Money was so Beth's natural element that hearing her diss it was like hearing fish dismiss the importance of water. "You'll have a third of Dad's say when he retires."

"And like that's going to mean anything with Michael and Sam kissing up to you and Eric every time a vote's taken?"

"Michael doesn't kiss up to anybody."

"Yeah, but Sam does."

"Sam's a diplomat. You could take lessons from him." Amy set out bread and lettuce. "Tuna or sliced ham?"

"You wouldn't happen to have turkey, would you?"

"Nope. And no caviar or smoked salmon either."

"You don't have to get smart-assed. I was just asking. Mayo?"

"In the refrigerator. And you still didn't answer my question. Why are you here?"

She filled the coffeemaker with water, spooned coffee into the basket, and pushed the on button before fixing her younger sister with a stern eye. "Beth?"

"I told you. I quit the job."

"Then it seems to me you should have stayed in town and found a new one."

"I couldn't. My credit cards are maxed out, my cell phone's been cut off, and I'm behind on my rent."

Amy's jaw dropped. "How could you be behind? You've only been there two months. And didn't Dad pay the first month?"

"Look, I had to buy furniture, didn't I? And a bunch of new clothes to fit the corporate image, and clothes for Spain, and then, I don't know, it was all gone and there was nothing left for rent."

"You've been *evicted*?"

"Not exactly. I found someone to sublet it for six months. Mom said I could move back home for a while and she was going to give me enough to tide me over, but Dad found out and that's when the shit hit the fan last night."

Claire had been tiding her over one way or another since the moment she was born. Claire was a natural mother and probably should have had a dozen children. Dad, on the other hand, thought four kids were enough, and he had taken the necessary steps to ensure that Beth would be his last. Compensating for the babies she would never have, Claire had babied Beth in a way she'd never babied the boys or Amy, who was four when Dad remarried. From the time she was old enough to think about doing the math, Amy had assumed his quick marriage was because Claire was already pregnant with Sam. Now she wondered if he'd sensed what a good mother Claire would be to a little girl who could no longer remember her own mother. Certainly Claire had been as loving to her as to the two boys.

But Beth had been the child of her heart.

"So the blowup was over the apartment, not the job, right?"

She shrugged. "I guess."

"Okay, first thing in the morning, you're going to call Dad, grovel if necessary, and get your job back. Then you're going to—"

"Like hell," Beth said calmly. "He can go fuck himself."

She rotated her left shoulder, trying to get the kink out, then sat down at the big wooden table and took a bite of her ham sandwich. "Is that coffee ready yet?"

Amy took mugs from the cupboard and poured them each a cup. She brought sugar for Beth and set out the skim milk.

"No half-and-half? No, wait. I bet I know the answer—'No half-and-half and no crème fraîche, either.' Right?"

"Why are you here, Beth?"

"I told you why."

"No. I mean why come to me?"

"Hey, you're my sister."

Amy raised a skeptical eyebrow.

"Look, I'm broke, I don't have a job, all my worldly goods are out there in the car, and I don't have a place to live right now. You're down here trying to empty out this mausoleum by yourself, right? I need a job, you need help. It's a fit."

"You want to work for me?"

"Not *for* you, *with* you."

"No."

"C'mon, Amy. I really can't go crawling back to Dad right now."

"It won't work," she said. "*You* won't work."

"Yes I will. I promise."

"It's just scut work, anyhow, taping up boxes, filling out shipping labels."

"I'll do anything. Hey, I'll even do your laundry or scrub toilets, if that's what it takes to get you to say yes."

Beth scrub toilets? That would be the day. And yet, despite the surface flippancy, Amy sensed something genuine in her need.

"What's really going on here?" she asked.

Beth wouldn't meet her eyes.

"Beth?"

Her sister's head came up defiantly. "I think I may be pregnant."

"Think?"

"I'm nine days late."

"Aren't you on the pill?"

"Yeah, but I forgot to renew the prescription."

"Did you do a pregnancy test?"

"Three of them. The first one said no, but the other two were positive. And I've never been late in my life."

"Oh, Beth."

"Don't look like that. It's not the end of the world. I just need a place to crash till I decide what to do about it."

"Do about it?"

"Have an abortion or become a welfare mom. Those are my main options at the moment, aren't they?"

"What about the father? That guitarist?"

"Hugo?" She gave a sour snort. "Not in a million years."

"But you said you loved him, you asked Dad to give him a job, you wanted Eric to make a place for him in the video division."

"Oh, shit, Amy. That was just to twist Dad's tail. Hugo was fun to play with, but I'd never tie myself to such a loser."

"Except that you have."

"Like hell. In the first place, I don't necessarily plan to go through with this. And in the second place, even if I do, he's never going to know about it. I dumped him over a week ago. He's history." She looked at Amy beseechingly. "But I can't tell Dad and I really don't know what else to do. Please, Amy?"

With everything else to deal with—Eric, the house, Aunt Martha's odd behavior—coping with Beth was the last thing she needed. And yet, this was her sister.

Her pregnant sister.

"It's only for two or three weeks," she warned.

A relieved smile spread across Beth's pretty face. "Thanks. You won't be sorry, you'll see."

To demonstrate her reformation, she jumped up, put away

the sandwich makings, rinsed out her coffee mug, and wiped off the counter.

"Okay," said Amy as she unplugged the coffeemaker. "I guess we can give it a try. Go get what you need out of the car and we'll find you a bed."

At the doorway, Beth paused. "I should be worth twenty-five an hour, don't you think?"

"They're probably paying six-fifty at McDonald's."

"You'd pay your own sister minimum wage?"

"Plus free room and board."

"Okay, fifteen an hour."

"Ten."

"Done!"

"And the clock stops every time you do," Amy said sternly.

CHAPTER
15

Whether it was because the kitchen was at the opposite side of the house from Amy's bedroom or because Barkis had slept as soundly as she after getting Beth settled, Amy was surprised to go down to make coffee the next morning and find a blue pickup parked at the rear of the back yard. A man in jeans, tan work shirt, and an Atlanta Braves ball cap sat on the porch steps smoking a cigarette, a large black dog at his feet.

She opened the door and both man and dog came to their feet.

Barkis bounded out and immediately began to growl protectively, claiming his rights as resident canine. The black dog could have made two bites of the terrier, but he was mannerly enough to concede that this was indeed the smaller dog's territory and that he was just a visitor here himself.

"Good morning," said Amy. "May I help you?"

"I'm your cousin Curt," the man said shyly, resettling his cap. His hair was iron gray and his face was deeply tanned from working in the fields all summer. "I don't reckon you remember me, but Aunt Martha said you sent word about the figs?"

"Yes, of course. Let's see . . . you're Frannie and C.W.'s father, aren't you?"

"Yes, ma'am, and I'm real sorry about him and Paulie and Jimmy scaring you like that the other night."

"I'm pretty sure they didn't mean to," Amy said diplomatically.

"All the same, it won't right. C.W. said for me to tell you that if you need anything hauled to the dump, he'll be glad to take it for you. And if you need anything heavy moved, him and me can do that, too."

"That's very kind of you. I may take you up on it." She was both touched and amused by this country way of making amends. "I was about to pour myself a cup of coffee and pick a few figs for my breakfast. Can I pour you one, too?"

"Oh, that's all right. I wouldn't want you to go to any trouble."

"No trouble at all," Amy assured him. "What do you take in it?"

"A little milk would be nice, if you've got it."

"Be right back," she said.

By the time she returned with two mugs of coffee and a bowl to hold her figs, the dogs were romping together at the edge of the field and Curt was pulling back the net that covered the fig bush. She set the mugs on the tailgate of the truck and helped him open it up enough to let them get to the fruit.

He drank from the mug Amy offered him, set it back on the tailgate, then took a bucket out of the cab of the truck and began to pick. The sun was barely up and the big leathery fig leaves were still damp with morning dew. Amy knew it would be hot and steamy later, but here at sunrise it felt good to be outside.

She soon filled her bowl and poured it into his bucket.

"Aw, now, you don't need to do that."

She ignored his protest and said, "I met Frannie's husband

when he came over with Pauline to pick up the table. What's she up to these days?" Not that she really cared, but it would be rude not to ask. Frannie was five or six years older than she and well into boys and makeup by the time Amy started coming to the farm again, so they were never close. Especially since Grandmother did not encourage it. Grandmother still thought Mary had been presumptuous in naming her Frances without first asking.

"Not out of love for me," Grandmother had said, "but for my money."

From something Aunt Martha had said at the funeral, Amy suspected that the hundred dollars Grandmother had left "to my namesake, Frances Barbour Johnson" had been taken more as an insult than a bequest.

Precisely what Grandmother had intended, no doubt.

"Her and Jake live over in the edge of Raleigh. They've got just the one boy, Mike. He'll be starting at East Carolina next month. Going to study business, they tell me. I guess you never had no children?"

"No. Not yet, anyhow."

"That's right. I keep forgetting you're a lot younger than Frannie and C.W."

As they picked, Curt's shyness wore off a little and he offered comments on the weather, the size of the figs, and the recipe he used to preserve them.

With the two of them picking, it didn't take long for the bucket to fill.

"I reckon this is all I can use," he said after a while.

"Too bad you can't dig up this bush and take it with you," Amy said, biting into another sweet ripe fig.

"If I thought it'd live, I'd surely try, but I never had no luck growing figs of my own. Aunt Frances now, she just stuck this one in the ground back here and it took off like it had a rocket under it. She was a real willful woman, won't she?"

"Indeed," Amy said dryly. "I guess you'll be sad to leave and see all this go under."

"Naw. I'm ready. Been ready for a couple of years now. Be different if C.W. or Jimmy wanted to farm. Or Frannie's boy. But they don't. Farming's on the way out in this part of the state. Time to let the land do something different." He sat down on the tailgate and cupped the coffee mug in his big hands. "We do appreciate it that you're going to let the sale go through."

Amy shrugged. "I'm just sorry Grandmother held you up for so long."

These last couple of days had opened her eyes to what the sale meant to the rest of the family and she felt obscurely embarrassed that Grandmother had so disregarded the situation. Would she be alive now if she had acceded to the wishes of the others and agreed to sell?

"Well, now, as it turns out, it didn't hurt to wait," her cousin said. "The option we signed gives us about twice what we first got offered when we heard the interchange was coming."

"I've heard that the broker was getting a little desperate."

"D.C. Brown? Maybe a little bit." He took another swallow of coffee and cleared his throat awkwardly. "Aunt Martha says you think maybe it won't somebody on drugs that killed Aunt Frances. She says you think D.C. had something to do with it."

"I only asked if she thought it was possible."

"Is that what the SBI thinks?" he asked doggedly.

"They're pretty sure it wasn't a burglary." She repeated what Major Bryant and Agent Wilson had told her Thursday night. "There was silver, there was art, but they didn't take anything. And they walked right past Grandmother's sleeping pills, so they weren't really after drugs either. They think she was killed either for the land deal or for her money."

"Well, now," Curt said. For the first time, his eyes met hers squarely and shrewdly. "If it was for her land, that'd put it on us down here. If it was for her money, though . . ."

"Yes," Amy agreed. "That would put it on us in New York."

"They tell you which way they're leaning?"

"No."

He sat silently for a moment, then handed her back the mug, and whistled to his dog, who came running and jumped up in back. He slammed the tailgate shut.

"I thank you for the figs. I'll bring you over a jar when they're done."

"That'll be nice," said Amy.

"And don't you worry, shug. It may be they're way off base on this."

"I hope you're right," she said.

He was clearly ready to go, but Amy was reluctant to let him leave now that they had achieved a measure of ease. "Were you here when my mother died, Curt?"

"Naw." He pulled his cigarettes from his shirt pocket and patted his pants pockets for his lighter. "Naw," he said again, still not meeting her eyes. "I was housing tobacco that day. Me and all the kids. We didn't know nothing about it till we saw the sheriff's car come by."

He turned away to spread the net back over the bush and she took one side to help him get it up over the tallest branches.

"Who *was* here that day?" she asked.

"In the house?" He bent to weight the edge of the net down with a brick. "Best I remember, they said it was just Aunt Frances and Uncle Bailey, that German couple that worked for them, and you. Straightaway, soon as it happened, Aunt Frances called Aunt Martha and she came right over and took you to her house."

"She called Aunt Martha before she called a doctor or the sheriff?"

"Won't nothing neither of them could do for Maxie at that point, was there? I reckon she was thinking about you."

So the out-of-sight/out-of-mind forgetting started that very first day, thought Amy. "You and my mother were about the same age."

He nodded cautiously.

"Were you friends?"

"Like did we talk a lot? Can't say as we did. She was close with my sisters when they were girls. After she was grown, and they were off, she sort of kept to herself when she'd come visit."

"That German couple, the Hahnemanns—"

"Yeah, that was their name. I was trying to remember."

"They packed up and left the very next day, didn't they?"

"Yeah, I drove 'em to the train station myself."

"Did they quit or did Grandmother fire them?"

He shook his head. "I couldn't rightly say because *they* didn't say. Aunt Frances told everybody later that they up and quit on her and couldn't get away fast enough, but I remember Mrs. Hahnemann cried all the way to Raleigh, like she was sorry to be leaving."

He finished weighting down the edges of the net so as to keep the birds out, then stepped up into his truck. "It was a sad time here, shug. Took Aunt Frances and Aunt Martha a long time to get over it. Aunt Frances is gone now, but Aunt Martha's still here. I hope you ain't going to get her all upset again. I can understand how you might like to know every little thing, but it ain't going to change what happened, ain't going to bring Maxie back, is it?"

"I'll try not to upset her," Amy promised, "but I think I do have the right to know. I can't stop asking questions about Maxie's suicide any more than I can stop asking why Grandmother was killed."

Curt resettled his Braves cap on his gray head and turned the key in the ignition. His clear blue eyes met hers. "I guess you got a right to ask, but you might not like all the answers you're gonna get."

He eased off on the brake and moved slowly down the driveway. Amy and Barkis watched till the blue truck was out of sight.

*   *   *

By the time Beth struggled out of bed, bleary-eyed in an over-sized T-shirt that featured a band Amy had never heard of, Amy had already made a run to an office supply store in Garner.

"You feeling okay?"

"My shoulder's still stiff and I couldn't get to sleep for hours," Beth grumbled. "Too goddamned quiet. No horns, no sirens, how the hell do you stand it? Any coffee left?"

It was almost an hour before she reappeared in shorts and an-other cropped top, her tangled brown hair brushed to shining smoothness and tied back in an off-center ponytail. "So where do you want me to start?"

"By calling Claire."

"No."

"You have to, Beth. You know she'll be going crazy, worry-ing about you."

"Then she shouldn't have sided with that asshole."

"Either you do it or I will."

"I don't have the number there and I'm not calling his cell phone."

"It's on a pad by the wall phone in the kitchen."

When Beth came back upstairs a few minutes later, she said, "Okay. It's done."

"The others get there okay?"

"I didn't ask. And the call's on your clock, Bosslady. What's next?"

"Books." Amy handed her a three-pack of knocked-down shipping boxes, strapping tape, and a marker. Carrying more boxes herself, she led Beth into her grandmother's bedroom. "We're shipping all the Pink and Blue and Max books to the of-fice, so you can box them up first. The others are signed first editions and they—"

"Oh, wow!" said Beth, standing amazed in front of the por-trait. "*That's* Bailey Barbour?"

"Didn't you ever see any pictures?"

"Yeah, but in the photographs, he's just an okay-looking

middle-aged guy. I never knew he was such a hunk." She walked around the big room touching books and opening drawers with childlike curiosity. "How about a quick tour first? I almost got lost getting down to the kitchen this morning."

"Right," Amy said. "I keep forgetting you were never here."

As she explained the reason for Grandmother's open studio, it occurred to her how oddly different their childhood summers had been. The lake house was the only vacation spot the four of them had in common. Michael occasionally visited his father's people in Chicago, and the aunt who'd raised Claire on the Jersey shore would sometimes invite Michael and the younger two for a week in August, usually when Amy was down here so that Claire and Dad could get away together, but she herself had always come alone to Carolina every summer until she was old enough to have other interests. Grandmother was punctilious about sending them money at Christmas and for all their various birthdays, but otherwise concerned herself not at all with the other children, so, yes, of course this was the first time her sister had ever been in the house.

Because it was on the same end of the house as her own room, she had given Beth the room that Bailey's nurse had once used.

"And this is my room down here at the end."

"Nice bed for a kid," Beth commented slyly.

"Grandmother *did* come to the wedding," Amy reminded her.

They passed the grandfather clock and started down the steep end stairs.

"Is this where she was killed, or by the other staircase?" Beth asked.

"This one."

"Good thing you're not superstitious." Beth gave an exaggerated shiver. "Where did Max do it?"

Amy paused in midstep. "I don't know."

"Huh?"

"No one ever talked about it, at least not in front of me. And they didn't like it if I asked questions. I always assumed it was in her bedroom, one of the guestrooms on the other side of the house." She shook her head in bewilderment. "I can't believe I don't know something as basic as that. It was almost five years before they let me come back, though. They wanted me to forget and I guess I did."

"You don't remember anything about her?"

"Nothing."

"Not even her funeral?"

"I doubt they let me go."

"Weird," said Beth. "I can remember lots of things from when I was three."

"What things?" Amy challenged, nettled.

"Sam's birthday party when he was seven, for starters. That scary clown? And *Runaway Bunny*. I saw it there on your grandmother's bookcase. You used to read it to me."

"I did?"

"Don't you remember? When you and Mike used to baby-sit Sam and me? I always wanted you to read *Runaway Bunny* before you turned out the light because it was like a promise that Mom would be there in the morning."

"I remember baby-sitting and playing games, but not reading to you."

"Well, you did, so maybe it's not that nobody's telling you stuff, maybe it's just that you have a rotten memory."

They passed through the formal rooms downstairs and Beth said, "Cool furniture."

"You like it?"

"Yeah, I sort of do. I thought the house would be full of delicate antiques, but this is real. What would you call this style?"

"Mission oak or Arts and Crafts. Most of it's Roycroft. Made near Buffalo near the end of the eighteen-hundreds. There are books in the den if you're interested."

"I like the lines, but I'd ditch the yucky brown cushions. Do them in rich purples and blues and emeralds."

Amy frowned. "Prints?"

"God, no! Solids. In a coarse weave. Maybe hopsacking?"

Amy half closed her eyes and visualized it. Beth was right. Slipcovers for the old leather cushions wouldn't hurt the integrity of the pieces and would make them much more inviting. "Eric said I could keep some of these things, put them in storage till we find a place in the country."

"Generous of him," Beth said.

Amy flushed, but didn't rise to the bait. "And here we are back in the entrance hall. Sunroom past the arch, kitchen through there, service stairs to the guestrooms, pantries, laundry, and a small suite for the live-in couple they used to have. And here's where I let you get to work." She pulled car keys from her pocket and Barkis looked up alertly. "My aunt's going to show me some films from when Maxie and I used to visit."

"You're going to leave me here alone?"

"Barkis will keep you company."

"But I want to see the films, too. See what everyone looked like back then."

Barkis edged closer.

Dog and sister were looking at her so beseechingly that Amy caved and picked up the leash. "Oh, come on then."

She didn't bother with a purse, but Beth grabbed hers, a straw bag clearly bought with Spain or Sam's place in Mexico in mind, pulled out a pair of designer sunglasses, and slung the bag over her shoulder. "Want me to drive?"

The sturdy Volvo Dad had bought her for college after she wrecked her sporty little convertible was crammed front and back with clothes and suitcases and shopping bags full of the things she'd planned to transfer from her apartment back to her old room at Claire and Dad's place.

"Or maybe I'll drive," Amy said.

She opened the rear door for Barkis, who jumped in and im-

mediately stuck his head between them as if not to miss a word
while they drove.

"Did you recall seeing any cans of old films around the house?
Aunt Martha said Dad once owned a movie camera."

"Nope. Just videotapes from his camcorder. Didn't you hate
it at Christmas when we had to wait outside the living room
door till he was in position before we could see our presents?"

"And birthdays." She clicked her seatbelt and turned the ignition key. "Half the time the candles burned down into the
icing before he'd let us blow them out. Remember that time he
had you lean over to blow out the candles and your hair caught
fire?"

"Oh, God yes! You know what? We ought to sneak the tapes
out and get Eric to do a montage of birthday cakes through the
years for his next birthday."

"You plan to be talking to him by then?" Amy asked, glancing over at Beth with mock innocence.

"Yeah, yeah, I know what you're thinking. He's still a tight-
assed bastard, though." She pushed the terrier's face out of hers
and settled back into the seat. "This aunt of yours. Was she
around when Max shot herself?"

"On the farm? Yes. Not in the house, though."

"All the same, I bet she knows where it happened. Why don't
you ask her?"

CHAPTER

16

By golf cart across the fields, her aunt's house was only five or six minutes away. Driving the car meant going past several other farms to the end of the road, then taking the next two rights to reach the neat white clapboard house.

Aunt Martha seemed flustered when Amy rapped on her back door, but professed herself glad to see them both.

"Come in, come in! If you can squeeze through all this mess."

The "mess" consisted of half-filled movers' cartons that neatly lined one side of the kitchen and continued down the central hall to the bedrooms, where more cartons could be seen through the open doors.

"Paulie and I have started getting ready to move. Lord, the stuff that's accumulated in this house! I don't know how you're ever going to get through all of Frances's things. You don't need to tell me who this is. We met at the funeral, remember? Isn't this sweet of you to give up your vacation and come help your sister? Oh, Amy honey, don't worry about your dog. He's fine. The cats already had all they wanted, you know how picky cats are—oh my, he *was* thirsty wasn't he? No, no, you don't have to apologize. If it's on the floor, it's fair game. Let me get him some more water. Hot as it is, you don't want him getting dehydrated, do you? There, now! Let's all go into the den. I've already put in the tape of the first summer Frances and Bailey came after he gave us that movie camera. Just move that pillow if it's too much, honey. Let me see now. Paulie usually works the VCR, but I think if I . . . no, that's not . . . ah, here we go!"

From the faded colors and washed-out features that flickered across the television screen, Amy could tell that the original film had deteriorated almost past saving by the time it was transferred to video. Nor had Uncle James possessed a steady hand while filming. Nevertheless, she sat entranced as Aunt Martha narrated.

"That's me with Mama in front of the house when we were waiting for Bailey to get there. That's Pauline I'm holding, she wasn't even a year old. Can you believe I was ever that skinny? And there's your Aunt Kate, my brother Curtis William's widow? You remember her, don't you, honey? That's right, she's only been gone six or seven years. Somehow it seems longer. Those are my brother's children, Beth—Curt and his two sisters. I can never tell which girl's which in these films, they're just little towheaded Barbours, aren't they? Running around barefooted, nothing but shorts and shirts on. Kate had her babies like stairsteps. Not but eleven months between Jean and Vera. Can you believe that? If Curtis William hadn't got killed in the war, no telling how many she'd've popped out before it was over. And, look! Yonder comes their car. After those books started selling, Bailey bought himself a nice new one every year. Let me think now. It was the summer of 'forty-nine, so Maxine would have been ten. She and Curt were both born in the spring of 'thirty-nine. Wasn't she the cutest little thing? Paulie looked just like that when she was ten. Aw, look at that. Isn't that sweet how she comes over and kisses Mama and me and wants to hold the baby. Oh, and there's Bailey! So, so handsome, don't you think? And see how pretty Frances was. Kate and I, we always felt we were the country mice for sure when she came down from—"

They were interrupted by excited yips from Barkis out in the hall, followed by a crash of breaking glass and loud hisses.

Amy reached the hall door first and saw the dog standing in one of the half-filled cartons and trying to get to the cat that spat at him from atop a narrow bookcase. In jumping up to that safe spot, the cat had knocked over one of several small glass vases grouped at the end.

Apologizing like crazy, Amy grabbed the terrier's collar and pulled him into the den. "I am so, so sorry. I hope that vase wasn't something of your mother's?"

"Now don't you give it another thought," said Aunt Martha, coming with a portable hand vac to clean up the broken glass. "It was just a dimestore thing that we were thinking to put in our yard sale. When we're ready to move, Paulie's going to put an ad in the paper, 'Century Farm Moving Sale,' which is not a lie because the farm *has* been in the family more than a hundred years though of course not everything we're selling's been on the farm that long. But people from Cary and all those fancy houses over past Clayton? You wouldn't believe what they'll pay good money for."

Amy fastened Barkis to a railing on the back porch. They returned to the den and after a couple of tries Aunt Martha got the tape back to where the animals had interrupted them, and soon they saw adults lazing on the swings and rockers of the shady front porch.

"That was before Bailey got the house air-conditioned. And I still don't know but what air-conditioning's more trouble than it's worth. Seems like people have more summer colds than they used to, coming in and out of the cool so much. Makes the heat bother you more, too, don't you think? Since we got ours, I sure don't get out in the garden like I used to. And nobody sits on their porches anymore. Bailey must've been holding the camera then, 'cause there's James putting Paulie on her pallet. Paulie fusses at me every time she sees that, us putting one of Grandma Johnson's handmade quilts on the floor for her to spit up on, but how'd we know people would start calling them folk art and pay hundreds of dollars for old quilts like that?"

"Where's Max?" asked Beth after several minutes. They hadn't seen her since the arrival scene.

"Oh, she was always off playing with Jean and Vera or else watching grass grow. That's what Bailey called it. In fact, I believe it's along about here . . ." She fast-forwarded the tape, ran past where she meant to stop, rewound, and then began to play the tape at normal speed. "Bailey sneaked up on her here. She must've been a million miles away."

Young Maxie sat cross-legged on the grass beneath a large shady tree, her back to the camera, and she seemed to stare intently at the ground before her. To Amy, there was something touching in the tilt of the little girl's head as she leaned over the patch of sand. Occasionally she would pluck something from the ground and carefully place it on the sand.

"What's she doing?" Beth asked.

"Playing with doodlebugs or ants. She could sit like that for hours, talking to herself the way children do, only she was real quiet, never talked out loud, just sort of whispered to herself. Bailey did love to creep up on her and hear what she was saying. Some of it was so funny he'd put it in their storybooks."

At that instant, the child seemed to realize she was being filmed. She jumped up from the grass and with her bare foot brushed away whatever she'd been watching. Bailey must have told her to smile. Amy recognized that phony expression of happiness from years of being told the same thing whenever Dad picked up his camcorder. The screen went briefly white, then picked up again with a Christmas that didn't include the New York contingent.

"That's all for this tape. And I couldn't find any more of them till Maxine was about sixteen."

Again, it was a summer arrival scene and the colors were somewhat sharper.

"That's Paulie sitting on the steps. Look at that precious snaggle-toothed grin! She turned six and lost both her front teeth, all in the same week."

Amy's great-grandmother Virgie no longer stood to welcome her firstborn home. Instead, she had become a fragile old woman who had to be helped out of the door and into one of the porch rockers. But Bailey was vigorous and truly movie-star handsome as he stepped from the car in a pale blue nylon shirt that was unbuttoned at the throat.

Frances and Maxie both wore plaid Bermuda shorts and crisp white sleeveless shirts, with the collars turned up in the back, à la Elvis. Frances had better legs, though, and as the two came past the camera (Uncle James had developed a steadier hand) to greet those on the porch, her face was flawless, while Maxie's skin had erupted in teenage acne and her Barbour nose seemed much more prominent than before.

The camera swung around to the driveway at that point and Uncle James let his lens linger on the new Cadillac's sleek tail-fins while Bailey casually lounged against the front fender and lit a cigarette, then lifted his head and laughed into the camera, his white teeth flashing and those blue eyes glinting in the sunlight.

"There now," Aunt Martha sighed as the screen went white.

"Yeah," said Beth with a sigh of her own.

More fast-forwarding through a high school football game, and there they were again, the whole family, jammed in around the big dining table that Pauline had tried to remove Wednesday night. The camera panned across each face, lingered on the huge Thanksgiving turkey, and caught Bailey as he stood at the head of the table with carving knife and fork. There was only one quick glimpse of Maxie in a red turtleneck sweater.

"I'm afraid that's all till you were a baby," Aunt Martha apologized. She took another tape from a nearly empty shelf above the television set and put it in the player. This snippet of film had been shot on the terrace outside Grandmother's studio. Spring flowers overflowed the planters and the adults sat around a large glass-topped table. The chipped and rusting iron patio chairs were new and gleaming white in the film.

"Oh my God!" said Beth. "Disco Daddy in a powder blue polyester leisure suit? With *sideburns?* We have *got* to get a copy of this!"

And then Maxie walked through the French doors onto the terrace. She wore a very short, very tight yellow minidress that set off a sexy figure, and her shoulder-length blonde hair was flipped up at the ends. Her face glowed and she was almost beautiful as she held her baby up to the camera.

"And there you are," Aunt Martha said triumphantly.

Amy leaned forward eagerly. "Could you go back and put it on slow motion?"

Her aunt obliged, and Amy savored this first sight of her grown-up mother moving and smiling and showing off her baby, then dropping a light kiss on the baby's forehead—*My forehead!* Amy marveled—before tenderly placing the baby in the crook of a man's arms. When she stepped back, the seated man was revealed to be Bailey Barbour.

But what a change.

"Bless his heart," Aunt Martha said sadly. "This was after his first stroke. About ten years after Mama died and they'd fixed up the house. See how the side of his face is pulled down a little? It never did come back right. Not all the way. But he could walk with a cane and his mind was still sharp as ever. Frances did think you were so precious. See how she takes you away from him? And that's where you started crying 'cause you were hungry."

Again Maxie stepped into the picture and reached for her baby.

"Frances thought it was common of her to breast-feed you, but it was coming back into style then and they do say it's better for the baby, don't they? Of course, women were more modest about it thirty years ago. Maxine always took you off to their bedroom, not like Jimmy's wife. That Ethylene, she just pulls it out wherever she is like it's nothing more than a thumb to suck on. Embarrassed me half to death the other Sunday when the preacher was here for dinner."

The camera followed as Maxie walked back into the house, the top of Amy's tiny head just visible above her shoulder before the picture went to black.

Even with all the rewinding and fast-forwarding, the entire showing had taken less than forty minutes.

"That's all?" Amy asked. "I thought you said there was a lot of footage of my mother. And of Grandfather, too."

Aunt Martha gave a helpless shrug. "I thought there was, but I was wrong, honey. It got to where James just didn't carry the camera over when your folks came because they had one of the first video cameras. I reckon you're on some of our videos, but that was long after Maxine was gone, so you wouldn't be interested in those. Oh my goodness! I just realized: I never offered y'all a single thing to eat or drink, did I? Where on earth are my manners? And I said I was going to make popcorn. Beth, honey, what can I get you to drink?"

Before Beth could answer, Amy, who had spent enough time in the South to know that this was the polite equivalent of Here's-your-hat-what's-your-hurry?, said, "No, thank you, Aunt Martha, we should be getting back anyhow. Thank you for taking time to show us these films. May I borrow these three and let my husband make copies? I promise I'll get them back to you."

"Well, I don't know. I sort of hate to let them go. Tell you what. Vera's husband is who got them put on video. I'll tell him to make you copies, okay? With all you've got to do, you don't need to be worrying about maybe getting these tapes mixed up with things you're packing up over there. It'll be my Christmas present to you. How about that?"

"Wonderful," Amy lied.

At the back door, she retrieved the dog, but as her aunt

stepped aside to let them leave, she suddenly paused and handed her the leash. "Excuse me, Aunt Martha. I thought I could wait till I got home, but I'm afraid I'm going to have to use your bathroom. And sorry, Beth! I didn't mean to stick you with my purse all afternoon."

She pulled the straw bag from Beth's shoulder. "Oops! Wait a minute, it's caught in your hair."

She bent forward, pretending to free Beth's hair, and mouthed to her sister, "Keep her talking!"

Then she turned and headed back through the kitchen. "Be right back."

Earlier, when she was pulling Barkis away from the cat, she had noticed that one of the open packing cartons in the hall held a pile of videos. Most were musicals—*The Sound of Music, Seven Brides for Seven Brothers, Gigi,* and at least a half-dozen old Fred Astaire–Ginger Rogers movies. But there were also several labeled by hand: National Geographic specials, a Billy Graham revival, and yes, yes, *yes!* two more tapes labeled *Dad's Movies.* The date on one of them covered the year Maxie killed herself.

Without a second's hesitation, Amy grabbed up the tape, shuffled the ones remaining so that there was no obvious gap, slipped down to the bathroom, flushed the toilet, and stuck the tape in Beth's purse.

When she returned to the kitchen, Aunt Martha had a guilty look on her face as she handed over the dog's leash.

"Thanks again," Amy said, kissing her soft cheek.

"I'll be talking to you real soon," Aunt Martha promised. " 'Bye, Beth, honey. It was real good seeing you again."

"What was all that about?" asked Beth, grabbing her straw bag as soon as they were back on the road. Without waiting for an answer, she opened it and looked inside. "Well, I'll be damned. You stole a tape from that trusting little old woman? *You?*"

Amy nodded sheepishly.

"Gimme five!" Beth crowed. "There's hope for you yet."

"Thanks for keeping Aunt Martha distracted."

"You should thank me. She told me where Max killed herself, and you were right. It was in her and Dad's bedroom."

"Which was where?"

Beth shrugged. "Soon as she heard the toilet flush, she changed the subject. Said we ought not to talk about it in front of you."

CHAPTER
17

As soon as they reentered the house, Amy went straight to the VCR in the den, popped in the tape, and fast-forwarded it past people she didn't know until she came to familiar faces.

A much younger Aunt Martha beamed as she placed a birthday cake in front of a little boy who held up six fingers. Waiting with cake server and plates was Pauline, already a good twenty pounds overweight.

"Who's that?" asked Beth, sinking down into a nearby chair.

"Aunt Martha's daughter, so that's probably her grandson Jimmy."

The camera focused on that threesome during the singing of "Happy Birthday" and the blowing out of the candles. Again the boy held up six fingers. Almost immediately, the camera swung around to a toddler who sat in a high chair and held up two fingers of her own.

"There I am," said Amy. "Two years old."

"Cute," said Beth.

"And there's my mother."

Looking relaxed and happy, Maxie leaned forward to help Amy drink from a cup. Pauline put some cake on the high-chair tray and Amy watched her infant self poke her fingers in the cake, take a taste, then offer some to her mother.

The camera shifted back to the birthday boy and remained there the rest of the scene.

The movie camera's novelty appeared to be wearing thin for Uncle James, who evidently no longer filmed day-to-day events, only milestones and festivals. After the summer birthday came Christmas scenes peopled only by Aunt Martha's immediate family, followed by an Easter Egg hunt for the children of a local church, then here came Aunt Martha with yet another cake for Jimmy.

It appeared to be late summer and the table was spread under a shade tree outside this time. Instead of adults, several children crowded around the table for a real party, and all were dressed like cowboys, complete with vests, hats, holsters, and cap pistols. In the midst of them was Amy, who wore a little cowgirl hat and a fringed leather skirt with matching vest. Like the others, she lifted her cap pistol in the air and fired it when Jimmy blew out the seven candles.

Except for a brief pan of the adults when the cake was being brought out, Uncle James had kept the camera on the children. Using the rewind and slow-motion buttons, Amy eventually located her parents and froze the frame so that she could examine them in detail.

Maxie wore a sleeveless green dress. Her lips were parted in laughter. Dad stood beside her and he, too, was laughing.

"Look what he's holding," Amy said. "A movie camera."

"Look what *you're* holding," Beth countered. "Better not let Michael see this tape."

"Why?"

"It's probably the last documented time any of us ever held a toy gun after Max shot herself. Michael held a grudge for years about his cap pistols."

"I don't understand."

"When Dad married Mom, Michael was what? Eight? And he

had a nice pair of cap pistols that Mom threw out because Dad didn't want pistols of any kind in the house. They told him you were terrified of guns, that they gave you nightmares, and if he would please be a good boy and never mention them in front of you, Dad would buy him any toy he wanted. Michael was sorry your mother shot herself, but he didn't see why he had to give up those neat guns because of it."

"He told you that?"

"Oh, yeah. I heard about Max as soon as I was old enough to understand that you and Michael and I had different parents. Sam and I were always warned not to talk to you about her but we pumped Michael for everything he knew. Those damn cap pistols *always* came up."

Bemused, Amy shook her head. "If I ever had nightmares about guns, that's something else I've forgotten."

On the screen, the tape moved, molasses-like, past the adults and back to the children. She watched her three-year-old self galloping around with the others, shooting away till the air was blue with smoke. At one point, a bigger child tried to take her hat and they got into a shoving match that ended with Amy pushing her down.

"That is *so* not you," said Beth.

"What do you mean?"

"I never saw you get physical about anything. You barely fight with words."

"Three-year-olds aren't known for verbal skills," Amy said mildly, yet even as she spoke, she realized that her words only confirmed Beth's low opinion of her assertiveness.

The sequence ended as abruptly as all the others, and she ran the tape back to Maxie and Dad again. According to Dad, the three of them had come down for their usual summer visit. A month later, Grandfather's second stroke brought them back to Carolina while he stayed in New York. A few days after that, Maxie was dead.

She stared at the figures on the screen and wished she could step into the frame and ask her mother why. What happened in that short six weeks to change her from this laughing woman into a woman who would put a gun against her head and pull the trigger?

With a sigh, she fast-forwarded the tape through two Christmases in a row. The first was over at Aunt Martha's and was attended by only her family and Aunt Kate's. No sign of Bailey or Frances. The second Christmas was here. Both her grandparents had aged years. Bailey came to the festive table in a wheelchair, and she didn't need audio to know that he must be slurring his words. His left hand curled uselessly in his lap, and when the camera circled the table after Curt Junior had carved the turkey, she noticed that Grandmother was cutting up the meat on Bailey's plate. There were dark circles under her eyes, and although she appeared to be carrying on a cheerful conversation with the others, passing bowls of vegetables and cranberry relish, to Amy's eyes she looked tired and sad.

Well, God knows she'd had enough to sadden her in the last year, between Bailey's physical deterioration and Maxie's death. The rest of the tape held nothing of interest to her and she pushed the rewind button.

"So what was so bad about those two birthday parties that your aunt lied to you about it?" asked Beth.

Amy shook her head. It bothered her, too, that Aunt Martha would try to keep her from seeing them. "I almost feel like calling Dad and asking him where his home movies are."

"Yeah, right," Beth jeered. "Like he'd tell you over the phone when he's never mentioned them all these years." She sank back lazily in the comfortable old Mission chair and propped her feet on the matching stool. "Why don't you fly up and search the apartment before they get back?"

Amy smiled at the absurdity of that.

"I'm serious. You have a right to know."

"Or I could wait till they get back to ask him," Amy said lightly. She got up, ejected the tape, and put it back in its box.

"I don't expect the films to tell me anything about Maxie's state of mind. But maybe they could help me remember her."

Beth yawned and stood, too. "He probably dumped them when he married Mom. I certainly never saw them around. What are we doing about lunch?"

"I'm not hungry, but there's salad and sandwich stuff in the refrigerator. I'm going back to work."

Yet, once upstairs, Amy did not go immediately to the stack of boxes awaiting her. These last few days had aroused so many conflicting emotions that she longed to escape from the squirrel cage her mind had become, to put heart and brain on idle, to become like the spider that hung upside down outside this window, thinking nothing, content merely to be.

She found a sketch pad in Grandmother's studio, sharpened a drawing pencil, and went out onto the terrace to take a closer look at the creature from its top side. The glass walls faced north-northwest, and although the far end of the terrace was in sunlight most of the day, the area next to the house was always shaded. Today was even hotter than yesterday. Happily, a light breeze made the terrace not only bearable but almost pleasant once her body adjusted from the air-conditioning inside.

Thanks to that book last night, she knew that orb weavers had bad vision, poor hearing, and did not willingly leave their webs. Emboldened by the knowledge that this spider would not be leaping off the web and into her hair or face, she pulled a patio chair close to the web and looked carefully at all its separate parts before she put pencil to paper.

Since walking out of the final exam for a required biology class in college, she had not given a moment's thought to the anatomy of arachnids; but that field guide had dredged up some of the old terminology, and she now recalled that unlike insects with their clearly defined head, thorax, and abdomen sections, spiders had only two: an abdomen and a fused head and thorax, where the eight legs were attached. Only, now that she looked closer, this spider seemed to have a fifth pair of legs, much shorter than the others, on either side of what would be its head.

Now that can't be right, she thought. Spiders are arachnids. Arachnids have only eight legs, not ten.

She laid down the sketch pad and slipped back into the house to retrieve the book from her bedside table. There was a simplified diagram in the front of the book. Okay, not legs but "pedipalps."

She looked from the diagram to the spider itself, fixing the names of the body parts in her mind. The tapered abdomen had black-and-yellow markings, while the shorter front segment—the cephalothorax—was creamy white. Yellow and black banded the long thin legs.

She picked up the pad and began to sketch. As she drew, her thoughts turned inevitably back to the tape she had just watched. She had come south hoping to figure out where she was going, to find answers to where she had been. Instead, she'd found only more confusion, more questions. Eric and Lisl would have to wait. At the moment, her head was filled with that last glimpse of Maxie at Jimmy's seventh birthday party. The little cowgirl outfit that she'd worn. The cap pistols.

Dad had made Michael give his up. To help her forget how Maxie died?

Had she really come back from Maxie's death with a horror of guns? A horror that led to nightmares?

Her pencil moved across the paper as if it had a mind of its own, while these new bits of information reeled through her brain.

Odd that she had never noticed the household ban on toy guns. Her pencil sketched the outline of a revolver, the long barrel, the little sight guide at the tip, the trigger and trigger guard, the plastic handle with its rough texture that was meant to simulate bone. She closed her eyes, tried to feel the weight of the gun in her hand, the smell of gunpowder.

Into her mind floated a disconnected image.

"Bang-bang, Mommy!"

"Bang-bang, Amy!"

An adult's index finger extended toward her to form a mock gun barrel as Amy giggled and pointed her gun to fire back. "Bang-bang, Mommy!"

The terrace door opened, scattering the synapses of memory.

"No wonder you didn't hear me calling," Beth said impatiently. "Why are you sitting out here in this heat?"

Her eyes fell on the huge spider. Startled, she hastily stepped back and half closed the door. "Jesus, Amy! Get away before it jumps on you!"

Irritated by her sister's interruption at the very moment of remembering, Amy snapped, "It doesn't jump and it's not poisonous. What do you want?"

"Well, excuse me!" Beth snapped back. "There's a woman downstairs. Says she's your cousin Jean. You don't want to see her? Fine. I'll tell her to leave."

She slammed the door and stomped away.

Sighing, Amy rose and hurried downstairs.

Beth was nowhere in sight, but a slender woman with short gray hair stood in the entry hall. She wore a turquoise silk shirt knotted at the waist above white cotton slacks and straw sandals, and she smiled as Amy came down the steps.

"Amy? Oh my goodness. They said you grew up beautiful and they didn't exaggerate."

Amy held out her hand to the woman, who exuded an air of brisk competence. "Jean?"

"Jean Barbour, honey. Your mother and I were first cousins. I'm your Aunt Kate and Uncle Curtis William's middle child."

"Yes, I know. Your brother was here this morning. I was trying to remember when I last saw you. Not at Grandmother's funeral?"

"No, and I was so sorry to miss it, but I was on sabbatical in Brazil then. Vera E'd me and I should have written you, but I'm awful when it comes to the social niceties."

"Not at all," Amy said inanely and gestured toward the sunroom that lay immediately under the upper terrace. Waist-level banks of clear windows on all three sides flooded the room with light, and it was furnished in comfortable brown wicker sofas and chairs that complemented the Arts and Crafts decor of the other rooms on this level. "Please, won't you have a seat? Can I get you something to drink?"

"Water would be great."

Out in the kitchen, Amy saw that Beth had left her plate and glass on the table, alongside some open books on Roycroft furniture. The dirty dishes didn't surprise her, but the books did. Evidently Beth wasn't blowing smoke about liking the furniture.

When Amy returned to the sunroom with a pitcher of ice water and two glasses on a tray, Jean Barbour stood by the east windows, looking out across the grounds.

"Sad to think all this is soon going to be paved over for another shopping mall."

"You're the first one who's said that. All the others seem to be glad."

"Probably because they've had to live out here and wring a living from the land," Jean said with a wry smile. "It's those of us who left a long time ago who can afford the luxury of regret."

Amy poured a glass of water and Jean Barbour held it up to the window before drinking. "A simple thing like pure well water from the ground. It'll soon be gone, too. Nothing but treated reservoir water with no more individuality than the parts per million of chlorine or fluoride." She gestured toward the sketch pad Amy had dropped on the table. "You have Maxie's interest in spiders?"

"I didn't know she had an interest. This is one I found on the upper terrace. I never looked at any up close before."

"They fascinated Maxie. Spiders, dirt daubers, potter wasps. She could watch them for hours."

"Really?" Amy sat down on a nearby chaise and tucked her legs beneath her.

"Oh, yes. We were going to be the female American equivalent of Fabre."

"Who?"

"J. Henri Fabre? The great French entomologist?"

The name meant nothing to Amy. "Sorry. I majored in art. What did he do?"

"He was a high school teacher, but when he retired, he bought a little place in the country and spent the final thirty-odd years of his life observing the insects and spiders that lived around him. Nobody had really done that before—just sat and watched a single insect over several seasons to see how and what it did. His observations filled about ten volumes before he finally died in nineteen-fifteen. Maxie had some of the translations, and when I was ten and Vera was nine, she read us passages that so captured our imagination that we spent the next six or eight summers documenting the insects and spiders around the farm. She had us raising caterpillars to see how they pupate and emerge from the chrysalis. If it hadn't been for your mother, Amy, I don't know if we'd have even gone to college, much less made careers in science."

"Aunt Martha said you teach at State?"

She nodded. "Entomology. And Vera's a plant pathologist at the Arboretum. Maxie opened our eyes to what was around us, and as soon as she said she was going to become a biologist, it made me want to be one, too."

"But she never did."

Jean's face clouded. "No. She never did."

"Why? If she loved it, if she studied it in school—?"

"I used to wonder if she didn't choose biology for all the wrong reasons: not because it was the love of her life, but because it was so far from the art and poetry of Aunt Frances and Uncle Bailey. Can you remember Uncle Bailey before the last strokes?"

"No."

"Too bad. He was one of those larger-than-life men, like Byron or Keats must have been. There was something magnetic about him, a way of making your world seem brighter or more glamorous just because he was in it. Women adored him, especially the women of this family—Grandma, Aunt Martha, Aunt Frances. Even my own mother used to say she wished she'd met Bailey before she met my father."

"Not you, though," Amy said shrewdly.

"And not Maxie. Or so she said. Of course, part of her problem was that he so seldom turned his charm on her. I always thought that Aunt Frances and Uncle Bailey were so wrapped up in each other that they had no room for Maxie. They were golden and they made her feel like lead."

"That's not why she killed herself, though, was it?"

"Ah," said Jean, glancing over to the drawing pad. "I wondered about that gun."

"This feels like my last chance to finally know once and for all. After the house is gone, there'll be nothing left of her. If you were her friend—?"

"I'm sorry," Jean said. "I'd tell you if I knew, honey. Vera and I have gone around and around about it, but it's all speculative."

"Was she so terribly unhappy?"

"I didn't think so at the time." Jean hesitated. "Did you know that your mom and dad had marital problems?"

"That he had other women? Yes."

"Did you also know she was planning to divorce him?"

"*What?*"

"He was cheating on her," Jean said. "Had been for ages."

"I know. Grandmother told me that a few years ago, and Dad admitted it last month, too. But he said that the women didn't affect their marriage and that Maxie knew he'd never leave her."

Jean rolled her eyes. "Of course he'd never leave her! Give up what he had? Frances and Bailey could turn a blind eye as long as he stayed married to Maxie, but if he divorced her for someone else, that would make it a matter of family pride and he'd have been out on his ear. Maxie almost left him once before, but he whisked her off for a second honeymoon and she came home pregnant with you."

"She stayed in an unhappy marriage because of me?"

"I don't think it was unhappy, at least not for the first couple of years after you were born. He was sweet with you, attentive to her. She thought he'd changed, but he hadn't. He just got a little more discreet. But she was through looking the other way. She was going to divorce him and then go back to school, become a nature writer."

"She wanted to write?" Amy was bewildered. "They always said she wasn't creative."

"They were wrong," Jean said flatly. "She showed me some of her essays and they were really good—clear, insightful, even a neat little touch of humor between the lines. She never told anyone else because she was afraid they'd make fun of her—your dad, her parents. She said it was something of her own, something Aunt Frances and Uncle Bailey couldn't take."

" 'Couldn't take'?"

"The way they took Pink and Blue away from her. Those first stories grew out of personalities *she* had given the stuffed animals."

"No," said Amy, who had grown up hearing how Grandfather had been so amused by the way Maxie chattered to her toys that he had created adventures around them.

"Yes," Jean said inexorably. "In the beginning, Uncle Bailey just parroted them back, but she didn't care. She was just happy that he'd written them down in letters addressed to her. She thought it meant that he loved her and that she was special. Then he came home from the war and the new stories weren't for her. They were for other kids—for money— You never knew any of this?"

Amy shook her head. "I mean, I knew the books started with her toys, but Grandmother always said he wrote the stories so

Maxie would have something to remember him by in case he was killed."

"Oh for God's sake!" Jean said. "He was never in any physical danger, although you'd never know it to hear Aunt Frances go on and on about how frightened she was the whole time he was gone. That was the two of them playing out a Grade B movie. He was the handsome, sensitive hero who goes off to save the world and she was the brave and beautiful heroine he's left behind to cherish his memory. My dad was a plain and simple dirt farmer who knew how to shoot a rifle and he was killed in the landing on Guadalcanal. Uncle Bailey knew how to type, so they gave him a staff job well behind the lines."

Amy was dumbfounded. All her life she had pictured those letters as written from a foxhole between bursts of mortar fire and machine guns.

"Anyhow," Jean continued, "Maxie had it all worked out in her head. She'd already applied to a couple of schools and she planned to speak to a lawyer when she got back to New York. We were sitting right here in this room the last time I saw her. You were asleep on the sofa there with your head in her lap and she looked down at you and said, 'Amy's the best thing that ever happened to me, Jean. If I don't do this, if I can't gain my own self-respect, then I'm not fit to be her mother.' A week later, she was gone."

"You must have been stunned when you heard she'd shot herself."

"Yes and no," Jean said slowly. "Her relationship with Aunt Frances and Uncle Bailey? It was such a love/hate thing. She tried to pretend she didn't care, but I think she really needed their approval. I couldn't help wondering if she'd told them what she planned to do and they shot down those dreams, too. Maybe they threatened to cut her off financially. Or to side with Jeffrey in a custody battle over you."

Distressed, Amy remembered how dismissive Grandmother had always been of Maxie.

How Maxie had always been blamed for being a child, as if her interruptions had kept Bailey from becoming a serious poet.

How Dad had said, "I think you and Bailey were probably the only two people Frances ever loved."

How even those pristine children's books in Grandmother's bedroom bore mute testimony to Dad's assessment, books signed by their authors "For Maxine Barbour—Hope you enjoy it!" Unlike the raggedy old much-read and much-loved books Claire had read to Beth, Sam, and her, those books were in such mint condition that it was clear they'd never been read to Maxie.

Jean set her glass back on the tray and leaned over to touch Amy's hand. "I'm sorry, honey. Maybe I shouldn't have spoken so bluntly."

"No, I'm glad you did. It's the first halfway logical explanation I've heard yet. Poor Maxie. I guess no one ever really loved her for herself alone."

"Not true," Jean said gently. "You loved her, Amy. Completely and unconditionally. And that did make a difference. If she could just have held on for a little longer . . ."

They both sighed for all the might-have-beens and Amy squeezed her cousin's hand. "Thanks, Jean."

"Any time, kid." Then, with returning briskness, she glanced at her watch and stood up. "I'm probably keeping you from things you need to be doing, but Aunt Martha said you'd asked her to ask Vera and me if we wanted anything from the house?"

"Sure." Amy jumped to her feet. "Down here or upstairs?"

"Upstairs, unless it's been moved. There was a writing desk in Maxie's old room that had a secret compartment. That's what Vera would like unless it was something you were going to keep?"

"Oh, no, I'm glad for her to take it." The desk was in her room at the moment and Amy had always liked the secret compartment, too, but if the piece had special meaning for her mother's cousin, then better it go to her.

Together they walked up the wide curving staircase to the landing.

"As long as you're here, let me show you my spider," Amy said, crossing over to the terrace window. "See?"

"Ah, yes. *Argiope aurantia*. Have you fed her today?"

"Fed her? No. How would I do that?"

"Simple," said Jean and stepped out onto the terrace.

Past Grandfather's old room, through the open door into Grandmother's room, Amy saw Beth slide a handful of books into a carton and reach for another. She had been busy in the last half-hour and that section of shelves was almost empty. Now she gave Amy a wary look across the width of both rooms.

"Jean's going to feed my spider," Amy said, offering a flag of truce. "Want to see?"

"Yuck!" said Beth. Nevertheless, she put down the books and came to watch.

The older woman had gone down to one of the end planters that was overgrown with weeds. She studied the plants intently, then they saw her hand dart out.

"Got it!" she called triumphantly. Upon seeing Beth, she said, "Hi, again."

Amy performed belated introductions and Beth said, "What's that you caught?"

"The arachnid equivalent of a Big Mac." She held a small green-and-brown grasshopper by the head with one hand and gently teased open its two strong hind legs till they were fully extended up over its back. Then, holding the insect by those two legs so that its front legs wiggled futilely, she approached the web.

"The trick is to entangle the grasshopper's legs enough so it's caught, but not to disturb the web so much that we scare her off."

She leaned forward and deftly, delicately gave a half twist of the insect against the web so that its front legs were held by the thin filaments. As soon as she released the back legs, they automatically kicked and they, too, were trapped.

The spider was instantly alert, and when the grasshopper kicked again, she raced across the web and seized it with her front legs.

"Oh, my God!" Beth gasped. "Look at that!"

From tiny tubes at the pointed end of the spider's abdomen, it was pulling a sheet of silk at least a half-inch wide with its back legs, looping the silk first around those strong kicking legs, then around the doomed insect's whole body until it was cocooned in white silk.

"Now watch," said Jean. "When she bites it, she actually injects a venom that paralyzes the creature, then some digestive juices to dissolve its internal organs. Argiopes can't do much chewing, so the food has to become liquid."

"You keep calling it 'she,' " said Amy. "How do you know it's female?"

"The size for starters. Males are much smaller. But the pedipalps are the real giveaway."

"Those two things near the head that look like short legs," Amy told Beth.

Jean grinned. "Very good, class! In males, the tips are clubbed." She made a fist to illustrate.

"Why?"

"Well, if you were one of my students, you'd probably say he has a permanent hard-on."

"Huh?" asked Beth.

"They don't mate like mammals, you know. When the male is sexually mature, he deposits his sperm on a little web, sucks it up in his pedipalps, and then goes looking for a female. At that point, he's nothing but a single-minded sperm delivery machine."

"I've known guys like that," Beth said darkly.

"Anyhow," said Jean. "You should feed her once a day if she hasn't caught anything on her own."

"That's so cruel," Beth objected.

"You a vegetarian?"

"Well, no, but—"

"Ever visited what's euphemistically called a chicken process-ing plant?"

"That's not the same."

"It sure isn't," Jean said cheerfully.

They reentered the house and Amy headed down the hall. "The desk is in my room now. I'll show you."

Beth followed. "Amy and I were wondering, Jean. Which room was Max's?"

"Why, this one," said Jean as Amy opened the door to her room.

"No," said Amy. "Beth means the one where she and Dad stayed when they came to visit after they were married."

"This one," Jean said again. "It's the only room she ever used."

"But that's crazy," Amy said. "After all the trouble they took to make sure I would forget everything, why would Grand-mother give me the room where my mother killed herself?"

"She didn't," said Jean. "Where did you get that idea?"

"Aunt Martha." She turned to Beth. "That *is* what she said, right?"

Beth nodded. "I asked her if Max did it in her bedroom and she said yes."

"Really?" Now it was Jean who looked confused. "I always thought it was out on the terrace."

CHAPTER
18

Is Aunt Martha losing it?" Amy asked plaintively. "First she lied about a perfectly innocuous piece of film and now to say that Maxie killed herself here in my bedroom?"

"She's pushing eighty," Jean Barbour said. "But I haven't heard that her mind's slipping. What was the film?"

Amy described the two birthday parties and Jean seemed equally perplexed. "Unless she thought seeing Maxie would trigger bad memories."

"I'm so tired of hearing that. I was three years old! If I'd actually seen her shoot herself, why wouldn't I already remember something that traumatic?"

"Because Dad and Frances did a number on you," Beth said. "No guns, no films, no visits back here."

"And you *were* here in the house when it happened," Jean said, "so you must have seen or heard *some*thing."

"But those last scenes with Maxie and me were filmed over at Aunt Martha's house."

"You'll just have to ask her, then," said Jean.

"That would be a little awkward," Beth said with a grin, and

Amy explained how she'd taken the tape without their aunt's knowledge.

"Now I have to figure out how to sneak it back."

"Give it to me," Jean said. "Curt and Mary are expecting me for supper, but I can drop by Aunt Martha's on my way and put it back without her noticing."

She walked over to the desk that sat in the dormer beneath a window that looked out over the back gardens. "Yes, this is the one Vera wanted. You're sure you don't mind?"

"Absolutely."

"Good. I'll get C.W. to come by with his pickup tomorrow or the next day, if that's all right?"

"Fine, but what about you? Can't I give you something?"

"Not furniture," Jean said decisively. "I already have enough of Mother's to open an antique store."

"What then?"

"You may want to keep it yourself and I'll certainly understand if that's the case, but what would mean the most to me is the journal we wrote with Maxie when we were kids."

"Journal? What did it look like? I haven't come across any of her things here. And if it was in New York—" She shook her head helplessly. "I don't think Dad kept much after he married Claire." She looked at Beth for confirmation.

Beth shrugged. "I never saw anything of hers at home."

"We called it our summer journal," Jean said, "and we only wrote in it when Maxie was here. I wonder if it's still in the attic?"

With Beth trailing along, they rode up to the attic, where Jean paused to get her bearings. "The elevator wasn't here when we were girls. We had to use those stairs down there and we set up as far away from them as we could."

The attic was neither heated in winter nor cooled in summer. Ventilators along the peak released some of the heat, but the air was so hot and still up here that when they stepped out of the cool elevator, it was like being slowly smothered under heavy wool, which was why Amy never played here as a child. The elevator may have been her space capsule but the attic was always too hot even for a pretend alien planet.

After a moment's hesitation, Jean confidently led the way between boxes and cartons and miscellaneous seasonal items that had been stored here. Amy followed, excited by the possibility of finding Maxie's girlhood journal.

"Uncle Bailey used to snoop around up here once in a while, but Aunt Frances almost never came up," Jean said.

As they moved further away from the elevator and stairs, the boxes thinned out a little, and when they reached the far gable end, Amy saw that a wide arc had once been cleared beneath the windows in the end wall. Dormer windows on opposite sides gave more light. The space was occupied by a round wooden table, two mismatched chairs, a tall stool, and a set of shelves cobbled together from boards and bricks. Over the years some boxes had encroached upon the area, and a few were even stacked on the chairs and table, but Jean easily moved them out of her way.

"Our laboratory," she said. "And there's our microscope and magnifying glasses."

A small crowbar hung from a nail beside the window, and with the familiarity of memory, Jean immediately used it to pry open the balky end windows as well as a window in each of the adjacent dormers. Soon fresh air flowed through and they could breathe easily again.

The shelves held snail shells, a hornet's nest, several varieties of acorns and pine cones, a hummingbird skull, the skeleton of a fish mounted on a piece of stiff cardboard, and at least a dozen more natural objects that had caught the eyes of those observant young girls. Thumbtacked to the wall above the shelves were multicolored feathers from wild and domestic fowls, a pressed leaf from every type of tree that grew on the farm, desiccated butterflies and moths, and a long transparent skin shed by a snake at least fifty years earlier. Each item was neatly labeled by both its common and its Latin name.

The snakeskin swayed sinuously in the crosscurrents of air and one of the small labels fell to the floor.

Jean shook her head in wonder. "I can't believe it's all still here."

"No journal, though," Amy said mournfully.

"Wait," said her cousin.

The floor was made up of long boards that ran the length of the attic, but the dormers had been pieced with shorter boards. Crowbar in hand, Jean went over to the dormer directly above Amy's room, slipped the pry end into a narrow crack between two of those boards, and flipped one of them up. There in the space between the joists were a long narrow ledger book bound in pale green cloth, an open pack of cigarettes, and a box of wooden matches.

Amy laughed. "More experiments?"

"Better than what a lot of kids are trying today," Jean said, bending for the journal.

Silverfish had nibbled the borders of some pages to lace, but all the writing seemed intact. With Amy and Beth looking over her shoulder, Jean gently turned the pages. They saw diagrams of beetle wings, grasshopper legs, wasp stingers, and a sketch of a velvet ant in the act of using a stick as a tamper to firm down the dirt above the underground chamber where the ant had just laid her eggs in the paralyzed body of a captured insect.

"We had read that only humans used tools," said Jean. "The first time we saw a velvet ant do this, I wanted to run through the neighborhood shouting, 'They've evolved! They've evolved!' Fortunately, Maxie talked me into waiting till we'd made further observations."

"That's all the journal is?" Amy asked. "A nature log? Nothing personal?"

"I'm sorry, honey," Jean said. "Were you expecting a diary?"

Amy nodded, too disappointed to speak.

"If she ever kept a diary, I never saw it. On the other hand, Maxie was real good about guarding her privacy, so who knows?"

"Wonder if there are any other loose boards?" said Beth, reaching for the crowbar.

While Beth tapped and probed her way around the attic perimeter and Amy leafed through the journal one page at a time, Jean stood before the old collection of natural objects, lost in nostalgia for the days in which these things had been solemnly gathered, sorted, and meticulously identified. At last she sighed and turned back to Amy. "Do you want to hang on to the journal for a while? Or I could get it photocopied."

"No," said Amy. "You can have it. There's nothing in it for me."

Beth rejoined them, her hands and shorts dirty from the boxes she'd moved, her face flushed with heat, her shirt damp with perspiration. "No luck," she said and hung the crowbar back on its nail.

After Jean had driven away with the videotape and the journal, Beth went back to packing books and Amy began to dismantle Grandmother's studio.

She decided to put the easels and drawing table in storage against the day when she and Eric bought a summer home where she could have a studio of her own.

When they bought a summer home? More like *if*.

She had managed to hold thoughts of Eric and Lisl at bay all day, but now grief and anger tore at her heart. How *could* she have been so stupid? His feigned impatience with Lisl's screwups? His phony threats to fire her? Why hadn't she recognized them for what they were?

She looked at the double portrait that Grandmother had begun and knew that she was too conflicted to decide right now what to do with it. Finish it? Toss it? Either choice had merit.

Instead she began to fill a box with canvas, bundles of stretchers, and odd lengths of framing. Brushes, drawing supplies, tubes of paint, boxes of powdered pigments and such went into another box. When C.W. came with his truck to pick up the desk for Vera, maybe she would ask him to take some of these boxes over to the local high school art department.

In midafternoon, Beth came through on her way to the kitchen. "I saw some tomato juice in the refrigerator before. You want a glass?"

"That sounds good," Amy said, realizing that she was starting to feel empty. "Thanks."

"If you'll tell me where the vodka is, I bet I could even mix us up a couple of decent Bloody Marys."

Amy was ready to agree that Bloody Marys sounded even better, but then she recalled why this was not a good idea. "Wait a minute! You can't drink. You're pregnant, remember?"

"Oh, shit," said Beth. "This is going to be such a bummer."

As she spoke, the cell phone rang. Amy pressed the proper button and held it to her ear. "Hello?"

"Amy? Is that you?"

"Oh, hi, Claire. How's the lake?"

"It's fine, although we're missing you and Eric. This is the first year you've missed and I hope it's going to be the last."

"I'm sorry, Claire, but there's so much to do here that—"

"I understand, sweetie, and that's not why I called. You haven't by any chance heard from Beth lately, have you?"

"Beth?" she temporized, raising an eyebrow at her sister.

"I'm not here," Beth said and escaped down the stairs. Barkis jumped up from his spot over the air vent and trotted after her.

"She and Dad had a terrible fight Thursday night and they both stormed out." Claire sounded on the edge of tears. "I've called everyone I can think of, even Hugo the Horrid, and nobody's seen her. Her phone's not working either. What if she's been hurt? Wrecked her car? Or—"

"Calm down, Claire, she's fine. She's here."

"She's there?"

Claire sounded bewildered. And with good reason, thought Amy, considering that she and Beth had never been best buds.

"She got here last night."

"Last night?" Claire's fears turned to indignation. "And you didn't call me?"

"It was after midnight. Besides, I told her to call as soon as she got up and she said she had."

"And you believed her?"

"Silly me," Amy muttered.

"What did you say?"

"Hang on and I'll get her for you."

Down in the kitchen, she found Beth mixing tomato juice, Tabasco sauce, and slices of lime in a glass pitcher. She was just unscrewing the cap on a bottle of vodka, and Amy didn't know which irritated her more—that Beth had lied to her about calling Claire or that she planned to put her fetus at risk by drinking vodka. She grabbed the bottle and thrust the phone into Beth's hand.

"Here, talk to your mother."

With a dramatic huff at Amy, Beth said, "Mom?"

While they talked—or rather, while Claire talked and Beth responded in monosyllables, Amy put ice cubes in two glasses, filled them both with the Virgin Marys, and took a sip. Quite tasty. The lack of vodka didn't affect the taste, only the kick.

"No, I'm not talking to him," Beth said angrily. "You put him on and I'm hanging up. I—"

She abruptly handed the phone to Amy, grabbed the other glass of doctored tomato juice, and drank half of it without pausing.

"Hello?" said Amy.

"Amy? Where's Beth?"

"I'm sorry, Dad, she doesn't want to talk to you right now."

"Damn straight," Beth muttered from the other side of the kitchen.

"And you condone her childish behavior?"

"No," she said mildly, "I'm just stating the facts."

"Why did she run to you, anyhow?"

"I guess she felt she had no other options."

"Only because she's botched them all. I don't think you should encourage her in this, Amy, and I don't want you giving her money. It's time Beth took responsibility for her lack of self-discipline. You won't help by babying her."

"I'm not babying her."

"You're letting her stay with you, aren't you?"

"What was I supposed to do, Dad? Slam the door in her face?"

"Yes!" he snapped. "Oh, not literally, but I want you to send her back to New York first thing tomorrow morning."

"To live where? In her car? On the streets?"

"It might not hurt her to get a full dose of reality, but I don't suppose that's practical in this day and age. No, if she'll go back to New York and go back to work, I'll arrange for her to stay in the corporate apartment there till Claire and I get back. If she's acting more responsibly by then, I'll help her straighten out the financial mess she's in."

"I'll tell her, but don't be surprised if she won't do it."

"She has until Monday morning to decide. After that, my offer's withdrawn. And she needn't think she can get around me by going to Claire. That door's closed now. I'm just sorry you have to be the bearer of unpleasant ultimatums, my dear. Except for Beth, though, how's it going there?"

"It's going," Amy said.

"Good. Well then . . ."

"Dad?"

"Yes?"

"Aunt Martha showed me some home movies Uncle James took before Maxie died. She said you used to have a film camera, too."

When he didn't respond, she said, "Do you still have the films?"

"No. I'm afraid I didn't store them properly and they were in such bad shape that I threw them out years ago."

"You threw them out? How could you *do* that?" Frustration sharpened her voice. She hadn't realized how much she was looking forward to seeing those home movies. And now to hear that they were gone? It was enough to make her want to howl with rage.

"What's done is done, Amy, and I don't appreciate your tone of voice."

"I'm sorry, Dad, but—"

" 'Sorry, Dad. Forgive me, Dad. Excuse me for living, Dad,' " came Beth's mocking voice.

Something snapped in Amy. She felt as if she'd been apologizing her whole life—to Dad, to Claire, to Beth and the boys, to Eric—anything to keep peace and order, to avoid head-on confrontations.

"One thing more," she said calmly. "I heard today that Maxie was going to divorce you."

There was shocked silence at his end. At this end, Beth sat up and listened with interest.

"Who told you that?" he asked.

"It doesn't matter who told me. The real question is, why wasn't it you?"

Another pause. "Because frankly, my dear, it wasn't any of your business."

Even to Amy, his words sounded lame. "You lied to me. You said those other women didn't affect your marriage, and now you say the divorce isn't my business?"

"Other women?" squealed Beth.

"If I lied, Amy, it was to protect Max's memory. She wouldn't have gone through with any divorce, so what was the point in telling you?"

"What else haven't you told me? What other lies have I grown up believing?"

"I knew it was a mistake for you to go down there," her father said. "This isn't something to discuss over the telephone. If you really feel you must open up this old tragedy, we'll talk when I get back to New York. In the meantime, please give Beth my message."

Without giving her a chance to respond, he told her good-bye and hung up.

"Other women?" asked Beth. "He cheated on Max?"

"Yes." Already she regretted speaking so bluntly in front of Beth, who still didn't know that he'd once cheated on Claire.

She relayed his message and, as she expected, it only fueled Beth's earlier rage at him. "And anyhow, why did you tell Mom I was here? I covered for you with your aunt. Why couldn't you return the favor?"

"It wasn't the same thing at all, and you know it, Beth. Besides, you lied to me when you said you'd called her, so just chill, okay? Do something, don't do something, fine. But I'm through being lied to, understood?"

"Does that mean you're not kicking me out?" Beth asked meekly.

"And have to train a new assistant?" She gave a pointed glance at the clock. "Anyhow, break's over. Back to work."

"Whatever you say, Bosslady."

CHAPTER
19

Michael called about two hours later. Before he finished saying hello, he was interrupted by Sam on an extension. "Hey, what'd you say to piss Dad off? He's been stomping around here like he's found a pickle in his ice cream. Mom and Jane finally dragged him off to a decoy exhibit in town, but I don't think hand-carved ducks are going to do it. Which one of his chains did you rattle? And how come it's you he's so pissed at? That's usually Beth's job."

"Don't worry," said Amy, stepping out onto the terrace with the phone so that Beth wouldn't overhear. "She hasn't lost her knack."

"Why is she there, anyhow?" asked Michael.

"You heard about her fight with Dad when she tried to move back home Thursday?"

"Because of the mess she's made of her finances?" Had Michael written the Ten Commandments, one of them would have been *Thou shalt not exceed thy income.*

"And how Mom's got to stop enabling her? Oh yes," said Sam. "Ever since we got here. But you should have seen his face when he heard she'd run to you."

"I don't know why. After all, we *are* sisters."

"Yeah, but it's usually Beth and me against you guys. When did you two get tight?"

Sam was right, thought Amy. Early on in their parents' marriage and long before his epiphany at Tavern on the Green, she and Michael had formed a working alliance. "They *have* to stay married," he'd told her solemnly from the vast wisdom of his extra four years. "Every proper house has to have a mother and a father." "Proper" was the closest he could come to expressing the stability and security that had gone missing from his world after his own father died and Claire fell apart. Despite his "awesome Amy" jibes, he recognized that they were both outsiders in the Voygt family, compared to Sam and Beth, and while he wasn't above teasing her himself, he had usually taken her part against the other two.

"Anyhow," Michael persisted, "what did you say to set Dad off?"

"Get off the line, Sam," she said.

"Hey!" he protested. "Why?"

"Michael, make him get off and make him stay where you can see him," she said, knowing Sam was quite capable of eavesdropping.

Standing in the shaded part of the terrace near her spider, she heard Sam arguing, then an annoyed clash as his receiver was slammed back in its cradle. She was wryly amused at how quickly they could revert to childhood roles.

"Is this what I think it is?" asked Michael when it was just the two of them on the line.

"Yes."

"Oh."

Years ago, when they pieced together the reason Dad and Claire were fighting, back when they were afraid the fights were going to end in divorce, she and Michael had made a pact to keep Dad's philandering away from the younger two; and after he finally settled into monogamy with Claire, they saw no reason to tell. They seemed to have been successful. Beth had looked surprised to hear he'd cheated on Maxie and, so far as she knew, Sam still lived in ignorance. Now she quickly explained to Michael what she'd learned from Jean about the circumstances leading up to Maxie's death and how she'd confronted Dad with her knowledge that Maxie was going to divorce him.

"That's what made him angry—that I caught him in a lie. My cousin thinks Frances and Bailey would have fired him if there was a divorce," she said.

Michael was silent as he considered the situation. He wasn't as quick as Sam or Beth nor as brilliant as Eric, and there were times when his attention to detail exasperated them all, but his conclusions were usually dead on.

"They couldn't have fired him, Amy. He owned half the company. Of course, they owned the copyrights and the Pink and Blue trademark, so the company wouldn't have been worth much if it couldn't license the books from them. But would they have withheld the books? I mean, Dad really was the one who turned a cottage industry into a financial goldmine."

"Jean thinks that's one of the reasons why Maxie killed herself. That they would have sided with Dad if Maxie was the one to file for divorce."

"Look, Amy, maybe Dad's right this time. Maybe you really shouldn't keep digging at this. There's no way you're ever going to know why she did it. Is blaming him really going to help when there's no way you'll ever know for sure?"

"No," she said, reluctantly agreeing. But something new now gnawed at her, something so taken for granted, she'd never before questioned it. "Michael? How come you got to call him Dad but Claire never let me call her Mom?"

"Frances," he said promptly. "That first trip down to Carolina for Mom and me to meet them? Dad said something to you like, 'Let Mommy help you with that,' and Frances came down on them like a load of bricks. 'Amy must call her Claire,' she said.

'I will *not* have my granddaughter calling someone else Mommy.' You don't remember?"

"No."

"It doesn't matter, Amy. Really. Mom loves you. You know that."

"Yes."

"And listen, don't let Beth con you, okay? I'm not saying don't help her, but just take everything she says with a grain of salt because she's going to tell you what she thinks you want to hear."

"I know all her old tricks," Amy assured him.

"Yeah, but do you know all her new ones?"

She laughed.

"Hurry and get through down there and come on up to the lake," he said. "Jody wants to show you how he can dive off the high board now."

"If you let my only nephew break his neck—"

"Relax. Mom had it changed. The high board's only about three feet higher than the low one now."

Amy and Beth worked until seven, then showered and drove into Garner for dinner. Beth was on her best behavior, chatty and charming. It was almost like having a real sister, Amy thought wryly. Beth had taken one look at the only purse Amy had brought with her—an all-purpose black leather that worked fine with city clothes but looked dowdy with floral-printed capris—and insisted she take the colorful straw bag she'd claimed in front of Aunt Martha.

"I've decided I like this one better anyhow," Beth had said candidly, displaying a second bag that was almost identical to the one she was offering Amy. "Saks was having a fantastic summer sale and I couldn't decide which one I liked best, so I bought them both. Only seventy dollars, too."

Beth had looked at her so expectantly that she had obligingly handed over the money. No wonder Beth stayed broke. All the same, the bag would go great with all her casual summer clothes.

After dinner (for which she paid, of course), she even let Beth talk her into seeing a new thriller at the local multiplex, but with everything else going on in her head, the movie didn't stand a chance of holding her interest. On the drive back to the house, Beth's chatter about the actors, their various affairs and who was doing what with or to whom, passed right by her.

"Sorry," she said automatically when Beth called her on it. "I'm too tired to concentrate." Considering all that had happened since she stepped out of bed at dawn, she felt physically and emotionally drained.

At the house, Barkis was waiting patiently by the door and she held it open so he could go out.

"I'm really beat," she told Beth. "Would you let him back in and then lock up?"

Upstairs, she brushed her teeth, creamed her face, and fell into bed. Sleep came instantly, and she was so far under that the house phone by her bed trilled four times before she could come awake enough to answer. As she lifted the receiver to her ear, she heard Beth say, "Hello?"

The line was open, but no one spoke.

"Anybody there?" Beth asked impatiently.

"Go away," rasped a spooky whisper. "Go back where you came from before you get hurt, too."

"Oh, *please!*" Beth said disdainfully. "Just who the fuck do you think you're talking to?"

Dead air answered. Whoever it was had hung up.

"Beth?" Amy said. "I picked up the same time you did."

"You have caller ID or automatic callback?" asked her sister, still in her belligerent I-Am-Woman mode.

"On my cell phone. Not on this one. I didn't know I'd be needing it."

"Stupid kids."

When Amy didn't respond, Beth said, "That's all it is, isn't it? Hick kids? Big yucks?"

"Probably," she said, realizing that Beth didn't know Grandmother's death might be deliberate murder.

"I mean, you've only been here three days. Who could you piss off that quick?"

"No, you're right." The illuminated dial on her bedside radio read 11:33. "Is Barkis in?"

"Right here at my feet. And before you ask, yes, all the doors are locked. We're down here in the den watching *Saturday Night Live*. Your dog thinks Britney Spears is still hot."

Amy laughed, said goodnight again, and rolled onto her stomach to go back to sleep.

And found herself staring into darkness.

That raspy voice on the telephone just now was like something out of a Saturday morning cartoon, too clichéd to be taken seriously. It probably was only a couple of bored kids, dialing at random, hoping to spook someone. And yet—?

"Before you get hurt, too," the voice had said. *Too?* Meaning as Grandmother had been hurt? Was this a call from her killer?

She rolled back over as the red LED crystals blinked to 11:34.

A call from a possible murderer, but no call from her husband. And whose bed was *he* sleeping in tonight?

She reached out and touched her cell phone in the dark. So easy to press a few buttons and see if his phone was still switched off. "Don't want to break my concentration," he'd said.

It wasn't rocks he'd be concentrating on at this hour, was it?

Hard to remember a time before cell phones let everyone stay connected. The first year or so of their marriage, they had always called each other when one of them had to be away. When had they stopped? If this were four days ago, she would have called him tonight for some pillow talk without a second's hesitation. Now the thought that Lisl might be sharing his pillow was enough to keep her from picking up the phone.

11:44.

Think of something else. Think of Maxie, a woman labeled all her life as weak and uncreative. Think of Maxie making plans to become a nature writer, of divorcing Dad. Think of the lies of omission he'd let her believe all these years. And Grandmother's shading of the truth. Grandfather's nonexistent battle experiences. Did Dad know the real story behind *Pink and Blue and Max*?

"Something of her own," Jean had said. "Something Aunt Frances and Uncle Bailey couldn't take." The way they'd taken Pink and Blue from her?

What did they do, Blue? What did she think, Pink?

Jean again: "Uncle Bailey used to snoop around up here."

Aunt Martha: "Bailey did love to creep up on her and hear what she was saying. Some of it was so funny he'd put it in their storybooks."

And Maxie herself had written, "I will not turn the things Amy says to herself into anecdotes for your morning amusement."

As you two did to me, was her unspoken and unwritten implication.

Poor Maxie. Born to a mother and father so into each other that they could steal their daughter's imaginary playmates and turn them into their own little money machine without compunction or understanding, she had gone from a loveless childhood to a loveless marriage with a man who divided his energies between other women and gearing the machine to crank out even more money.

And what about her own marriage? Like mother, like daughter?

Like Eric and Lisl.

11:52.

Again her fingers hovered over the cell phone. Call? Don't call? A handful of numbers and she could reach him wherever he was—in a wilderness cabin or a Boston hotel.

Or a Washington hotel?

Startled, she realized that this had been nagging at her subconscious since late Wednesday night when those lawmen asked where Eric was when Grandmother was killed. In Washington, she'd told them. "I woke him up at his hotel."

In truth, he could have been in the next room or the next country because she had not gone through the hotel switchboard as Agent Wilson and that sheriff's deputy probably assumed. She had simply called his phone directly.

This was so crazy. Even at his angriest, Eric never got physically violent. Yes, he could get single-minded when working on a project. Yes, he could take her for granted and assume that her compliance with his plans meant she had none of her own. And yes, maybe he could commit adultery. But commit murder?

No, no, and *no!*

12:00 and the clock on the landing began to strike midnight.

Think of something else. Think of Aunt Martha freaking out over letting her see those birthday scenes. Her little cowgirl outfit. Cap pistols. The way poor Michael had to lose his toy guns so that her memories of that day would be lost, too.

Cap pistols . . . the smell of gunpowder . . . the way . . . she . . .

The clock's chimes evoked their usual Pavlovian response and Amy fell asleep before they finished counting the hour.

The caller hadn't expected that reaction. She was a woman, wasn't she? With no man in the house to comfort and protect her? She was supposed to have been scared. Her voice was supposed to shake. She certainly wasn't supposed to sound mad or start cussing as if she'd suddenly grown herself a spine. Coming back here like this. Asking all those questions. Getting Curt riled up so that he was starting to ask questions of his own, the real questions that she would never think of by herself.

There was still paraquat in the barn and glycol in the garage and Jimson weed still flourished along the edge of the back fields. The old folks used to say that half a teaspoon of the seeds were enough to kill a grown man.

Plenty of seeds in fig preserves.

Crush up a few more, who would notice?

CHAPTER
20

"Two messages for you," Beth said when Amy came down from the attic the next morning. "A woman who said her name was Ethylene Phillips? With a Y. Like the gas. I made her spell it for me, so I'm not making it up."

Amy smiled. "That would be Jimmy's wife."

"Jimmy?"

"The birthday boy on the film clips. Aunt Martha's grandson. What did she want?"

"Must be his birthday again. She's inviting you over for cake and ice cream this evening. And she said I'd be right welcome to come, too." Beth twanged the words in malicious mockery of Jimmy's wife. "I told her I was right honored, but that I'd already made plans for the evening."

Beth had always had a wicked talent for impersonations and her rendering of the local accent was so perfect that Amy had to smile. "You said two messages?"

"Right. Some guy named Jacob Grayson left a number and wants you to call him back as soon as you can."

As she handed over both phone numbers, Beth said, "That call last night. It spooked you, didn't it?"

"A little," Amy admitted.

"Is something going on here I don't know about?"

Sighing, Amy gave her the same abbreviated version she'd given Curt of the inconsistencies in Grandmother's death, which Agent Wilson had listed for her.

Beth's blue eyes grew wider with the telling. "You let me stay here when Frances was murdered on purpose?"

"If you remember, your being here wasn't my idea."

"You should have told me."

"Sorry." Having been so long on the receiving end, Amy couldn't resist giving Beth the needle for a change. "But hey! Your car's still packed, right? You could be on the road in an hour." She walked over to the house phone on Grandmother's desk and picked up the receiver. "In fact, if you hurry, I bet you could even make Dad's Monday morning deadline."

"Go to hell!" Beth said automatically.

Amy grinned and dialed her cousin Jimmy's number. When a woman answered, she said, "Ethylene? This is Amy. My sister gave me your message. It's not by any chance Jimmy's birthday, is it?"

"Why, yes it is!" the woman exclaimed. A baby wailed loudly in her ear. "Oops! Wait a sec, Amy. The baby just lost my nipple. There you go, sweetie pie. Now isn't that something, you re-membering Jimmy's birthday? Yeah, we thought we'd have cake and ice cream for everybody out at Miss Martha's. Our place isn't big enough. And it'll be squeezing to get us all in there, but she's got that deck if you don't mind the heat and since this may be the last time the whole family can be together before the farm's gone, we thought—"

Impulsively, Amy said, "Would you like to move the party over here? There's plenty of room."

"Oh, gee, I don't know. That's awfully nice of you, but . . ."

"It was nice of *you* to think of inviting me," Amy said, touched that this cousin by marriage would include her in a family gather-ing. "Please? Let it be my birthday gift to Jimmy."

"Well, if you're sure? I have to say it'd certainly be better to spread out and visit without worrying about heat and mosquitoes, specially since they're talking rain on the television. I've got all the paper plates and napkins, so you won't have to fix nothing."

"What about ice? Or coffee?"

"Coffee would be good, but we've already got four bags of ice in the freezer. I told everybody seven, but maybe Paulie and me'll come a little early to get things set up?"

"That'll be fine," Amy said.

"I'm real sorry your sister can't be there."

"I know Beth's sorry, too," Amy said sweetly. "Unfortunately, she's thinking of driving back to New York this afternoon."

Beth glowered at her, but she'd evidently had time to reconsider her options; and when Amy finished talking to Ethylene, she said, "You can't stay here alone with a killer on the loose. Why don't we both go home tomorrow? I promise I won't camp on you and Eric more than a couple of weeks."

"I can't leave until I finish what I came to do. And anyhow, why would you be camping on us when Dad said you could use the corporate apartment?" She had said it to tease, but Beth immediately flared up again.

"That fucking apartment comes with too many strings, as you damn well know."

Amy said nothing, just stood there with the phone in her hand, looking at her almost as if she were an inanimate object.

Beth stirred uneasily beneath her cool gaze. "What?" she said belligerently.

"I was just thinking how very tired I am of hearing that word. It's crude and it's juvenile."

"And like I give a flying fuck?" Beth said with insulting deliberateness.

"No, I guess you don't." She walked down the hall to her bedroom and came back carrying her checkbook.

"What are you doing?"

Amy sat down at Grandmother's desk and began to fill out a check. "Let's see. Two hours this morning, six hours yesterday, that's eight total. I can give you forty in cash and a check for the other forty."

She signed her name, tore it from the checkbook, and held it out to Beth along with a couple of twenty-dollar bills. "Good-bye, Beth. I'll see you back in New York. Or not."

"That's it? You're kicking me out because I say 'fuck' once in a while? Well, fuck you!" She grabbed the check and the money, then stormed down the hall to her room.

Barkis trotted along after her and got the door slammed in his face.

It was the first time Amy could ever remember standing her ground and confronting someone's anger head-on. And maybe it wasn't a fair fight since she held all the cards, but she'd held all the cards before and still backed off. This time she hadn't placated nor tried to be conciliatory, and to her surprise, it felt pretty good. Was it really this easy to face down an antagonist? She remembered the way she'd looked at the age of three after successfully defending her cowgirl hat—flushed and triumphant. That's exactly how she felt now.

Exhilarated, she dialed the appraiser's number.

"Grayson's Galleries," said a recording. It proceeded to list the antique store's hours and ended, "Please leave a message and we will return your call."

"This is Amy Steadman and I'm—"

Immediately, a man's voice cut in. "Mrs. Steadman! Jacob Grayson here. Thanks for returning my call. I've been looking at my schedule and tomorrow's going to be a little jammed for me. I was wondering if I could possibly come out this afternoon?"

"Certainly. When?"

"Actually, would now be too inconvenient?"

"Not at all." She gave him directions on how to get there and said she would expect him within the hour.

As she passed Beth's room on her way to freshen up for Mr. Grayson, Barkis paused to sniff at the door. Amy spoke sharply and the terrier immediately heeled.

She emerged from her bathroom ten minutes later to find Beth standing in the hall outside her open door. Her nose and eyes were red, as if she'd been crying.

"I'm sorry," she said. "I was way out of line. I don't know what's wrong with me these days. My nerves are shot to h—" She caught herself with a wry smile. "Shot to pieces. All this stuff with the baby. Maybe it's hormones that's making me so bitchy."

Beth had been bitchy all summer, beginning with her first full day of work at PBM, long before any pregnancy, but her apology seemed genuine and Amy was willing to let her salvage her pride. By the time Mr. Grayson rang the front doorbell, they were back to relative normality.

Most of the male antiques dealers Amy had met in New York were either old and courtly or else middle-aged and flamboyant. Jacob Grayson had short, curly red hair and the wiry muscularity of a tennis player, and despite a closely trimmed red beard, he didn't look a day over thirty. Instead of suit and tie, he wore white shorts, a black knit polo shirt, and thick leather sandals. A canvas backpack dangled from his hand.

"Oh, wow!" he said as soon as he stepped into the entrance hall and got a good look at the glass in both the door and its surround. "You said the house is coming down?"

"Yes," said Amy.

"What a shame. Will you be selling the glass, too, or taking it with you?"

"I hadn't thought about it one way or the other. Is it worth saving?"

"It sure is. I'll give you the name of a colleague who specializes in salvaging architectural antiques—doors, windows, hardware. It'd be a crime to let all this good stuff get bulldozed."

He craned his neck at the wrought-iron chandelier overhead and Amy saw his eyes widen as Beth appeared at the top of the steps and came down to join them. A sarong printed in bright red, orange, and yellow rode low on her slender hips and a lime green top left the rest of her midriff bare. More of her Spanish wardrobe, no doubt. She was barefooted and her light brown hair fell loosely around her pretty face. Here amid the monochromatic ivory and cream walls and the heavy dark furniture, she looked as deceptively fragile as a rare and colorful parrot from some tropical rainforest.

"My sister, Beth Voygt," Amy said. "Beth, this is—"

"Jacob Grayson," he said, stepping past her with his hand extended to Beth. "Will you marry me and become the mother of my sons?"

Beth laughed. "How many?"

"Six?" he said with a hopeful air.

"Sorry. But cut it to two and make one of them a girl and I might reconsider."

"Ah, a shrewd negotiator. I like that. Useful for the shop. What do you know about antiques?"

"Not much, but I *have* started reading about Roycroft."

"Smart woman. Arts and Crafts are really hot now and—omigod! Look at all this stuff!"

Bemused, Amy followed them into the front parlor, where Grayson began turning metaphorical cartwheels over the range and quality of Grandmother's furniture. He raced from one room to another, exclaiming, admiring, and, in his own words, "drooling" over what was here.

His hands caressed the wood and lingered on the hardware, and when Beth asked him a technical question on the construction of glass cabinet doors inlaid with copper, he answered with the enthusiasm of a born teacher.

Amy interrupted long enough to tell him which of the main pieces she planned to keep, then left them to it while she went out to the kitchen to tidy up for the party.

Although she hadn't cooked anything since Eric left—was that really only two days ago?— the sink and counters were littered with cups and glasses, plates, and silverware she and Beth had used. So much for Beth's reformation. She put everything in the dishwasher, wiped down all the counters, and brought out a large coffee urn from the pantry. One cupboard held a collection of mugs imprinted with the logos of book and toy stores from across the world that had been sent to Frances through the years. Amy set a dozen or so on the counter along with a cream pitcher and sugar bowl.

There was no longer a table in the dining room, but she doubted if her cousins would mind serving themselves in the kitchen. She had to unfold several cloths in the linen press before she found one to fit the big round table here. From the garden, she brought in blue hydrangeas and white gardenias and arranged them in a large, hammered copper bowl, which she set amid five matching candleholders of varying heights. It took her a while to locate appropriate candles, but when she'd finished, the table looked festive enough for a birthday.

"Nice," Beth said approvingly when she and Grayson came out for something to drink. He immediately upended one of the copper candleholders to look for the maker's mark and beamed when he found it.

"There's way more here than I expected," he said. "I need to run back to the shop for more inventory sheets and to check out some prices on the Internet. Shouldn't take us long."

"Us?" asked Amy, noting that Beth's bare feet now sported a red thong on one foot and a yellow on the other.

Her sister gave a graceful shrug. "Jacob's invited me to come see his store."

"And we'll probably stop by the house I'm restoring in the Oakwood section of Raleigh since that's where we'll be living after the wedding. I think she ought to have a say about the wallpaper in our bedroom, don't you?"

"Absolutely," Amy agreed solemnly.

"We'll be back in a couple of hours. Don't worry."

Amy didn't. Not about Beth, anyhow. Beth had been breaking hearts since she was ten. She did, however, spare a moment of concern for Jacob Grayson.

CHAPTER
21

The phone rang a few minutes after Beth and Grayson left.

"Amy?" Anxiety and pleasure mingled in Aunt Martha's voice. "You're just so sweet to tell Ethylene she could have Jimmy's birthday party over there. Are you sure you want to do it though? There's right many of us."

"No problem," said Amy. "Um, how many's 'right many'?"

"Well, there's Jimmy and Ethylene and the baby, of course. Me and Paulie. Curt Junior and Mary and C.W. I don't know if you heard that C.W.'s wife left him for a Greyhound bus driver last year? But he's got the two children this weekend. That's nine, if you don't count the baby. Then Frannie and her husband and son. I believe you met Jake when he and Paulie went for the table? Jean said she was coming with Vera and her crowd. I don't think Vera's daughter's coming, but she and George'll have their three grandchildren, so that's nine more. Oh, and Pat will come and bring Herbert. Bless his heart, he won't hardly remember any of us, but he does seem to like getting out with folks. Pat and Mary take him to the Senior Center three mornings a week and it does him the best good, to be sure. Scares me sometimes when I look at him. He's not but four years older than me. Of course, his arteries have been hardening on him for more than five years and mine seem to be just fine, so maybe I'll be all right. Oh, shoot! I've lost count how many that is."

Amy had jotted each name on the notepad as Aunt Martha listed them, and before her aunt could begin all over again, she quickly added them up. "I think it's twenty-two, counting the baby and Vera's husband."

"And don't forget you and Beth. You're sure that's not too many?"

"The more the merrier," said Amy.

"That's just what Bailey used to say. He did love a party so much. Mama and Daddy, too. I'm so glad you're doing this, honey. I'm going to call everybody right now and tell them to be sure and bring their cameras. Our last party in the home-place. The little ones won't remember, but the bigger ones will."

"Yes," said Amy, thinking of how much she didn't remember, thinking of those films Aunt Martha hadn't wanted her to see. Tonight, one way or another, she was going to make her aunt tell exactly where Maxie died.

When Aunt Martha finally said good-bye, Amy took a stack of hand towels from the linen closet and carried them down to the lavatory off the entry hall, then went back to the kitchen and laid out more mugs and all the spoons and forks she could find. No way did she have enough coffee on hand, though.

She slung her new straw bag over her shoulder and jingled her car keys at Barkis. "Want to ride?"

He beat her to the side door and happily jumped into the car as soon as she opened it. The car was an oven—"Hot enough to bake biscuits," Pat would say—but the air conditioner soon gave blessed relief. At the grocery store, she parked in the shade and left all the windows cracked while she darted inside for coffee, several cans of mixed nuts, and a handful of helium-filled Mylar birthday balloons, which she bought on impulse and which afforded Barkis much amusement when she returned and tried to get them into her car.

By two o'clock, she was back at the house with all her hostess chores completed and at least four full hours to sort through or pack up more boxes before Jimmy's wife and mother arrived.

Despite everything, they were making a dent in the place, and she saw that for all Beth's shirking of kitchen duties, she had accomplished a surprising amount of work in the brief time she'd been here. All the books in Grandmother's bedroom were now neatly sealed in clearly labeled cartons awaiting pickup from one of the parcel services.

Grandmother's closet and dresser drawers had also been emptied. Beth, who was slightly taller than she, though by no means as tall as Grandmother, had asked for some of the silk lingerie and a couple of shirts. Amy had put aside a couple of items for herself. Maybe Aunt Martha would like something. If not, there must be local charities that would.

Happily, Grandmother hadn't been sentimental about clothes. When Grandfather died, she'd sent all his things to Goodwill, not to the attic. Beth had prowled through the cartons stored up there, hoping for funky vintage clothing, but so far had found only a trunk stuffed with ancient baby clothes and a box of hats from the forties and fifties that had probably belonged to Great-grandmother Virgie as well.

For all that Beth had accomplished, however, Amy could point to even more. The studio was stripped nearly bare. She had carried a half-dozen black plastic garbage bags down to the back porch, intending to take C.W. up on his offer to haul stuff to the Dumpster for her. Here on the landing, sealed cartons designated for what she was already mentally calling the Frances and Bailey Barbour Collection were ranged chest high along one long wall. As soon as Dr. Mills's shipping labels arrived, she could start them on their way, too.

Not bad, she thought. At this rate, she might actually make it up to the lake while Dad and Claire were still there.

Thoughts of New Hampshire inevitably led to thoughts of Boston. She checked her cell phone to make sure it was turned on, not that she expected Eric to call before nightfall when, presumably, it would be too dark to use rock climbing as an excuse for keeping his own phone turned off.

Feeling bereft and unloved, she sighed and wandered over to the terrace window. On her drive to and from the grocery store, she'd heard predictions of scattered showers and thundershowers, but at the moment, the only clouds she could see were fluffy and white. Closer to earth, her writing spider hung quietly in its graceful web. The zig-zag "writing" that strengthened the center was crisp and white. There was no evidence of the grasshopper Jean had fed her yesterday, but a small silk-wrapped shape in an upper quadrant of the web assured Amy that she needn't worry about whether the spider was getting enough to eat. As she watched, she saw movement at the top of the web.

Another spider.

This one, however, was much smaller than hers. A juvenile? She looked closer and was thrilled to recognize a male Argiope. The tips of its pedipalps were so engorged that they did indeed look like tiny clenched fists. She watched in fascination as he edged along the side of the web. Knowing now how sensitive her spider was to the web's smallest movement, she was surprised that the female didn't react, but even more so that the male seemed immune to the web's stickiness. Any other small creature would have hopelessly ensnared itself by now.

She brought her sketch pad over to the window and began to draw. After exploring the edges of the web, the small male positioned himself upside down near the top and hung there as motionless as his intended mate. She wondered if spiders slept and if the dreams of sleeping spiders were as troubled as her own dreams.

At that moment, the sleeping dog that had been sprawled beside the cool air vent came to his feet, barked once, and trotted across the landing and down the staircase to the front door.

About time Beth and Jacob Grayson were getting back, she thought, glancing at her watch. Two hours, he'd said? It'd been closer to four.

The bell rang and Barkis answered with a sharp welcoming yip. Amy set her sketch pad on the floor and hurried downstairs. First thing tomorrow, she told herself, she would hunt up a set of keys for Beth.

His stub tail wagging furiously, Barkis was bouncing back and forth from her to the door.

She glanced through the glass and immediately opened it with a smile.

"Agent Wilson?"

He stooped to pat the terrier, who was trying to lick his face in extravagant welcome. When he stood again, she saw that he was dressed more formally today in a light brown sports jacket, soft shirt and tie, as if for an official call. "Hope you don't mind me dropping by like this, Miz Steadman, but first your line was busy and then you didn't answer."

"I ran out for a few groceries and I keep forgetting to reset Grandmother's answering machine. Come in." Her eyes were drawn to the thick manila file envelope he carried. "Is that what I hope it is?"

"Your mother's case file? Yes, ma'am. Even though it's Sunday, soon as I told Major Bryant about the checks Mrs. Barbour wrote to that live-in couple, he got interested enough to meet me at the courthouse and root it out for me." He saw the balloons that she'd tied to the bannisters on each side of the stairs. "Am I interrupting?"

"Not for another two or three hours," she assured him.

The kitchen table was the only one large enough to spread files out on downstairs and it was already dressed for the party, so Amy led him up to her grandmother's studio. She lowered the angled top of the drawing table until it was flat while he rolled an extra stool over next to hers and began pulling documents from the folder, explaining each as he went.

Here was the first responding officer's report, laboriously printed by hand, in the death of Maxine Barbour Voygt, Caucasian female, age thirty-six. The officer had arrived at the house at 3:55 P.M. Subject was DOA and the cause of death was "consistent with a self-inflicted gunshot wound to the chest."

"Chest?" asked Amy. "I always thought she put the gun to her head."

"That's the usual method," Wilson agreed, "but sometimes people aim for the heart instead. The ME's report is there. She took out her pulmonary artery. Death would have been instantaneous."

"This is so weird," Amy said, reading further. "This says she died up here on the landing."

Wilson raised an eyebrow. "So?"

"Yesterday, Aunt Martha said it was in the bedroom, the same room my grandmother gave me when I first came back to the farm, which would have been totally illogical after all the trouble they took to make me forget. Jean says she thought it happened out on the terrace."

"Jean?"

"Jean Barbour. One of my cousin Curt's sisters. They're the children of Curtis William, the brother that was killed in the Second World War. She and Maxie were first cousins and fairly close."

"They say why they think your mother did it?"

"Mmm?" Amy was now deep in the report written out by the sheriff, who seemed to have arrived about a half-hour after the first officer. He had personally interviewed Grandmother, who told him that Maxie had been seriously depressed at the time, although not in the care of a psychiatrist.

"Your aunt and your cousin," said Terry Wilson. "Were they living here on the farm at the time?"

"My aunt was. My cousin lived in Raleigh."

"Either of them have a theory?"

"Aunt Martha doesn't want to discuss it all and Jean says

Maxie was *not* depressed. In fact, she was planning to divorce my father and strike out on her own. And look at this! Statements by the people present in the house: Karl Hahnemann, Anna Hahnemann, Frances Barbour, and Bailey Barbour. The Hahnemanns say that Grandmother was down in the kitchen with them and that Grandfather was asleep up here."

As always, the former sick room stood with its wide double doors folded back.

"His hospital bed was over there," she said, gesturing, "so that they were always in each other's view when she was painting here in the studio."

She looked back down at the report. "They say they heard the shot and came running up and found Maxie dead there on the landing between the studio and his room. There's no mention of me."

"Yes there is."

He reached across to turn the pages, and as his hand brushed hers, Amy was abruptly aware of his physical closeness, his maleness, his clean smell of soap and aftershave, his size.

Eric was only a few inches taller than she, with a slender build. This man was big. Big and muscular. Being small herself, she had never been attracted to large men, and yet, here and now, a wave of primitive animal lust swept through her, shocking her with its intensity and leaving her consumed with desire. Was this what Eric felt with Lisl? This sudden irresistible attraction to someone totally different?

"See?" He pointed to a paragraph near the end of the page and read, " 'Decedent's three-year-old daughter Amy was away at the time, at the house of decedent's aunt, Martha Barbour Lee.' "

Amy gave her errant libido a stern command to *Sit!* but it was far less obedient than Barkis. She turned her head slightly and looked up at his face as he read. It wasn't a particularly handsome face. His nose was too long, the lids of his hazel eyes drooped a little, his brown hair was beginning to thin. But it was a strong face with laugh lines at the corners of his eyes and firm lips that probably smiled more often than they frowned. How would those lips feel against hers?

"Miz Steadman?" His voice seemed to come from far away.

"Amy," she said. "Call me Amy."

He looked down into her face so close to his and whatever he saw there made his own face go very still.

She reached up and drew him down to her level, her eyes closing as her lips neared his.

Abruptly, his strong hands were on her shoulders, holding her away. "No," he said.

She opened her eyes. His breathing was as ragged as hers. "Don't you want to?" she whispered.

"Want?" He groaned in frustration. "Of course, I want. But I can't."

"Because I'm a suspect?"

"You're not a suspect. You were in a symphony hall surrounded by eight hundred people, including your father and your stepmother."

"Then—?"

"You're off limits for me till this case is over."

"When the case is over, I'll go back to New York."

"Will you?"

She looked deep into his eyes. "Will I?"

He didn't answer.

"Are you with someone now?" she asked. "Are you married?"

"No, but you are."

"Yes."

"When you called him that morning, did you call the hotel's number or his cell phone?"

Now it was her turn to not answer.

"We checked the phone records," he said gently. "Washington's less than a five-hour drive. He and his cell phone could have been anywhere."

"Eric didn't kill my grandmother, Terry."

He let his name hang there in the air between them, then took a deep breath. "Are you absolutely sure of that, Miz Steadman?"

"Yes."

She felt her eyes fill with sudden tears and ducked her head, hoping he hadn't noticed. "Show me again where I'm mentioned," she said and her voice barely wobbled at all.

"Here at the end." His voice wasn't all that steady either. "You spent the whole afternoon with your aunt."

"No," she said, forcing herself to concentrate on the reports, not on his rejection. "That was a deliberate lie. I was here in the house."

"You remember that?"

"No, but my cousin Curt does. He was working on the farm that day. He says that as soon as it happened, even before Grandmother phoned for a doctor or the police, she called Aunt Martha to come and get me and take me back to her house. Then she lied to the sheriff and said I wasn't here at all."

"And the Hahnemanns went along with her story. For a price." His breathing was almost back to normal.

"Is there any way to trace them? Find out if they're still alive?"

"If you can give me a Social Security number, I can try."

Her grandmother's tax records had already been packed up, but she had jotted the contents on the outside of each box and it was a simple matter to locate the box and then the folders for the taxes on each full-time employee. While she hunted for them, Amy said, "What was my grandfather's statement?"

"He doesn't seem to have made much of one. The sheriff noted that he seemed confused and disoriented and unable to give a coherent account. Makes sense. A stroke victim. Asleep. Then to be blasted awake by the sound of a shot just fifteen feet away and see his daughter lying dead . . ." He frowned and scanned through the forms again. "I'm surprised there's no nurse mentioned. Didn't he have one?"

"Not then. He'd had a second stroke and spent some time in

a rehab facility afterwards, but he'd been home about a week. That's why we were here: Maxie came down to help out when he first came out of rehab. He wasn't completely bedridden till after his third stroke. He could still get himself out of bed and back and forth to the bathroom with his walker and the house was set up so he could go anywhere in his wheelchair."

"His mind wasn't affected?"

"I don't know. The last Pink and Blue book came out the following year, but to guess how much of it was done after that second stroke?" She shrugged. "I just don't know. Aunt Martha could probably say. She might even tell you if you ask her. Every time I try, I just get more of the old 'You don't need to remember that, honey' that she and Dad and Grandmother have given me since it happened. I must have been here, though."

She described the films she and Beth had watched the day before and how cap guns had been banned from their toy box when they were growing up. "What sort of gun did Maxie use?"

"A snub-nosed .357 Magnum revolver with an ivory handle." He continued reading. "Your grandparents kept it in a drawer beside their bed. For protection, Mrs. Barbour said. She kept the bullets in a separate drawer, but said that her daughter knew that." He paused to visualize the gun in his mind. "Ivory handle? Except for the weight and the short barrel, it would have looked a lot like a kid's cap pistol. That's probably why they kept toy guns away from you kids."

"Grandmother came up to New York to see me nearly every month, and she took me with her on trips during school vacations, but it was almost five years before she let me come back here. Till I'd forgotten everything. Even my own mother."

"How old were you when your dad remarried?"

"Four."

"Was she good to you?"

"Yes. Claire's incapable of treating any child coldly. She was a loving mother."

"But?" he asked shrewdly.

"But I was never allowed to call her Mom, and that kept me aware that I wasn't really her daughter, that I'd had a different mother, one that didn't love me enough to keep living."

Her voice was so matter-of-fact that a less perceptive listener would have missed the heartbreak beneath her words. It took every ounce of Wilson's restraint not to put his arms around her and try to comfort her.

"You knew about her suicide?"

"Oh, yes. They never hid that from me. It's like being adopted. You assume the child's going to learn the truth some-day—another child blabs, or she finds the adoption papers—so you tell her she's adopted from the beginning and there's no huge traumatic shock."

"Except?"

"Except that eventually she grows up to realize there are more questions than they have answers for. That's why so many adoptees go looking for their biological parents."

"And that's why you've come here yourself rather than hiring someone to empty the house."

"Yes."

He straightened the papers and put them neatly back into the file envelope.

"Okay," he said at last. "I'm in. I'll find the Hahnemanns and I'll talk to your aunt."

CHAPTER
22

The party began with a bang as angry black clouds rolled in from the west.

Beth and Jacob Grayson arrived at the front door minutes before the rain and only seconds after Ethylene arrived at the back door, which meant that Amy had no time to hear Grayson's explanation of where they'd been all afternoon because Ethylene had followed her out and immediately began to gush about how happy she was Beth hadn't gone back to New York after all and of course her friend must stay for the party, plenty of cake and ice cream for everyone, and speaking of ice cream, where did Amy want her to put the two churns because with this many people one churn wasn't enough and of course they were going to leak salt water, so maybe out on the back porch? And oh, my goodness, just look at that pretty table! And balloons, too? If Amy didn't just beat all!

Ethylene had, by her own admission, "never seen a stranger." And God knows she certainly fit right into Jimmy's family of female talkers, thought Amy.

Curt and Mary blew in as the wind was picking up. Curt carried a box of half-pint canning jars filled with the fig preserves he'd made the day before and which he'd brought over to share with everyone. "One here for you, too," he told Amy jovially as they headed back out to the porch to wait for the others. Mary followed silently.

Amy had caught a strong smell of whiskey when he greeted her, but she didn't know Mary well enough to know if that was the reason she was so short-spoken this evening or if taciturnity was a family trait she shared with her sister Pat and nothing more.

The skies continued to darken, thunder rumbled and boomed, and lightning popped all around, but that didn't stop the Barbour clan. Cars pulled in close to the wide front porch and people laden with gaily wrapped presents dashed through the downpour and up the shallow steps to stand shaking rain from hair and shoes like dogs shaking water from their fur.

C.W. parked his truck under a tall magnolia tree and hastily splashed across the drive with a nine-year-old girl under one arm and a six-year-old boy under the other like two sacks of chicken feed.

The storm was so dramatic that no one wanted to stay inside. As soon as they'd relieved themselves of their presents and bags and found something to drink, people automatically returned to the deep porch where swings and wicker rockers offered comfortable seats from which to enjoy the vivid streaks of lightning.

"It's a million-dollar rain for farmers," Curt said happily. "Gonna weight up the last two primings on tobacco and save the cotton crop."

"Good thing you asked us to move the party over here," said Pauline. "Mama's deck wouldn't have been a bit of use to us tonight."

Vera's husband George, bald and jovial, came bounding through the rain in a silly hat that was actually a small umbrella, to the delight of his grandchildren, three little stairsteps in hooded yellow rain jackets, who ranged from three to six in age. Vera and Jean followed more decorously under a big blue umbrella until a sudden gust of wind grabbed it and sent it cart-wheeling across the lawn and the gray-haired sisters scampering for the porch.

Unable to resist, Barkis dashed out into the rain to chase after the umbrella, barking joyously as the wind caught the blue fabric and sailed it down the long drive.

Jean and Vera made it to the haven of the porch just as another downpour let loose. Lightning forked from a black cloud directly overhead and, in the same instant, a deafening clap of thunder brought them all to their feet.

Two of the children started to cry as the adults exclaimed and pointed to the magnolia. A bright white gash now ran the full length of the seventy-foot tree's trunk, and blasted twigs and leaves rained down on C.W.'s truck.

"Holy shit!" said Beth.

"Amen, sister!" said an equally awed George.

A terrified Barkis came flying up the drive and almost tore through the screen door trying to get inside to safety.

Frannie and her husband and eighteen-year-old son drove in about then and the boy ran onto the porch wide-eyed with excitement. "Man, did y'all *see* that?"

More lightning split the black clouds. The sky got even darker and rain fell so heavily that when Jimmy arrived with Aunt Martha and his baby son, they had to wait in his truck until it abated enough for someone to go out with umbrellas and ferry them in.

"Whose umbrella did we run over?" Aunt Martha asked. "The rain was coming down so hard we didn't see it till it was too late to stop."

The baby was crying and Ethylene just unbuttoned her shirt and held him to her breast without losing the thread of her conversation. Aunt Martha gave Amy an expressive look, but no one else seemed to notice.

Last to arrive were Pat with Herbert Raynor. C.W. and Frannie's son went out to help their grandfather from the car and up the two shallow steps, where they installed him in a high-seated rocker. Pat was drenched and more than a little annoyed.

"I couldn't get him to get his leg in so I could close his door," she said. "You'd think he was the one with the bad knee instead of me."

While Mary helped her towel off in the lavatory, Amy ran up to her room for a hair dryer and Mary seemed surprised when she came back with it.

Heretofore, Mary had kept her distance whenever Amy visited and she had started out cool this evening. Amy suspected that Mary and others on the farm regarded her as a stiff-necked extension of Grandmother, who had held herself aloof from the younger generations of Grandfather's family and had not encouraged familiarity. Aunt Martha was the only exemption—because she had kept her mouth shut about Maxie's death? Like many self-made people, Frances Barbour disdained those who had not made it, and Amy was increasingly aware that Grandmother had not hidden that disdain.

No wonder the others were wary of her. Except for Jean and Aunt Martha, the other relatives had barely spoken to her since she was a child, and knowing what she knew now, Amy couldn't really blame them for their wariness. Grandmother might have hostessed holiday dinners here while Bailey was alive, and she might have chosen to live here after he died, but she had never quit thinking of herself as a New Yorker and she had never opened the house to a purely family party like the one tonight.

The small act of offering a hair dryer to Pat seemed to breach Mary's prickly defenses, however. "I appreciate you letting Curt come get figs yesterday. He does love his preserves."

"I hope he kept enough for you two."

"Oh, he's the only one that eats them at our house. Too sweet for me." She hesitated, as if making nice was making her awkward. "Pat told me you wanted some help with the house? I wish I could come, but we're packing up, too, you know."

"That's okay. I spoke to her before I knew Beth was going to be here. We're managing fine."

"I feel bad not to help you. Especially since Aunt Martha told me you were going to chip in for Dad, too."

"It's only fair," said Amy. "He and Pat earned it."

C.W.'s little girl skidded up to Amy with a message from Pauline. "She says do you have a great big plate?"

Out in the kitchen, Pauline was ready to assemble the enormous birthday cake that Aunt Martha had baked and decorated in three separate pieces. "I don't know how we forgot to bring Grandma's turkey platter. That's what we usually use."

Amy opened and closed several cupboard doors, but nothing of the right size immediately presented itself. "Let's ask Pat. She'll know."

Only a little damp around the edges still, Patricia Raynor came out to the kitchen and went straight to the pantry where party supplies were kept, emerging with a large round platter of cut crystal in her workworn hands. When the kitchen lights hit it, each facet of the design became a prism that shot off refractions of the rainbow.

"This is almost too pretty to use," said Pauline, tilting it back and forth to enjoy the colorful sparks.

"It's Austrian," Aunt Martha told them. "Bailey gave it to Frances for their anniversary one year with airplane tickets for Vienna. He was always so romantic."

"Did they take Maxie to Vienna, too?" Amy asked curiously.

"Oh, no. She was usually in school when they traveled."

Now why does that not surprise me? thought Amy. She turned to Pauline. "Would you like to have the plate?"

"Really?"

"Why not? You guys seem to celebrate a lot of birthdays and I don't know when I'd ever use it."

"It'll certainly get used with us," Pauline agreed. "Thank you."

They put the cake together, topped it with candles, and gathered everyone into the big kitchen. The birthday boy stood by the cake with a self-conscious smile while cameras flashed and a couple of camcorders rolled as everyone, even Beth and Jacob Grayson, sang "Happy Birthday" and watched Jimmy blow out his candles.

The ice cream churns were brought inside and generous scoops of homemade peach ice cream topped each slice of cake.

With the long table gone from the dining room—"I'd've left it if I'd known," Pauline lamented—the children clustered around the glass and wicker coffee table in the sunroom while most of the adults went back to the porch to eat. Thunder and lightning seemed to be over, the sky brightened to a dirty gray, but the rain had settled in as if it meant to go on till morning.

"Temperature's dropped at least ten degrees," said Curt, who had brought a large dish of ice cream out to Herbert Raynor.

The five younger children quickly finished eating and soon became bored. Unable to run off their energy outside, they raced through the house, making C.W. and Vera apprehensive about the damage they might do unsupervised, especially since Amy had explained who Jacob Grayson was and why he was here. With an official appraiser in the house, they were acutely aware that these sturdy chairs and chests, these cabinets and settles, were now items of serious value, not monkey bars to be climbed upon or banged into.

Knowing that their exuberance would drive Vera and Jean into leaving early if she didn't divert them, Amy herded the children into the elevator, showed them how to operate it, and took them up to the attic. The rain had dropped the temperature here, too, and as soon as she switched on the lights, they spotted the old toys and games and dived right in.

"Thanks, Amy," said Vera when she returned. "I adore those kids, but they do wear me out."

"Tell me about it!" said Mary, who helped C.W. with his two children whenever it was his weekend to have them.

"That's why God gives babies to young mothers," Aunt

Martha said comfortably. Her great-grandson slept in her arms and she rocked gently back and forth.

"What's bad is when you have to be mother to your own parents," said Pat, as they watched Curt silently feed his father-in-law ice cream. Earlier in the evening, Curt had been chatty and sociable, but as the evening wore on and talk turned to future plans, he'd grown quieter and quieter, as if all that mattered was emptying the bowl one spoonful at a time. Herbert Raynor opened his mouth obediently as a bird and seemed to be enjoying the sweetness.

"You've been good to him, Aunt Pat," said Frannie, "but it's going to be so much easier on you and Mom when he goes into Rosewood."

"Is that where you've decided on?" asked Aunt Martha. "I thought that looked the best of all the pictures you showed me."

"Soon as the money comes through," said Mary.

George got up to go smoke a cigarette with C.W. at the edge of the porch and Amy took his seat next to Vera on the swing. A packet of travel brochures for Australia and China had dropped from his pocket and she handed them to Vera. "Are you planning a vacation?"

"Planning our retirement," said her cousin. On her the Barbour nose was slightly more prominent than on Jean and Curt. "George and I have spent most of our lives working with exotics at the Arboretum. Now we're finally going to get to see them in their native habitats. I can't tell you how excited we are about it."

"You've never been?" asked Amy, who'd flown out to the Far East with Jeffrey several times and had made the side excursion to Australia at least twice.

"There was never enough money before," Vera said cheerfully. "Our daughter's medical expenses just about broke us."

Amy vaguely remembered hearing Grandmother speak of

Vera's daughter, who had made a rash marriage and whose husband abandoned her with three children when she got sick.

"But the scans have come back clean three years in a row now," said Vera, "and she finally got a job with benefits, thank God, so George and I are going to take early retirement and go see the gardens of the world."

Yet another dream deferred by Grandmother's disregard, thought Amy.

Jean had shown her sister the journal they'd compiled with Maxie, and Amy listened quietly while Vera reminisced about those long-gone days and how seriously they'd taken their amateur observations.

"Remember the summer we catalogued all the pines, Jean?"

"I couldn't tell you a loblolly from a swamp pine," said Frannie's husband. "A longleaf's the only one I've ever been sure of."

"That's me with oaks," said Jimmy. "I know jack oaks and willow oaks and that's about all."

"If y'all are going to open a lawn service, you better let me show you how to key leaves and twigs through a field guide," said Vera.

As Jimmy and C.W. began to discuss which pieces of equipment they would keep from the farm and the new mowers and edgers they wanted to buy "soon as the money comes through," old Herbert Raynor swallowed wrong and began to cough. Mary and Pat both jumped up to bring him water and a napkin. Curt relinquished the spoon to his wife and joined his sisters and Amy.

"Yep," he said, as if picking up a conversation already in progress, "real lucky for all of us that Aunt Frances got killed when she did, wasn't it?"

Everyone looked at him with shocked faces.

"Really, Curt!" Vera said sharply.

"There's an eight-hundred-pound gorilla on this porch," he

told her belligerently. "Just thought maybe somebody ought to notice it."

"Have you been drinking?" Jean asked her brother.

"Yep. And when I get home, I might just have some more. Wash the bad taste of her murder out of my mouth."

"Curt, honey, you ought not to be talking like this," Aunt Martha scolded. "Not here. Not in front of Amy."

"Sorry, Aunt Martha, but Amy already knows. She's the one told me."

"Hey, now," said George. "What's that supposed to mean?"

"Somebody killed Aunt Frances, George. Somebody murdered her. Her and poor old King, too."

"We know that, bo. Some burglar—"

"Not a burglar." Curt might have had a drink or two, but his words were clear and precise. "Nothing was taken. Not her money, not her jewelry, not even her sleeping pills. Just her life. Somebody couldn't wait any longer."

For a moment, the steadily falling rain was the only sound on the porch, then Mary said, "That's enough, Curt."

His eyes met hers for a long moment. "I guess you're right, Mary. You usually are."

C.W. stirred uneasily. "Dad . . ."

Curt brushed his son away and stood up. "Keep your seat, C.W. I'm going. Sorry if I messed up your birthday, Jimmy, but you'll have lots more. Maybe next year, I'll give you a Cadillac."

"Curt!" Vera protested.

"Don't worry, little sister. Me and the gorilla are going." He stepped off the porch and into the rain. "You coming, Mary?"

"I'll ride with Pat or C.W.," she said coldly.

He took a couple of unsteady steps, then turned and looked back at them. "Look," he said. "I understand. I'm glad for the money, too. But damn it all, we'd've found a way to pay back the option money or get the money for anything else that was really needful. She didn't have to be killed like that. King neither."

Rain streamed down Curt's face and darkened his shirt. He stood there with his hands outstretched for a moment, but when no one spoke, he shrugged and walked around the house to his truck parked at the back. They heard the engine catch, then a flash of headlights swept the side bushes as the truck swung around and headed back home through the farm lanes.

As if a switch had suddenly been flipped, everyone seemed to talk at once.

"What's he thinking?"

"It was the whiskey talking."

"Amy, I'm so sorry."

"He saying one of us—?"

"Curt never could handle liquor."

"—not a burglary?"

In an effort to rescue the evening, Ethylene asked Jimmy, "What do you think, honey? You ready to open some presents while the baby's still asleep?"

"You start and I'll go get the coffee," said Amy, already fleeing toward the front door.

Out in the kitchen, the big coffee urn had finished perking. Beth had followed her. "God, it's like a freaking made-for-television reality show! The Beverly Hillbillies do Hercule Poirot. 'My li'l ol' gray cells say y'all must be the killer, ma'am.' "

Normally, Amy found Beth's impressions amusing. Not tonight. " 'Y'all' is never singular," she snapped.

"Dammit, Amy, that guy as much as said somebody out there on that porch killed Frances."

"He was drunk."

"In vino veritas."

Beth might have said more, but Jacob Grayson had come down the back stairs, a camera around his neck. He slid the inventory sheets into his backpack and zipped it up. "I think I've seen everything and I'll try to get you some hard figures by the middle of the week."

"Thank you, Mr. Grayson."

"Call me Jacob," he said with a grin. "I'm going to be your brother-in-law one of these days, remember?"

Beth rolled her eyes.

Amy put a sugar bowl and spoons on a large tray, added a pitcher of milk, and filled the tray with the steaming mugs. When she took the milk carton from the refrigerator, she noticed that someone—Curt?—had set a jar of those fig preserves on the top shelf. Tomorrow's breakfast.

"Coffee?" asked Beth.

Grayson shook his head. "There's an estate sale in Wilmington tomorrow morning and I need to be on the road early. Want to come? I'll be passing right by around eight."

"Sorry, I'm working here," she said virtuously.

Amy left them discussing it and carried the tray out to the porch. The floor around Jimmy's chair was littered with birthday paper and a nearby chair held new shirts, CDs, a recent video release, and a set of socket wrenches. George took the heavy tray from her hands and Jean helped pass around the milk and sugar.

Despite Ethylene's efforts, the earlier festive mood had vanished, although Pauline tried gamely to restore it, making bright comments on each present Jimmy unwrapped. She had saved hers for last, and when he unwrapped it, it was a digital camera.

"That's so you can e-mail Mama and me pictures of the baby every week after we move to Beaufort," she said happily.

Soon as the money comes through, thought Amy and saw that same thought reflected in other eyes around her.

"It's been a very nice party," said Jean, and the others gratefully seized upon this signal to disperse.

"Yeah, real nice. Thanks, Ethylene. Thanks, Amy."

"Better call the kids down."

"Yeah, time we were getting back to Raleigh, too."

"Oh, y'all don't have to leave just because we are."

Amy suddenly remembered Grandmother's clothes and asked if anyone was interested. The women were torn between wanting to leave and curiosity about the rooms upstairs, which most of them had seldom, if ever, seen.

Curiosity won.

As they crossed the entry hall, the elevator descended, its door opened, and children spilled out, laughing and chattering. All wore hats. C.W.'s son had a derby on his head and a holster belted around his waist. His sister had on a floppy garden hat and she clicked an empty cap pistol at him.

Amy stared, frozen. Vera's youngest grandchild, a towheaded little girl, ran toward them. She was wearing the same cowgirl outfit Amy had seen in the film she'd taken from Aunt Martha's: a fringed vest and skirt, even the hat Amy had once defended. But there were dark blotches on the skirt and vest that had not been there in the film. With her index finger extended to form the barrel of a pistol, the child laughed and "shot" at Amy. "Ka-pow! You're dead!"

"Oh my Lord!" Aunt Martha gasped. Her coffee mug slipped from her fingers and smashed on the hardwood floor.

In that instant, Amy knew that Maxie's death had not been suicide and she knew why Grandmother and Aunt Martha had bundled her out of the house before the police arrived that long-ago day.

"Bang-bang, Mommy!"

"Bang-bang, Amy!"

I shot my mother, didn't I?"

"No, no, no!" Aunt Martha moaned.

"It's all right, Mama," said Pauline. "Now, you young'uns, step back away from the glass."

Amid the squealing children and the bustling women, who automatically hurried for paper towels, dustpans, and brooms, only Aunt Martha had heard Amy's stunned question; and Pauline took her mother's protest as dismay over the broken mug.

"Where are your own clothes?" Vera asked her granddaughter. "Upstairs?"

The child nodded while the others capered around the hall in the hats.

"Okay, y'all," C.W. said to his two. "Time to go." He took off their hats and handed them to Amy along with the holster and cap pistol.

Still in a daze, Amy found herself in the elevator with Vera and the little girl and more hats. In the attic, the box that had held them was tipped over on its side.

"That's where the Jessie Cowgirl things were," said the child as

Vera helped her change into her own clothes. "Way down at the bottom."

Vera looked at the scattered toys and tumbled hats. "I'll get the kids to come pick all this up."

"Don't bother," said Amy.

She hefted the cap pistol in her hand and concentrated, desperately trying to remember.

"Amy? You okay?" asked Vera.

"Yes."

"You look a little green. Too much ice cream?"

"No, I'm fine. You go ahead, Vera. I'll be right down."

When Vera and her granddaughter were gone, Amy slowly went over to the little fringed skirt and vest that had been carelessly tossed over a box. The splotches on the fawn-colored suede had not been her imagination, but they don't have to be Maxie's blood, she told herself. They could be oil, chocolate syrup, fruit stains, a dozen different things.

(What do you think, Pink?)

According to the reports Terry Wilson showed her, "Mrs. Barbour stated that the gun was normally kept in her bedside table."

Three-year-olds can open drawers.

"She said that the bullets were kept in a separate drawer."

Possible.

"The gun was always unloaded."

Oh, please! If the gun is for your protection against a possible break-in, you certainly don't plan to waste precious moments rummaging for bullets.

(What'll we do, Blue?)

She carried the whole outfit, cap pistol and hat, too, to her bedroom and stashed them in the bottom drawer of her dresser, then went down to find Aunt Martha.

In the kitchen, Pauline busily packed up the remnants of the cake. Jean stood at the sink washing coffee mugs, and Ethylene came from the front porch with a full bag of party trash.

"I'll just stick it out on the back porch with the rest of those bags, Amy. All that's trash, isn't it? And Jimmy'll come take everything to the dump tomorrow. He can pick up the ice cream churns then, too."

"Here," said Jean. "Let me add the coffee grounds before you tie it up."

"Where's Aunt Martha?" Amy asked.

Pauline licked a speck of frosting from her fingers and said, "Oh, honey, she was so upset about breaking that cup that she got C.W. to take her home when he left with the children. It wasn't a special cup or anything, was it?"

"No."

"And the floor's going to go when the rest of the house is pulled down. I told her that, but she was almost shaking. Mama's always been so strong, I have to keep reminding myself that she's going to be eighty soon."

Out on the porch, Pat and Mary had reboxed Jimmy's birthday presents and stacked them neatly. George had backed his and Vera's SUV up close to the steps, which made Amy remember that she'd told Vera earlier that they could take the little desk this evening.

"I'm so happy to have it," Vera told Amy again as George and Jimmy loaded it into the back of the van. Her hand brushed Amy's cheek affectionately. "You're very like her, you know. I wish she could have seen you grow up."

She herded the children into the van and called to Jean, who came hurrying out, then stopped and impulsively hugged Amy. "Please keep in touch, honey. You're all we have left of Maxie."

The rain had dwindled to a light drizzle and Pat decided she might as well go, too, so that she could get Herbert in and out of the car without getting drenched again.

"I'll ride with you then," said Mary. "I already said goodnight to Paulie and Ethylene. Thanks for having us, Amy. And I do apologize for Curt."

"That's all right."

"He really liked Aunt Frances."

Amy almost had to smile, for Mary's tone was one of bafflement. But then this was the woman who never understood why Grandmother wasn't flattered that Frannie had been named for her.

As soon as they had driven off, Jimmy pulled his own truck in close to the steps and put his presents inside the cab, then stood on the porch looking out into the rainy darkness. Amy was too keyed up to make small talk, and after a few moments, Jimmy said, "Don't know what got into ol' Curt tonight. Unless—" He hesitated. "What he said? About you being the one told him Aunt Frances was, you know, murdered? Was that right?"

"Did I tell him what the SBI agent told me? Yes."

"Oh, Lordy," he sighed.

"Now you tell me something," she said. "You were seven when my mother died and you grew up here on the farm, right?"

"We weren't here right when it happened. Mom and Dad were still married then and we lived in Fuquay till I was ten." His broad face was wary. "Why?"

"What were you told about it?"

He shrugged. "That she shot herself with Uncle Bailey's gun because she was unhappy."

"Did you ever hear what she was unhappy about?"

"Well, naw. We young'uns did wonder about it when we got older. I mean, there she was with lots of money to do whatever she wanted, good-looking husband, you. We couldn't never figure what she had to be so unhappy about. That was before all the talk shows educated us about depression and stuff like that."

"But what did the adults say? Aunt Martha, your mother, Curt and Mary?"

"They didn't never talk about it much. 'Specially not Grandma. Her and Uncle Bailey and Aunt Frances were real close and it just hurt too much, I reckon."

"You never heard anyone suggest that maybe Maxie didn't shoot herself?"

"Huh?" He shook his head vigorously. "No. Never. Why you asking that?" He looked at her sharply. "You thinking the same person as killed Aunt Frances killed Maxie way back then?"

"What on earth are you two talking about?" asked Pauline, who had come to the door unnoticed by either of them. "Maxie shot herself. Everybody knows that. You can ask Mama."

"She was there?"

"Well, no, but she went right over, soon as Aunt Frances called, and brought you back to the house with her."

"That's not what she told the sheriff. She said I was with her when it happened. That I'd spent the whole afternoon with her."

Pauline looked perplexed. "Now that can't be right. I'm sure she told me she went and got you so you wouldn't have to see or hear anything."

"Grandmother told them the same thing, and so did that couple that worked for her. That I was at Aunt Martha's all afternoon. I read the coroner's report today."

"Really? Well then, maybe I got it mixed up."

"No, you had it straight. Curt told me that Grandmother did call your mother to come get me out of the house."

"Oh, well, Curt. You heard him tonight. You can't go by what Curt says."

"It's not just Curt, Mom," Jimmy said. "Amy says it's what the SBI's saying."

"Well, that's the silliest thing I ever heard of."

"Which?" asked Amy. "That Grandmother and Aunt Martha lied about where I was or that Grandmother was killed by someone she knew?"

"Both," Pauline said firmly. "Leave it to the police, honey. And don't go getting Mama all upset about this, okay? Jimmy, Ethylene says her and the baby are ready to go. If you'll pull the truck around to the back and help me load up my car, we can get on home."

She turned and went back into the house.

Jimmy looked at Amy, gave a what-can-I-tell-you? shrug, and got into his truck to do as he was told.

When all the Barbours had driven away, Amy whistled Barkis back inside, locked the doors, and went upstairs. Beth met her on the landing. Although it was only a little after ten, she was already in the oversized T-shirt that served as her nightgown.

"Is it safe to come out?"

"They're all gone, if that's what you mean."

"You look beat. I brought a bottle of wine up to my room. Want some?"

"You're drinking wine?"

"One small glass. It's not going to hurt the baby. French women drink wine all through pregnancy and their babies turn out fine. Want some or not?"

"Okay."

While Beth went to get it, Amy walked over to the terrace window and turned on the outside light. There was no sign of either spider and only shreds of a web so tattered from the wind and rain that it was almost unrecognizable.

"Hope you don't mind a water glass," said Beth. She poured a generous amount for Amy and topped her own small goblet, then sat down across from Amy with a determined look on her pretty face.

Amy smiled wanly. "You look exactly like Dad when he's about to tell us something for our own good."

"Laugh if you want, but it's quit being funny. Somebody killed Frances. Somebody made a threatening phone call. Somebody doesn't want you here asking questions. Does Eric know about this?"

"He knows."

"Then he's crazy, too, to let you stay here. I really, really think we ought to leave, go home. You don't need this. *I* don't need this." She gave her flat abdomen an exaggerated pat.

"I don't like it any more than you, Beth, but I can't leave without knowing all the answers. You don't have to stay, though. In fact, you probably should go. Look, let me call Dad and—"

"No! If you're staying, I'm staying, so forget about calling him." She took another swallow of wine and settled back into the deep chair. "Anyhow, he doesn't call the shots anymore."

"He doesn't?"

"Nope. You do. Or you could. Now that Frances is gone, you have controlling interest, remember?"

Startled, Amy realized that yes, she did. She had known it, of course. The trust had been explained to her long before Grand-mother died, and Dad had reminded her of it only two weeks ago when he urged her to stand up to her siblings and to plan on tak-ing his place when he retired. Knowing something in the abstract was one thing, however; knowing it in the concrete and practical was something else, especially since she had always resisted that knowledge, had always tried to pretend she was no different from Michael, Sam, and Beth. But yes, if she wanted to, she could be Grandmother now and overrule Dad right down the line. She could give Beth back her job, she could let her stay in the corpo-rate apartment without any strings, she could even sell the com-pany to that German company that had made such an incredible offer back in the spring, an offer that had interested Dad, Sam, and Eric, but not Grandmother or Michael.

Nor her, either, not that anyone had asked her opinion.

"Anyhow," Beth said, "you've taken care of most of her papers, I've done the books, and Jacob's seen enough to give you an ap-praisal on the furniture. That's all you really care about, isn't it?"

"Jacob. Right. So how was Raleigh?"

"Raleigh was actually pretty cool, but you're changing the sub-ject."

"So are you. Jacob seems nice. Flaky but nice."

"He is."

"But—?"

"But nothing. The man's a fruitcake. A mental case. A—" She gave a frustrated swipe of her hand as if to brush Jacob Grayson off the face of the earth. "It's all a joke with him. Forget about him. I'm serious, Amy. Let's go home before something bad happens. Please?" She suddenly looked very young and very scared.

Amy put out her hand. "Nothing's going to happen. We're not standing in anyone's way. Tomorrow I'll sign the papers, everybody will have whatever it is they want, and we'll be safe."

"Will we?" She sounded lost and uncertain.

"Of course we will."

"I know you're getting off on this family business, but you're no farm girl and neither am I. We don't belong here. *You* don't belong here. It's changing you and it's trying to change me. You're a city person. Concerts, plays, good restaurants."

Amy looked at Beth in bewilderment. "Where did you get the idea that I'd want to stay here after the farm is sold?"

Unbidden, one reason to stay floated into her thoughts. The reason had a homely, basset hound face: SBI Agent Terry Wilson, who had made it so clear that he didn't want to get entangled that she flushed with remembered humiliation.

"Why are you blushing?" Beth asked.

"Am I? I don't know. Hot flashes? Early menopause?"

"At thirty?" Beth stood up. "I'm going to check out the refrigerator. Bring you some toast or something?"

Amy finished her wine and handed Beth the empty glass. "No, I'm going to bed. If you get into Curt's figs, leave me enough for breakfast, okay?"

"Okay."

As she started down the hall, Amy touched Beth's shoulder. "Thanks."

"For what?"

"For staying. For caring."

"For being a pain in the butt?" Beth said mockingly.

Amy smiled. "Well, I was going to say for being a sister, but I guess it's the same thing."

"Go to bed before we both get sloppy," said Beth.

CHAPTER
24

For a moment, Amy almost turned back to confide in Beth, as if they really were sisters who had grown up sharing secrets, but the lifelong habit of keeping her own counsel was too firmly ingrained. Besides, where to start?

With the day she killed her own mother?

The day Grandmother told her that Dad was unfaithful to Maxie?

Her suspicion that Eric now cheated on her as Dad used to cheat on Claire?

Instead, she wearily closed the bedroom door, kicked off her sandals, and changed into her nightgown. The bottom drawer of the old oak dresser clamored for her attention. Much as she really did not want to, she knelt and took out the garments she had been small enough to wear twenty-seven years ago—the little fringed vest, the matching skirt, both of buttery soft, fawn-colored suede. The label indicated that the outfit had come from an exclusive store in Dallas, as did the small felt cowgirl hat with silver conchos that were now tarnished nearly black. Maybe something Dad had brought back from one of his business trips?

The cap pistol, holster, and belt set were probably a Kmart buy and nothing special.

Her fingers touched the old stains and splotches. Her mother's lifeblood. Against her will, a mental videotape began to play in her head. She watched herself at three, an inquisitive little girl who had probably been told never to go into Grandmother's room uninvited and certainly never to open drawers.

But Grandmother is downstairs, Grandfather is asleep, and Mommy is on the landing with a magazine. She opens the bedside drawer and there is the gun.

She eagerly reaches for it. Another gun! Now she and Mommy can each have one. She hurries down the hallway, detouring around Grandfather's room because she's supposed to be quiet when he sleeps. There's Mommy on the couch.

She giggles, thinking how surprised Mommy will be. She raises the new gun and points it. "Bang-bang, Mommy!"

Mommy's reading. Absentmindedly, her eyes still on the magazine in her lap, she points her index finger at Amy and says, "Bang-bang, Amy."

As Amy gets closer, Mommy finally looks up and her indulgent smile turns to horror. "Amy, no!"

But it's too late. Laughing, Amy pulls the trigger and her world explodes in her face.

Grandfather wakes with a roar as she herself screams in terror from the unexpected blast. Mommy falls out of the chair onto the floor and there's blood everywhere. She's still screaming and Mommy doesn't get up to comfort her or to swoop her into her sheltering arms. Grandmother and the Hahnemanns come running.

"Mein Gott!"

"Someone call an ambulance!" cries Grandmother.

At this point, the tape in Amy's mental video snarled around the posts, because Grandmother did not call an ambulance or the rescue squad or whatever emergency help was available back then. Instead, she called Aunt Martha. Someone must have stripped off her blood-splattered costume and redressed her in normal summer play clothes while they waited for Aunt Martha. Someone had hastily carried the cowgirl things up to the attic and buried them deep in a box under a bunch of old hats where they would not be discovered by a cursory search of the house when the police came, one of the Hahnemanns probably, since Grandmother would have long since disposed of them if she'd known they were there.

There was a curious, almost touching logic in their actions. Maxie was dead. Nothing was going to bring her back. And there she was. Three years old and crying inconsolably for a mother who would never again stand up, never tuck her in at night, never kiss her good morning. What adult wouldn't lie if it protected a child from growing up under such a terrible, terrible burden of guilt?

She had wanted to know why Maxie died and her wish had been granted, but Dad was right. She should have left it alone. Too late now to put the genie back into the bottle.

Amy held the plastic-handled cap gun in her small hand and laid the cool metal barrel against her hot face. Tomorrow, she would have to call Terry Wilson and tell him he needn't bother tracing the Hahnemanns. Not tonight, though. She couldn't deal with any more emotion tonight.

She closed the dresser drawer and went over to the dormer window where Maxie's desk had stood. Undoing the lock, she tried to open the window, thinking that the cool fresh air and the gentle drumbeat of raindrops against the roof shingles would lull her to sleep. But the window refused to budge. What she needed was the small crowbar Jean had used to open the attic windows and lever up the board that had hidden that summer journal.

Board?

She looked down at her bare feet and at the short floorboards upon which she stood and felt a shiver run down her spine. This dormer was directly beneath the attic dormer with the loose board.

She pulled a lamp closer. Was it her imagination or were those faint tool marks at the edge of that board nearest the window? Fingernails were useless here. She found a metal nailfile in her cosmetic bag, inserted the pointed end in the crack between the boards, and felt the board shift ever so slightly. Unfortunately, the file bent before she could get enough leverage. It would have to be the crowbar.

There was no sign of Beth when she crossed the landing and took the elevator to the attic, but she heard the television down in the den as she returned with the crowbar in hand.

Back in her room, she tried again, and this time the board slipped up and away and there between the joists lay a diary bound in red cardboard, a sheaf of typewritten pages, and a pale green ledger book similar to the one Jean had taken.

She lifted them gently from their hiding place and carried them over to her bed, where she sat cross-legged on the coverlet to examine her find. The typewritten pages appeared to be drafts of nature essays. One of the ledger books was labeled "Field Notes and Observations" and, from the date of the first entries, had been begun about three years before her birth.

Scrawled on the flysheet in the red diary was an almost illegible inscription. "Happy Birthday" was clear enough, but she couldn't make out the signature.

Maxie had begun recording her thoughts on the third of February. "Today is my 10th birthday and this is one of my presents. I got new skates, hair ribbons, two dresses, new saddle shoes, a dollar from Grandma and a quarter from Mrs. H. next door. I really wanted a party but Mother and Father are working on another book, so I told her couldn't we have cupcakes because everybody else's mother brings cupcakes for their birthday and she rang Mrs. Feinburg who has the bakery around the corner from the school and gave me the money so Mrs. Feinburg brought up chocolate cupcakes with pink icing. She put a pink candle on mine and everyone sang Happy Birthday. Oh, and a book from Miss Templeton. I love Miss Templeton. She's so pretty and she never calls me Max. I wish I could still be in her class. It's called *Grassroot Jungle* by Mr. Edwin Way Teale. I'm going to read it all the way through and take it with me to Grandma Virgie's this summer and see if I can find a praying mantis."

The next few pages were conscientiously filled with school and homework and "Miss Templeton is going to take four of us to the Museum of Natural History next Sunday. She is so good and nice." By the end of February, Maxie was skipping at least one page a week. In March, more pages were blank than not, and the only entry for April was an impassioned, "I hate-Hate-HATE school and I HATE Faye and Marjorie and I HATE Pink and Blue and Max most of all. Every time they got near me today Faye would say What's that stink, Pink? and Marjorie would look at me and hold her nose and say Pee-yew, Blue! and everybody laughed and they kept saying Relax, Max. I wish I could change my name. I wish I'd never seen those stupid toys. I wish Father would write poems like he's always saying and not these stupid baby books that everyone makes fun of me about. I wish I wasn't so ugly."

April began with a more mature hand and the handwritten date was for mid-June four years later. "If some people go prying into other people's private diaries when he"—here the word "he" had been crossed out and changed to "they"—"when they shouldn't, then if they read something they don't like, it's their own DAMN fault."

"Damn" was not only capitalized but underlined three times.

"Why does he always have to snoop? Why can't he just talk to me—ask me what he wants to know? It's like he doesn't care what I think or feel if I say it straight out to him—no, he wants to catch my subconscious unaware—that's what he says anyhow. And she's just as bad. 'He's a poet, Max, and everything is grist for a writer's mill. You have to accept that. Besides, why would you write anything you'd be ashamed to have him read?' "

There were several pages of hot resentment along those lines, then a despairing "Sometimes I think the only reason they're glad they had me is because I used to whisper to my animal friends and that made Father write those damn books."

Skimming through the rest of the diary, Amy saw that Maxie had written in it only when she was here at the farm. She must have brought it down with her when she was fourteen and left it hidden here, where it was safe from Bailey's eyes. Each new return began with a recap of the time away before plunging into the dailyness of life on the farm with Grandma Virgie and her cousins. Here were all the passions and emotions, the opinions and reactions that had been missing from her letters. The small triumphs, the big disappointments. And always a yearning for a closeness with Frances and Bailey that never materialized.

Then came a completely joyous entry: "My first visit back since Jeffrey and I were married. Married! I've always felt so ugly. Jeffrey tells me I'm beautiful. I guess love really is blind!"

Four years later: "Stupid to think he could love me for myself alone. I wish I hadn't found out. He doesn't know I know. Father's never looked at another woman. Of course, Mother is still beautiful and clever and I've never been either. Ironic that I can't even get pregnant, while Mother had at least two abortions before they decided to have me. 'Your father wanted a son,' she told me, 'but once was enough, thank you very much, and I had my tubes tied even though you were a girl.' I think this must be the only thing she ever denied him. Of course, if exposing girl babies had been legal here, who knows?"

After Bailey's first stroke and the move to North Carolina: "I can't divorce Jeffrey now. The company depends on him. Mother and Father, too. I know it's partly my fault that he keeps finding new women. In the beginning we could talk about anything and everything and I made him laugh. Now everything I say or do bores him silly. When he still made love to me, it was as if he did it out of duty. It's been almost six months. Not since the night I told him I knew about Louise and all the others."

It was during those years that she began secretly writing a series of essays drawn from her journals. Slowly she began to formulate a plan to leave. "There's no reason to stay. The marriage is dead. Might as well bury it and get on with life."

And then came their reconciliation and her own personal miracle: "She's so tiny. So perfect. So beautiful. Amy. Jeffrey wanted to name her Samantha or Alison. I would never name a daughter of mine something that could be shortened to a man's nickname. Amy will always be Amy. It means beloved and she is. O God, she is!"

For the next two years, the diary was devoted to her baby's growth and development. Love and wonder suffused those pages and Amy read them with a growing sorrow that nearly choked her. To think what she had missed, what had been destroyed by Grandmother's carelessness and her own disobedience!

Near the end, though, there came a final explosion of hurt and rage: "I cannot *believe* that he did it again. When we have been so happy these last three years? When Amy adores him? How *could* he? I told my lawyer to draw up the papers. We'll file them as soon as I get back to New York. If it means the company must be sold, then so be it! He can have it all. All except Amy. I'll fight him to the last breath of my being for her and I don't care what Mother says. Or Father either. They'll never miss me."

The telephone on her bedside table shrilled so unexpectedly that Amy jumped. Her first impulse was to let Beth get it. Then she glanced at her watch. Almost midnight.

Eric?

On the third ring, she picked up. "Hello?"

Above the bad connection and the sound of Beth's television program, she heard a creepy raspy whisper. "Go back to New York. Now. Or your husband's gonna be taking y'all home in a pine box."

On the extension, Beth said, "Listen, you jerk-off! You think you can—"

There was a click and then an immediate dial tone.

Beth said, "Amy? This is really starting to creep me out. Please. Can't we go home?"

That night, Amy did something she hadn't done since she was seventeen and Claire and Jeffrey had flown down to Miami for a three-day toy trade show. Nine-year-old Beth had picked up a miserable head cold that made her miss Claire more than usual. At bedtime she'd had a meltdown, crying until her eyes and nose streamed. Michael was away at college, Sam was already asleep in his room on the far side of the apartment, and the current housekeeper's English was almost as nonexistent as Amy's Spanish.

But Amy remembered a scene from a book she'd once read, and she'd bundled Beth into her bathroom, turned the hot shower on full blast so that the room filled up with steam that unclogged her little sister's nose and let her breathe easier. Then she'd brought Beth into her own bed and rubbed the child's back until she fell asleep.

"I'm not nine anymore," Beth said when Amy suggested a repeat, but it was only a half-hearted protest, and she and Barkis snuggled into their half of the bed with no further argument.

Amy brushed her teeth, turned out the lamp, and slid under the sheet. Barkis tried to kiss her goodnight, but was easily deflected. Beth was another story. Lying here together in the darkness seemed to be dredging up memories of teenage slumber parties, a time for asking questions that might never be asked in daylight.

"Amy?"

"Mmm?"

"Is everything okay between you and Eric?"

"Why?"

"I don't know. He hasn't called since I've been here, has he?"

"He went rock climbing this weekend."

"No cellular service where he went?"

Amy described the danger of breaking one's concentration on a sheer rock face.

"It's just that you guys always seem joined at the hip. But you're down here and he's up in Boston."

"We're married, Beth, not manacled."

"Being married's like being manacled, though, isn't it? In a nice way? If the marriage is working, I mean? Jane leads Michael around by the nose and Eric tells you what to do and both of you seem to like it. While Mom and Dad—" She rolled over to prop on one elbow and face Amy. "What you said to him this morning about cheating on Max? He's cheated on Mom, too, you know?"

"That was years ago. Ancient history."

"I don't call year before last ancient history."

"What?"

"Some bimbo in Records. That's what Sam said, anyhow."

"Does Claire know?"

"I don't think so. Sam said Michael and Eric eased her out before it got messy. Didn't Eric tell you?"

"No."

"Probably thought you wouldn't want to know that either."

"What does that mean?"

Amy could feel Beth's shrug as she lay back on the pillow.

"He knows you don't like fights or upsets so he's sort of like a broom man or whatever they call them."

"Broom man?"

"You know that dumb game they sometimes show on winter sports programs? Where they slide a round stone slowly across the ice?"

"Curling?"

"I guess. Anyhow, there's always someone out in front of it with a broom sweeping the ice smooth so that the stone can slide right into the target area." She yawned widely. "That's

Eric. Smoothing it out for you so you can slide along with no friction."

"Nonsense," said Amy.

"All the same," she said drowsily, "it must be nice to have somebody watching out for you."

Amy patted her sister's arm. "Go to sleep," she said and turned over to discourage further talk.

But as soon as she closed her eyes, her mind was assailed by images of Eric and Lisl, of Maxie and handguns, of Aunt Martha's panicky denials, of Curt's implied accusations, of Maxie's pain and humiliation, of her own small hands opening Grandmother's drawers. And somewhere in the mix was Terry Wilson and his disturbing masculinity.

Beside her, Barkis and Beth both slept. Through the open window came the soft patter of cool rain. Amy matched her breaths to Beth's and eventually drifted off, too.

CHAPTER
25

Amy woke with the sun and she and Barkis eased out of bed so quietly that Beth did not stir.

When she opened the side door downstairs to let the terrier out for his morning run, the air felt cool and clean. She was not fooled, though. This was still early August and it was still North Carolina. Before midday, opening an outer door could very well feel like opening a sauna. She continued on out to the kitchen, started the coffee, and had poured her first cup before Barkis scratched on the door to be let back in.

She carried her coffee up to the landing and was delighted to see that both spiders had survived the storm after all. The black-and-yellow female hung upside down in a fresh new web while the smaller male strolled around the perimeter with cocky confidence. The new web was slightly higher on the plate glass wall and angled over to the projecting corner of an exterior pilaster. She went out onto the terrace, caught a bedraggled grasshopper in one of the neglected planters, and tried to hook it onto the web as Jean had showed her. Unfortunately, she was not as deft as Jean and the spider was so frightened by her clumsiness that it fled to the top of the web, and from there, on up to the awning overhang. After making sure that the grasshopper was completely entangled, Amy went back inside to sip her coffee and watch.

Several minutes passed before the spider felt safe enough to return. Once she realized that food was trapped in her web, though, she rushed over, wrapped it well, and immediately began her breakfast.

"Morning," said Beth from the hallway. "What's happening?"

"I just fed my spider."

"Oh, yuck. You're really getting into this nature stuff, aren't you?"

"It's interesting."

Beth came over and peered through the window. "Tarzan convinced her she's Jane yet?"

"Tarzan?"

"The way he drops off the web if she gets too near and then hauls himself back up, it's like he's got a set of vines to swing from."

Amy smiled. "So you've been watching them, too?"

Beth shrugged. "It makes a change from boxing stuff. Any more coffee?"

"A whole pot. I think I'll try some of those figs on a piece of toast. Want some?"

"Actually, what I'd really like is bacon and eggs," said Beth.

"Sorry, but—"

"Yeah, yeah, I know."

Amy laughed. "That wasn't what I was going to say. I have to drive in to Raleigh to sign those papers at Grandmother's lawyer's office, but there's a diner in Garner where we could go for breakfast, if you want."

"Quick jump in the shower first?"

"Take your time. I want one, myself." She glanced at her watch. "I'll call and tell him I'll be there at ten."

*　　*　　*

In less than forty minutes, they were both ready to roll. Barkis, too. He was vastly disappointed when Amy shut the door on him and left him behind, but no way was she going to leave him locked in a hot car while she ran errands.

She gave Beth a key to the house and said, "You want to follow me?"

"Why don't I go on into town with you? I need to pick up a few things myself. Girls' day out?"

That was what Claire used to say when she whisked Amy off for lunch and shopping when Amy was a child.

"What?" said Beth.

"Nothing. I was just thinking that it's been a long time since you and I and Claire went out for lunch together. Maybe when we're all back in the city." She handed Beth a map of Raleigh and pointed to where she wanted to go. "I'm fine till we hit the South Saunders Street exit right here. From there, though, you'll have to navigate."

"Aye, aye, Captain! Course laid in, all systems go."

As she headed for I-40, Amy said, "When you and Dad had that blowup the other night, you didn't say anything about his affair with that records clerk, did you?"

"Not with Mom there."

"That was nice of you."

"Damn straight. But I didn't do it for him. I did it for Mom. She would just die if she knew."

"That's what I meant," said Amy, deciding there was hope for her sister after all. Angry as she must have been at both of them, Beth had still managed to spare Claire that humiliation.

Instead of a diner in Garner, they wound up at a Raleigh pancake house where Beth ordered the special: orange juice, two eggs over easy, sausage, grits, biscuits, and regular coffee.

"She's eating for two," Amy told the waitress.

"Hey, these are the first eggs I've had in weeks," Beth protested.

"No morning sickness yet?" asked Amy, who had opted for a child-size order of pancakes made with fresh plump blueberries and a big glass of milk.

"Nope. Just lucky, I guess."

Their breakfast conversation stayed in the shallows. Beth didn't want to talk about whether or not she was going to carry the baby to term, which eliminated discussion of any long-range career plans. Nor did she want to discuss Jacob Grayson. The list of things Amy would rather not discuss would have reached out to the sidewalk. That left the weather or Grandmother's death and they had disposed of the weather on the drive into town.

Dissecting Curt's odd words the night before took them through most of the meal.

"He must have been drunk," Amy said finally. "He and his sisters will enjoy the money from the sale and so will Aunt Martha and her family, but none of them were hurting for it and their lives aren't going to change all that dramatically. Not enough to kill Grandmother for, certainly."

"Maybe whoever it was came over to try to talk her into selling and then lost their temper when she wouldn't. Maybe they didn't really mean to kill her after all."

"The door was smashed open," Amy reminded her. "And they killed Grandmother's poor old dog, too. That was totally unnecessary. To me, that sounds like they came planning to do exactly what they did. Cold-blooded. Not in any heat of the moment."

"Didn't someone say that the broker stood to lose his front money and his backing if Frances kept holding up the sale till his options ran out?"

"Yes, but I don't know how much money was involved."

"Wouldn't have to be an awful lot," said Beth as Amy pulled a ballpoint pen from her pocket and began doodling dollar signs on a paper napkin. "The thing with you, Amy, is that you've never had to worry about money. What's pocket change for you might be a fortune to someone else."

"You sound like a deprived orphan talking to a billionaire," Amy objected. The dollar signs turned into pigtails that framed the face of a weeping child. "Eric and I draw less salary than Michael and we live on what we make."

"Yeah, but that's what you choose to do, not what you have to. And it all comes down to Mr. Micawber's sixpence, doesn't it? Sixpence left over and you're rich; sixpence short and you face financial ruin. Maybe that front money is the broker's six-pence."

"Well, he's about to get his sixpence," Amy said, glancing at her watch. Although listening to Beth lecture her about the value of money was certainly a novel experience, it was almost ten o'clock. "You finished?"

Beth speared the last of her sausage as Amy crumpled the nap-kin and got up to pay the check.

The attorney's office was but a short drive away, over in Cameron Village in a block of small stores and shops.

Amy found a parking space almost in front of the office and hooked her straw bag on her shoulder as she got out. "This shouldn't take long, but I'll leave the car unlocked in case you get back first."

"Wait a minute," said Beth. "You've got my bag. Here's yours."

They exchanged the colorful purses, then Amy hurried into the low office building. She had expected Grandmother's per-sonal attorney to be an elderly gentleman, but when she was shown into his office, he proved to be even younger than she.

"You're Mr. Howe? Blanton Howe?"

"Rodney Howe, Mrs. Steadman," he said, rising from behind his desk to shake hands and offer her a chair. "I took over after my grandfather retired last year. He continued to deal with Mrs. Barbour, but I did all the actual work."

"I see." She looked inquiringly at the second man in the room, a man who had also stood when she entered the room.

"This is D.C. Brown," said Howe, "the broker on this deal."

"Ma'am, I hope you're about to make me a very happy man? I been hiding out from my creditors down in Makely all week, and when Howe here called to tell me you were coming, I just about broke the sound barrier getting up to Raleigh this morning."

Mr. Brown appeared to be in his late fifties, with steel gray hair and the leathery face of an outdoor man beneath a neatly clipped short gray beard. He held her hand a moment longer than was strictly necessary. "I see you inherited more than your grandmother's estate, Mrs. Steadman."

"Excuse me?"

"Meeting you makes me understand how beautiful Mrs. Barbour must have been in her younger days."

Amy took her hand back from this man who could have been her grandmother's killer. "I was told that you threatened to burn her house down."

"Me? Never!" He managed to looked shocked and hurt at the same time, but an involuntary narrowing of his suddenly baleful eyes let her know that he was more than the innocuous good old boy he was trying to play that morning.

"Last night, my cousin Curt Barbour said something about having to pay back option money. What did he mean?"

"I had a closed-end option on the farm with a contingency clause," D.C. Brown said.

Realizing the man was only one step away from asking her if her pretty little head could understand his big words, Amy said, "What were the terms?"

"The owners of two parts of the farm took my money and signed an agreement that they'd persuade the owner of the third part—Mrs. Frances Barbour—to sell to me within a certain period or else they'd have to pay back the money and the deal was through."

Amy abruptly remembered Aunt Martha's optimistic "I'd

been working on Frances and I do believe she was starting to come around."

"When does your option expire?"

"Actually, it expired the end of July, but we renewed it for another six months till her estate could be settled and I could tender my offer to you through Mr. Howe here."

"So if I said no, you'd be out a lot of money?"

"If you call ten thousand a lot of money, yes, ma'am. That's what I paid the two families for signing. That part I'd've had to eat and it wouldn't be fun, but that's the price of doing business. Your kinfolks though? They might've had a problem."

"I don't understand."

"See, in addition to the non-refundable signing bonus, I advanced them fifty thousand dollars, twenty-five on each parcel. They were so sure Miss Martha could talk Miss Frances into selling. But it didn't look like it was going to happen, so they were going to have to pay me back that fifty K. Yeah, I'd be out the interest I might could've made on that money and the ten K, too, but I got the feeling your people had already spent most of it and were going to be strapped to come up with it in July."

"I see." Now that she understood Curt's words, she realized what a motive for murder it meant. From the things they'd said last night, her cousins might well have had a difficult time paying back the option money. Grandmother had stood between them and a brighter future and her doctor had just given her a clean bill of health. That self-centered old woman could have blocked the sale for years.

Amy was so absorbed in her thoughts that Brown exchanged an uneasy glance with Howe.

"Ma'am?" he said at last. "You're not going to make everybody jump through more hoops, are you?"

She considered it. However self-centered Frances had been, however lacking as a mother, she had been a loving grandmother and had tried to protect Amy from ever knowing the truth behind Maxie's death. Didn't she owe it to Grandmother to hold off until Terry Wilson or Major Bryant found the killer? If she didn't sign, though, would that drive the killer to do something more than make threatening phone calls? This was someone cold-blooded enough to go further, and it wasn't just her safety at stake, it was now Beth's, too.

She looked him straight in the eye and asked, "Where were you the night my grandmother was killed?"

His bearded jaw clenched, but he met her eyes without wavering. "The police already asked me that and I'll tell you what I told them. I was home in bed that night. And, yeah, I've been known to stretch the truth at times, but you ask anybody that knows her and they'll tell you my wife's never told a lie in her whole life. Do I want this deal? Hell, yes! Would I kill for it? Hell, no!"

Oddly enough, she believed him.

She gave Mr. Howe the documents he had sent to her attorneys in the city and which they had sent down to her. He called in his secretary to witness and notarize her signature, Mr. Brown handed over the check, and she arranged for Howe's secretary to express it to the O'Days. The whole business took less than twenty minutes.

Beth was just emerging from a drugstore halfway down the block when Amy got back to the car.

"Guess what?" she said. "There's a day spa here!"

"So?"

"So my shoulder's still sore from Friday and they can take us both right now."

"For what?"

"For massages, of course. Ever since I fell on my skis last winter, a good massage is the only thing that puts my shoulder right. Come on, Amy. You've been uptight all weekend. A little hedonism will do you good, too."

"I've never had a massage," Amy admitted.

Beth looked at her in disbelief. "You're kidding, right? Everybody gets massages."

"Not me. Not a professional one, anyhow."

Beth giggled. "Husbands don't count. Come on. We'll initiate you with a full body treatment. You'll love it."

A half-hour later, Amy was ready to admit that Beth was right. She lay on her stomach, naked as a newborn except for a towel across her hips. New Age music, a combination of shimmering strings and rushing water, played softly in the dimly lighted room. The warm oil had a sweetly soothing smell that blended jasmine and sandalwood. Amy was grateful for the masseuse's silence and she relaxed completely as strong hands rubbed and kneaded up and down her body, loosening the knotted muscles and nerves in her neck, down her spine. She gave herself up to the sensuous experience of having each toe gently manipulated, the calves of her legs, her thighs and buttocks.

Halfway through the session, the masseuse said, "Turn over, please," and Amy experienced a moment of hesitancy.

Sensing her reluctance, the woman said, "Some ladies prefer not to have their breasts touched."

"No, that's okay," said Amy. If she was going to do this, she would do it all the way.

She closed her eyes again and willed the tension from her body as the masseuse smoothed warm oil across her breasts and began the circular motions. There was nothing erotic in what happened next. Indeed, it began with the half-drowsy thought that she had never in her life been caressed so intimately except in sexual foreplay. And yet . . . ?

It was as if her skin had its own set of memories, memories of an earlier, similar experience. She did not try to force those memories, but let herself drift backward along time's stream, through disconnected images that gently coalesced. She was a toddler again, being lifted up out of her bubbly bath onto a towel-covered lap. Loving hands dried each fold and crevice of her chubby little body, then held her close and tenderly stroked her arms and legs. She looked up into her mother's face and the light in those eyes seemed to warm her very skin. She reached up to touch her mother's smile and felt a kiss on her small fingers, heard soft murmurs: *"My precious baby. So dear. So—"*

"Mommy?" she moaned. "Oh, Mommy!" And suddenly she was wracked with sobs that seemed to be torn from the very core of her being.

"Ma'am? Are you all right?"

Amy's eyes flew open. Instead of Maxie's face, she saw only the concerned masseuse's. She nodded, then rolled back onto her stomach to hide her own face, too choked with emotion to answer or explain. All the bottled-up grief that Frances and Jeffrey had tried to pretend away came spilling out, as fresh in its pain and hurt as if it were only this morning that Maxie had died.

After a moment, the masseuse began to massage her back and shoulders again and the firm rhythmical pattern eventually brought calmness. Her grief was still there, but so was a deep and growing happiness, a happiness rooted in the knowledge that she had experienced her first real and authentic memory of Maxie and that she would carry that memory with her for the rest of her life.

Sometime later, the masseuse finished and covered her with a sheet. "You have the room for another fifteen minutes," she said, "so there's no hurry if you want to meditate awhile."

"Thank you," Amy murmured.

When she finally rose from the table, dressed, and stepped out into the hall, Beth was coming down the hallway, too, and Amy felt a sudden rush of love for her sister such as she hadn't felt since Beth was a child, before they grew apart. And yes, Beth had wanted a massage herself, but without Beth pushing for it, Amy knew that she might never have recovered this clear memory of Maxie.

"How's your shoulder?"

Beth rotated it happily. "All the soreness is gone. How'd you like it?"

"Wonderful. Thanks for talking me into it."

"That good, huh?"

"Better."

As they walked out into the reception area, Amy noticed that Beth was barefooted. "Weren't you wearing sandals before?"

"Oh, hell! I left them back there. Here, hold my purse. I'll be right back."

At the desk, Amy set both bags on the counter and asked how much the total was.

"I'm paying for both of us," she said and opened the nearer bag to get her credit card. Instantly she realized she'd once again muddled Beth's with hers and hastily closed it.

By the time Beth returned, Amy had given both masseuses generous cash tips and was signing the credit slip.

"Where now?" Beth asked brightly when they were back out on the street. Heat radiated from the sidewalk. "Want to check out some of the sales?"

"That's right. You'll soon be needing maternity things, won't you?"

"Oh, I'm months away from that," Beth said airily. "Let's go look at shoes."

"Actually, I was thinking that we ought to find a walk-in clinic and get a doctor to check you out. Let's ask in the drugstore here. They'll know where one is. And you should probably be taking vitamin supplements, too."

"Vitamins, yes," Beth agreed, following her inside, "but no doctor. Not yet. Not till I've decided what I want to do."

Amy left her reading vitamin labels and prowled the aisles in search of a certain product. When Beth caught up with her, virtuously holding a large bottle of tablets, she found Amy weighing the merits of two different brands.

"Pregnancy tests? You, too, Amy?"

"Not me. You. There's a restroom at the back of the store. Which of these sticks you want to pee on, Beth?"

"What are you talking about? I already did three of them, remember?"

"Then you shouldn't mind one more."

"What is this?"

"I can't believe you're still lying to me. That you'd make up a phony pregnancy so I'd let you stay." She kept her voice low, but her face was tight with such rage that Beth automatically stepped back.

"I opened your purse by mistake just now," Amy said. "There's a freshly opened box of tampons in it."

"Now wait just a damn minute here!"

"No. I'm through waiting. I want the truth and I want it now. Do I really have to buy one of these kits?"

All around them, shoppers were beginning to stop and stare, but for once, Amy didn't care.

"Look, I didn't lie to you," Beth said. "I really did think I was pregnant when I got here. I was as surprised as you are when I started bleeding yesterday. I—"

"From the moment you got here, you've lied to me and tried to manipulate me and— Oh God! That was you on the phone last night, wasn't it? Southerners never say 'y'all' to just one person. And you don't get a dial tone that quickly when a caller hangs up on you. It's only when you're the one who breaks the connection—and to pretend you were too afraid to sleep by yourself? Why?"

"I thought if you were afraid, too, we could both go back to New York," Beth said sulkily.

"Oh, you're going back to New York, all right," said Amy. "Come on! I'll drive you back to the house and you can get in your car and—"

"And you can go fuck yourself!"

They glared at each other, then Amy whirled and ran from the store. She didn't look back until she reached her car, and when she did, Beth was nowhere in sight.

Once inside, she lowered the windows and sat there fuming. Still no sign of Beth.

She reached into her purse to turn on her cell phone, but it wasn't there, although she could distinctly remember sliding it in beside her wallet. The straw bag had no zipper, only a flap that folded loosely over the top and was caught with a single snap on the front. She checked to see if it had fallen out between the seats.

Nothing.

Maybe under the seat?

She got out and made a thorough search.

As she bent to check in the backseat, a teenage boy came out to get into a car parked two spaces down from her right.

"Excuse me, ma'am?" he said. "That's not what you're looking for, is it?" He pointed to a crushed cell phone a few inches from the curb.

"My lucky day," she said, realizing that it must have fallen out of her bag and under the car that had been parked there when they arrived.

"There's a Radio Shack over yonder," said the boy. "If your SIM card's not damaged, they can probably fix you right up."

"Thanks," she said and reached down for the phone. As her fingers closed around it, sudden pain erupted and bright red blood oozed from the tips of her index and third fingers. Her phone had covered most of a thin, sharp piece of broken glass until she tried to pick it up. She hastily found tissues in her purse and stanched the blood. Amazing how much could flow from such small cuts.

Sighing, she carefully picked up the phone with her left hand and trudged across the street. And yes, the SIM card was bent and scratched beyond hope.

Definitely not her day.

Freud had said that there was no such thing as an accident,

she told herself. He said that all so-called accidents were deliberate acts by one's subconscious. So did her subconscious cut
her fingers as punishment for coming down so hard on Beth?

The phone had been smashed at least an hour before she
thought to turn it on so that Beth could call her. Therefore, her
present anger wasn't the reason she'd dropped it. Was it so she
wouldn't have to talk to Eric? Or Dad?

Well, the hell with all of them, she decided. Let them call her
on the house phone. And if she wasn't there to answer, let them
wonder.

All the same, her fingers were beginning to throb and she
wished Beth would quit sulking and come to the car.

She waited another fifteen minutes in the suffocating heat,
then drove back to the farm alone.

C H A P T E R
26

As soon as she got into the house, Amy let Barkis out, then headed straight to the medicine cabinet in Grandmother's bedroom, where she drenched her fingers in peroxide and clumsily bandaged them with her left hand.

Next she went down to the den, plugged in the answering machine, and reprogrammed the message.

Finally, she called Agent Wilson's number. He wasn't there, but when she gave her name, the person who had answered said, "Mrs. Steadman? He left two messages for you in case you called. One: do not under any circumstances eat any fig preserves. Two: he wants you to call his pager."

Amy copied down the number. "What's wrong with the preserves?"

"Sorry, ma'am, I don't have to understand the messages. All I have to do is relay them."

She laughed and dialed the pager number.

Within two minutes, Wilson called back. "Where are you?"

"Here at the house. 'Don't eat preserves'? Why?"

"You haven't talked to any of your relatives this morning?"

"No, I've been gone since eight. What's happened?"

"Your cousin Curt's been poisoned. Someone put Jimson weed seeds in his fig preserves."

"Weed seeds? Is that bad?"

"Yeah, it's bad." His rumbling voice was grim. "The doctors aren't sure he's going to make it."

"Oh, no! Where is he?"

"Wake Med. Do you know where that is?"

"Raleigh?"

"Yeah, just off the Beltline, east side of town, on New Bern Avenue."

"Is that where you are?"

"No, I'm at his house. We've got a crime scene unit here. If you don't mind, I'm going to come over and pick up your jar of figs. His wife Mary? She said he left a jar at your house last night."

"Yes."

"And his sister-in-law, Patricia Raynor, says that as soon as Mrs. Barbour called her from the hospital, she went over and left you a note on the back door."

"I came in the side door, so I missed it."

"It's probably fine. We've got back all the jars he passed out last night except yours and they're clean, but it doesn't hurt to check. Anyhow, I need to hear your version of what went on at that party last night."

"Okay."

"I'll be there in about ten minutes. Oh, and Miz Steadman?"

"Yes?"

"Please don't touch that jar. We'll want to print it."

Terry Wilson arrived in less than five minutes while Amy was still on the back porch with the note in her hand. In big block letters, Pat had written, AMY—DO NOT EAT CURT'S FIGS!!!!! MAY HAVE POISON!!!!! "Not" was underlined twice.

Barkis recognized the car and danced around until the big SBI agent opened the door and gave him a friendly ear scratch.

"Is Curt really in danger? What happened?" she asked as Wilson stepped from the car and followed her into the kitchen.

"I was hoping you could tell me." His former folksiness was gone. Ignoring the terrier, he was all business. "The whole family was here last night, right?"

"Yes."

"And Mr. Barbour said something that made his wife so mad that she went home with her sister last night?"

"Yes. He all but accused the family of wanting Grandmother dead."

"Anybody in particular?"

"Not that I could tell. He'd been drinking. Anyhow, it embarrassed Mary. He left early and she stayed here."

Amy opened the refrigerator and showed him the jar of preserves that sat on the top shelf. It was a plain Mason jar with a flat metal lid secured by a ridged canning ring. Even though the ring wouldn't hold fingerprints, Wilson put on latex gloves before lifting it out by the ring.

"I probably touched it last night when I put the milk away," Amy said.

"I need to get your fingerprints then."

They both glanced down at her bandaged fingers.

"What happened?" he asked.

She explained about her cell phone and the broken glass.

"You had a tetanus shot lately?"

She nodded. "Oh, and my sister may have touched the jar, too."

"Sister?"

"She drove down late Friday night."

He looked around as if expecting to see her.

"She's not here at the moment."

"When do you expect her back? I'll want her prints, too."

"I'm not sure. But that cup on the counter is the one she used this morning. Can you get them from that?"

"If we have to." He took the jar over to the window and tilted it back and forth. "Oh yeah. See there? Looks like the same crushed black seeds that were in the preserves your cousin ate."

He set the jar on the kitchen table and pulled a small tape recorder from the pocket of his sports jacket. "Let's talk about your party last night."

Amy sat down at the table and he placed the recorder between them.

He began with the time and date, gave his name and hers, then said, "Mrs. Steadman, would you please name the people who were here last night?"

Trying to match his professionalism, Amy listed them in the order of their arrival, beginning with Pauline and her daughter-in-law and ending with Pat Raynor and her father Herbert.

"You say that Mr. Curt Barbour arrived carrying a box of his figs?"

"Yes. He set them on the counter there and told everyone to take a jar home with them. So far as I could tell, he had one for each household, and they must have taken them because I saw Ethylene carry the empty box out to the porch with the rest of the party trash. Jimmy was supposed to come take it to the dump this morning, but the bags are still there. Is he at the hospital?"

Terry Wilson nodded.

"I can't believe this. Curt was so proud of those preserves. He told me he could eat half a jar at a time."

"He wasn't lying. According to his wife, that pint jar was almost half full when she put it in their refrigerator after breakfast yesterday. It was sitting empty in the sink this morning."

"Was it Mary who found him?"

"No, she stayed the night at her sister's. It was your cousin Pauline and your Aunt Martha. He crashed his truck into a big tree in their yard around six this morning."

"Crashed? But if he was poisoned—?"

"Jimson weed's a powerful and deadly hallucinogenic. We don't know if he crashed because his head was messed up or because of cardiovascular collapse. Mrs. Phillips being an LPN, she thinks he was coming to her for help. She called an ambulance and they came right away, but it was almost nine before he was diagnosed and we got the word."

"Poor Curt," Amy whispered.

"Yeah," he said. "So who put this jar in your refrigerator?"

"I don't know. It was already there when I came down to help clear away."

"Okay, then, which of your guests were in the kitchen last night?"

"All of them. This is where the food was. The birthday cake. The men were in and out with the ice cream freezers and they set the extra ice cream in the refrigerator after everyone had been served. People were back and forth for coffee. And all the women helped with the cleanup except for maybe Aunt Martha."

"That's right. She said she left early. Immediately after Mr. Barbour. With Mr. Barbour's son, C.W. That she was upset because she broke a cup?"

"Is that what she told you?"

He heard the difference in her tone. "Actually, I believe it was Dr. Jean Barbour who mentioned the cup. Why?"

"Let's finish this first," she said tightly.

"Okay. They say that Mr. Barbour alluded to your grand-mother's death, that you had told them what Major Bryant and I told you Wednesday night."

"Was it a secret?"

"Not really."

She repeated Curt's words and the shocked reaction they had brought.

"And you're sure no one else knew who he suspected?"

"No, I don't think Curt had anyone particular in mind. Only what it would mean to each of them if the option they'd signed expired before Grandmother agreed to sell. Did you and Major Bryant know about that contingency option?"

"Sure. Didn't you?"

"Not the details. Not that it meant each family would have to come up with its twenty-five thousand dollars by the end of July if Grandmother still wouldn't sell."

"Sorry," he said. "I assumed you knew."

"It makes a strong reason to want her dead, doesn't it?"

"I'm afraid so."

"Aren't any of them in the clear?"

"For which? The poisoning or your grandmother?"

"Either. Both."

"If the same person did both, then your husband and your brothers are. I can't see them knowing about your cousin's preserves."

"You suspected Michael and Sam, too?"

He shrugged. "We look at everyone. Your sister was pulled over for speeding that night up in Binghamton."

"Beth?"

"She stands to get a piece of PBM Enterprises, doesn't she?"

"Not from Grandmother. I'm the only one in New York who profits directly. But what about my relatives down here?"

"Mrs. Barbour was struck down in the middle of the night. They all claim to have been in their beds asleep. The married ones alibi each other, the rest sleep alone." He shrugged. "Who's to say who's lying?"

"Maybe you and Major Bryant are wrong. Maybe it really was a random thing."

"You knew your grandmother. If it wasn't someone familiar, why did she come downstairs? The phone line wasn't cut. Why didn't she call 911? She was wearing a personal alarm. Why didn't she push it?"

"Because she didn't feel threatened?"

"Exactly. Like we told you the other night, she even had her back turned to the killer. She wouldn't have turned her back on someone she didn't know."

"No. You're right," said Amy. "But those seeds. Where do you get them?"

"Jimson weed? It grows wild all over the eastern part of the country."

"Here on the farm, too?"

He nodded. "Your cousin Vera said she saw some here back in June. She's coming out later to show us. Not that we expect to find any shoe tracks after all that rain yesterday."

Amy thought of the summer journal that Jean had taken. Vera was a botanist and just last night she'd talked about cataloguing all the farm's pines. They must have identified most of the flowering plants as well.

"We've rounded up all the other jars that Mr. Barbour brought over last night. His sisters live there in Raleigh and they brought theirs to the hospital. His daughter's family doesn't like them, so she didn't take one, and we've eyeballed all the other jars here on the farm. Mr. Barbour's and now yours are the only ones with Jimson weed seeds. I'm afraid somebody doesn't like you, Miz Steadman."

"Besides you?" she asked, then immediately flushed so hotly that she reached out and switched off the recorder. "I'm sorry. I shouldn't have said that."

He looked at her with sad, wise eyes. "Rough day?"

"Yes."

"Want to tell me about it?"

She wanted to tell someone, she just wasn't sure he should be the one. Not as conflicted as she felt right now. Not when she couldn't trust herself to keep her emotions in check. If Eric were here—but Eric wasn't here and not likely to be here anytime soon. He hadn't called last night. He hadn't called this morning. Beth was sulking God knows where. Terry Wilson was her only here-and-now.

"I don't suppose you had any luck tracing the Hahnemanns?"

"Actually, I did. Both are dead, though. Eleven years ago for him; four years ago for her. No children, no siblings so far as we can tell. The director of the nursing home up in Pennsylvania where she died said she thought there used to be a cousin out in California, but she'd had no visitors for years. I'm sorry."

"That's okay. I figured it out. Wait, I'll show you."

She went up to her bedroom and brought down the blood-splattered garments and explained how they were found last night and how she had pieced together what must have happened. "That's what spooked Aunt Martha. I told her that I knew I was the one who shot Maxie. That's why they lied about where I was."

Against her will, her eyes filled up and she turned away and went over to the sink to run a glass of cold water.

"You were a baby," he said gently. "It wasn't your fault."

"Today, for the very first time, I finally remembered her." Her back was to him so that her tears were hidden, but she couldn't keep her voice from wobbling. "She was so gentle. So loving. And I killed her."

His chair scraped on the kitchen floor. "Hey, now," he said, and then his arms were around her, turning her to him and enfolding her as she wept against his chest.

"Tell me," he said, smoothing her fine soft hair with his big hand.

So she told him how Beth had talked her into having a massage and how it had evoked a memory buried so deeply she never knew it was there till now.

"I *never* cry," she said when she was in control again. "But for the last two days . . ."

"You've had a lot coming at you, shug."

She looked up into his face and this time he did not pull away when her lips lifted to his.

"Everything I touch falls apart," she whispered, clinging to him. "If Curt dies, it'll be my fault for repeating what you told me."

"No it won't." His arms tightened around her. "Bryant and I were planning to come out and hit them with it today, start another round of questioning. We figured your being here might've stirred them up a little, maybe got them thinking and—"

He broke off as the cell phone on his belt rang. "Wilson here . . . Oh? When? Okay. Thanks."

His shoulders slumped.

"What?" she asked.

"I'm sorry, Amy. Your cousin Curt died about fifteen minutes ago."

CHAPTER
27

When his crime scene technicians arrived to fingerprint Amy and lift Beth's prints from her coffee mug, Major Bryant was with them.

"I'm real sorry about your cousin, Mrs. Steadman." He looked over at Terry Wilson, who now sat across the table from her. "You already ask her about last night?"

Wilson nodded and Bryant said, "Hope you don't mind going over it again with me, Mrs. Steadman?"

Numbly, Amy once more went through all the details she could recall. As she spoke, she picked up a pen from the table and began sketching aimlessly on the back of Pat's warning note. The adhesive strips on her fingers made her less dextrous, but sketching had always helped focus her thoughts. Even though she hadn't known him very well, she still couldn't believe that Curt was dead, deliberately poisoned with his own preserves. "Several people had cameras last night, and there were at least two video cameras."

"Yeah, we've got somebody taking a closer look at the tapes, but the quick-and-dirty didn't show anything."

Bryant was slightly more thorough than Terry Wilson. He

asked about her conversation with Curt when they were picking figs Saturday morning, and who was around when he brought the preserves into the house and knew that she would be getting some?

"There were so many people in and out of this kitchen last night, I suppose any of them could have done it, but how did they get to Curt's jar?"

"Mrs. Barbour said she put it back in the refrigerator when she cleaned up the kitchen before church yesterday. She went by and picked up her sister, and your cousin stayed with old Mr. Raynor, so they were both gone for at least two hours. Then last night, they were over here."

"Surely they didn't leave the house unlocked?" asked Amy.

" 'Fraid so," Terry told her. "Mrs. Barbour says they lost the key years ago and never bothered to get a duplicate. Only time they lock up's at night when they're asleep. They're back off behind some thick trees and they've got dogs. Unless you know the house is there, you don't notice it from the road and they've never been bothered."

"So it was unlocked from the time Mary and Curt drove over here till he went back home last night?"

"Looks like it," they told her.

"Could my jar have been doctored while it was still at Curt's?" she asked. "Maybe it wasn't meant for me at all. Maybe they were doubling up on him."

"Doubtful," said Terry. "What he planned to keep for himself was already shelved in their pantry and those look to be clean. His wife says he boxed the rest and put them on his truck to bring over here."

"Oh." Her pen paused in midstroke. It chilled her to realize that someone she had invited into this house last night had come prepared to poison her. Had methodically waited for an opportunity and then seized it.

She gave an involuntary shiver and the two men exchanged glances. They had seen this reaction from others many times, this awareness of a near brush with death. If she'd eaten from the jar that was even now being dusted for prints, she might not have ingested as much of the alkaloid as Curt Barbour, but she was a small woman and it wouldn't have taken very much.

"Here we go, Major!" said one of the officers who had been crawling around the floor with a flashlight, peering under the overhangs directly beneath the counter next to the refrigerator. She used a narrow paintbrush to sweep out something that she sealed in a small plastic bag, which she labeled before showing it to them. "Looks like crushed Jimson weed seeds to me."

"Why don't you search the other houses?" Amy asked. "Or at least make everyone who was here last night show you the clothes they were wearing? I'll bet somebody's pocket still has a few seeds in it."

"Give us a name, point us in a direction, show us some hard evidence," said Terry. "The Constitution protects us from unreasonable searches. Without probable cause, we'd never get a search warrant."

Having finished with Beth's cup and other items in the refrigerator that the poisoner might have touched, a member of the forensics team approached Amy and said, "May I?"

Mindful of her cuts, he gently unwrapped her bandages, rubbed a light touch of antiseptic cream on those two fingertips instead of ink, then rebandaged them for her when he was finished.

"Let me ask you this," said Bryant, leaning back in his chair as Amy cleaned the ink from the rest of her fingers. "You say Mr. Barbour's wife all but told him to shut up when he was talking about your grandmother's death?"

"Yes?"

"Did you get the impression he might've been talking about her?"

"*Mary?* You think Mary did this?"

"She's the one with the most opportunity," said Terry. "More victims are killed by their mates than by other relatives."

"But they've been married for thirty or forty years. Why now? And why include me?"

"Why does any wife or husband suddenly lose it? Maybe he started wondering if she was the one killed your grandmother. She got laid off from her job, their third of that twenty-five K was gone, debts were piling up. My guess is that your conversation with Mr. Barbour Saturday morning set him to thinking along new lines."

So much had happened these last few days, Amy had almost forgotten about that first phone call. The authentic one, before Beth started campaigning to leave.

"You've remembered something?" asked Bryant.

"Well," she said slowly, "I *did* get a threatening phone call Saturday night."

"Say what?" asked Terry. "You didn't tell me that."

Amy flushed, aware that Dwight Bryant's eyes were moving speculatively from her to Terry and back again. To avoid looking up, she resumed her sketching. Two canine shapes now appeared on the paper beneath her pen.

"You want to tell us about the call?" he said mildly.

"It was around eleven-thirty. I'd already gone to sleep but my sister was still downstairs and she picked up first."

Unlike Terry, Bryant did not question her about Beth. From what she'd seen of this lawman, Amy suspected that he'd noticed Beth's car as soon as he drove into the yard and had probably run the New York tags as an automatic reflex.

"We thought at first it was just some bored kid."

"Male or female?"

Amy shook her head. "The voice was just a whisper. Whoever it was told me to go back where I came from or I'd get hurt, too."

"Too?" they both asked.

"Yes."

They kicked it around a few more minutes, then the forensics team left and Bryant rose to go back to Curt and Mary's house, where the family would be gathering. He looked at Terry, who hadn't moved. "You coming?"

"I'll be along in a minute."

Bryant did not raise an eyebrow or make a comment, yet Amy felt herself going red again.

"He probably thinks we're sleeping together," she said, when they were alone.

"Dwight? Naw," said Terry. "He knows I'm a slow mover."

"Three wives don't sound very slow," Amy said, a smile working its way back to her lips.

"Just means I'm a slow learner." He stood and looked around vaguely. "You got a paper bag somewhere?"

"In the pantry behind you, why?"

"I thought I'd take your cowgirl things and let our lab have a look at it."

"Why?" she asked again.

"Well, for one thing, to make sure those splotches really are human blood."

"They are." Her voice was bleak.

"Probably, but I like to know things for sure."

When the others came, she had stuck the clothes over on a side counter. Now she watched Terry slide them into a brown grocery sack.

"Do you happen to know your mother's blood type?"

"A-positive, I think. And thank you for not bringing this up in front of Major Bryant."

"I'm gonna have to tell him sooner or later," Terry warned. "Dwight doesn't forget things."

He looked down at the sketch that still lay on the table and smiled. "That's Dwight all right. Worries things like a bone till he gets the answers."

To Amy's bemusement, she realized that she had unconsciously doodled a sharp-eyed German shepherd, his head cocked alertly toward the small Mason jar on the floor in front of him like a glass bone. Peering around his shoulder was a droopy basset hound.

Embarrassed, she started to crumple it, but he laughed and took it from her hand. "If you're just going to throw it away, I'd like to have it."

At the doorway, he paused and looked down at her. "Are you going over to your cousin's house?"

"Yes."

"You *will* keep in mind, won't you, that whoever's doing this may be starting to feel safe now that your cousin's dead? Try not to say anything to make them think you know more than you do, okay?"

"Okay."

There was a moment of awkwardness at the door. She had wanted—had *needed*—his kiss before, the physical comfort of his touch. Now, though, she was conflicted. A second kiss would up the ante and take them where she wasn't yet sure she wanted to go.

As if sensing her ambivalence, he gave her shoulder a friendly squeeze and promised to call if anything came up. "I'm glad your sister's here," he said. "At least you'll have one person you can trust with you."

Except that I don't, she almost said. But that would have taken more explanation than she wanted to give at the moment, so she stood quietly and watched him drive away, then called Barkis in and locked the door behind them.

Inside the big quiet house, the horror was only now beginning to sink in.

Excluding herself, Curt, Beth and Jacob Grayson, the preteen children, and old Herbert Raynor, who was pretty much a child himself now, there had been thirteen adults at Jimmy Phillips's birthday party last night. All of them were kin to Curt by birth or by marriage, yet one of those thirteen had poisoned Curt as cold-bloodedly as he—or she—had killed Grandmother.

But however awful it was for her to think these thoughts, it must be even worse for the others. Imagine being C.W. or Frannie and wondering if their mother had poisoned their father?

Or to be Mary and wonder if it were one of the children or Frannie's son or one of Curt's sisters?

Or Jean or Vera or Aunt Martha giving long, hard consideration to Pauline or Jimmy or Ethylene.

Was Pat over there at Mary's right now, wondering if Vera's husband George or Frannie's husband Jake had killed Frances so that their wives could share in the sale of the land?

She sighed and went to freshen up, torn between her obligation to go join the family and her worry for Beth, who was out there wandering around Raleigh. With her cell phone smashed, she realized there was no way for Beth to get in touch with her except on the house phone here.

She waited another hour and when the phone remained silent, she drove over to Curt and Mary's house.

The front and side yards were so full of cars that she had to pull on past the house and park almost out at the barn. Inside, the house was jammed not only with Curt's immediate relatives but with friends and neighbors who had come to offer condolences as soon as they heard. Further complicating things was the presence of uniformed sheriff's deputies as Dwight Bryant and his people co-opted an empty bedroom and took statements from each family member. There was no sign of Terry Wilson.

Amy made her way through the crowd to where Mary sat on a dark blue couch in the blue-and-white living room, her sister Pat on one side, her daughter Frannie on the other. She took Mary's hands and said how very sorry she was, but Mary seemed too dazed to register her words. Amy had thought her reserved and unemotional, yet her eyes were almost as red as Frannie's and she kept shaking her head as if denying that Curt was gone.

Amy found Jean and Vera in the den and they, too, were in disbelief. Or seemed to be. Both broke into tears as they embraced Amy.

For once, Pauline was without words, and even Ethylene was subdued.

Aunt Martha was out on the porch, and when someone got up to refill her tea glass, Amy slipped into the chair and put her arm around the old woman.

Tears streamed down Aunt Martha's face. "Oh, Amy, honey, isn't this just awful? Poor Curt. It was hard enough to see him lying there in the truck this morning, his face all bloody where his nose hit the steering wheel, but Paulie didn't think he was hurt that bad. And now to know that he was poisoned and that he came to us for help and we didn't help him—"

"You did what you could," Amy said soothingly. "I don't think anyone could have saved him at that point."

"And you, honey." She looked even more stricken and leaned closer to Amy so that no one else could hear. Not that anyone was paying them any attention. "What you said last night," she murmured. "It wasn't true."

"It's okay, Aunt Martha," Amy said, her lips close to her aunt's ear. "I figured it out. I know why you said Maxie shot herself and it's okay. Honest."

"You don't hold it against Frances and me?"

"Of course not. She was gone. There was nothing you could do to bring her back. It was natural to protect the living."

"Yes! You *do* understand, don't you, honey? Frances was going to tell them it was you, but I stood up to her that time and told her no. You couldn't grow up with that on you. That's why we made it look like Maxie did it to herself and I took you back to my house till the sheriff and all were through so you couldn't tell them and then—"

They were interrupted by Pauline. "Mama, you doing okay? Major Bryant wants to know if you feel like talking to him again now?"

"I reckon." Looking every one of her years, Aunt Martha put out her hand for Pauline to help her stand, then moved slowly down the porch to the doorway.

Amy stayed a few minutes longer, then slipped back out to her car and returned to the house. Her cut fingers were throbbing and she didn't know most of these people anyhow.

There were no messages from Beth on the answering machine, but Eric's amused voice said, "Amy? Don't tell me you've left your cell phone in the attic again?"

CHAPTER
28

Eric was the last person she wanted to speak to at the moment, and rationalizing that she shouldn't interrupt him in the middle of a work session, she called his voice mail and left an innocuous message.

By now her fingertips were hurting so badly that she daubed them with peroxide again. Experience told her that most of the soreness would be gone by tomorrow. Fingers healed quickly, but were a nuisance till they did. At least it wasn't a torn ligament or a broken bone or something equally incapacitating. To take her mind off some of the chaos around her, she found her notepad and went through the house listing which pieces of furniture she wanted to send to storage and which she would let Jacob Grayson dispose of for her.

Grayson? Of course! Relief flooded through her, letting her know she was more worried about her sister than she wanted to admit. Grayson must be the reason why Beth hadn't called. She was probably sitting in his shop this very moment.

Amy found his card in her purse and awkwardly dialed his number with her left hand. The store's answering machine kicked in on the first ring. "Thank you for calling Grayson's Galleries," a woman's voice said cheerfully. "We're open Tuesday through Friday from ten A.M. till six P.M. and Saturdays from ten A.M. till two P.M. Closed Sunday and Monday. Please call again during our regular business hours."

As she hung up, Amy remembered that Grayson had said he was going down to Wilmington for an estate sale today. So where the devil *was* Beth? And how long should she wait before consulting Terry or Dwight Bryant?

So many different emotions, so many new bits and pieces of information were roiling around in her head that she couldn't seem to settle into any task that took concentration. Curt's death. The poisoned jar in her own refrigerator. That comforting kiss from Terry Wilson. The disconcerting discovery that it was Aunt Martha's idea to protect her, not Grandmother's. The sweet and vivid memory of Maxie.

It was almost too much to process, but at least there were a few things she could do that didn't take any thought: she could finish the job Beth had begun and clean out Grandmother's closet and dressers. For the next hour she filled and labeled large plastic bags to be taken to a local charity's thrift shop, methodically checking the pockets of each garment. She found a grocery list and a silver pocket knife in one, a nickel and two quarters in another, and a fifty-dollar bill in a jacket pocket. Too bad Beth hadn't gotten this far. She could probably use fifty dollars about now for a taxi to bring her out from Raleigh so she could pick up her car.

She thought about Beth's lecture this morning: *"The thing with you, Amy, is that you've never had to worry about money. What's pocket change for you might be a fortune to someone else."*

The money her aunt and her cousins would get from selling the farm wasn't exactly pocket change. Nor was the fifty thousand they were going to have to pay back to D.C. Brown if Grandmother didn't agree to sell by July. But Grandmother was killed in May, when Aunt Martha was still optimistic about her power to persuade Frances to change her mind and well before the expiration of the option. So why was she killed then? Why not a month later?

That fifty-thousand option had been divided between the families of Grandfather's brother and sister. Aunt Martha would have received twenty-five; the other twenty-five would have been divided between Curt, Jean, and Vera— a little over eight thousand each. Eight thousand dollars really wasn't all that much, and maybe Jean and Vera could have scraped up their shares since both had steady jobs with the state, but a farm couple living as close to the edge as Curt and Mary did? When Mary had been laid off from work?

Eight thousand might well be enough motive for Mary. Especially if she didn't trust Aunt Martha's powers of persuasion.

And what about Aunt Martha? Had she kept the entire twenty-five herself or given part of it to Pauline or her grandson Jimmy? Not that she could see Aunt Martha as a killer, but Pauline was a nurse and must be somewhat hardened to the sight of blood and gore. And she would certainly know about the toxic properties of Jimson weed, wouldn't she?

The same for Pat Raynor. Farm-bred, she had helped the men at hog-killing time and she was probably familiar with Jimson weed, too. Of course, killing an old woman and her pet dog wasn't quite the same thing as seeing a pig slaughtered for sausage and ham. Moreover, Pat had nothing to gain from the sale of the farm unless getting Herbert into a nursing home and being free to take a new job could be considered gain.

As for Frannie and her family or Jimmy and his, she simply didn't know enough about them or their finances to say who was desperate enough to do what was done here last night.

And yet, something she'd seen or heard these last few days tugged at the edges of memory. She went back down her mental list of people one person at a time.

(Think, Pink!)

She might claim to have no head for balance sheets, but her years of waiting for Dad or Grandmother to drop clues that would help her piece together what Maxie was like and why she had killed herself had honed her listening skills and, yes, there was one small thing that suggested another . . . and yet another.

The closer she looked, the more there was to see.

She reached for the phone to call Terry Wilson, then hesitated. It was all supposition. She wasn't sure what "probable cause" entailed, but supposition alone probably wasn't enough for him to get a search warrant. It was going to take more. First things first, though.

She began by calling Eric's voice mail again, explained that she'd broken her cell phone and that she was going out again, but that she'd call him before nine in the morning. Then she sat down with her notepad to give serious thought to what she could do.

As twilight spread across the farm, she put her plan in play. It wasn't a great plan and there were lots of objections, but it was the best she could come up with and she was determined to go ahead.

After changing into black cotton slacks and a black polo shirt, she called Curt and Mary's number.

"Barbour residence," said a woman's voice.

"Is that Jean?"

"Yes?"

"Hi, Jean. It's Amy. I was wondering if I could order some food for everyone? Pizza? Or Chinese?"

"That's thoughtful of you, honey, but people have brought so much already there's no need for anything else. The women from Mary and Aunt Martha's church are just getting it ready. Why don't you come over and eat with us?"

"Okay. And I'll bring the rest of the peach ice cream that Ethylene left last night. There's at least three pints of it."

"That'll be good. See you in a few minutes, then?"

"Yes."

*　　*　　*

Over at the house, the cars had thinned considerably and most of the remaining ones belonged to family members. Pauline met her at the back door to take the ice cream and put it in Mary's freezer till it was wanted. The kitchen table was covered in platters and bowls of food that friends and neighbors had brought, and Aunt Martha was teary-eyed at seeing this country custom for one of the last times.

"It won't be like this when we move off and live among strangers," she said.

Mary sat in the dining room between C.W. and Frannie. She shook her head when Pat set a full plate in front of her, but Frannie said, "You've got to keep your strength up, Mom."

Vera and her husband George were there, too, and they brightened at the sight of Amy. Urged to join them, Amy put some fresh tomatoes and string beans on a plate and let one of the church women give her a slice of ham, too, then carried her plate back into the dining room. The others followed, and soon there were thirteen of them squeezed in around a table meant to seat eight.

Aunt Martha said grace while low sounds of the television came from the living room. Herbert Raynor was in there watching with C.W.'s two children.

From the strained air that hung over the dining room, Amy sensed that ugly questions were roiling just beneath the surface. Probably the only thing holding them in check was the presence of four or five outsiders. Once everyone was served, though, those women tactfully retired to the kitchen to give the family some time alone and to eat a little something themselves before cleaning up Mary's kitchen for her.

At first, the talk was mostly of food, who had brought what and "Did you get you some of that potato salad, Mama?" and "Who made this casserole?" or "Been a good year for tomatoes, hasn't it?"

Curt's eight-hundred-pound gorilla was cavorting all around them, thought Amy. She could feel its hot breath on her neck.

"What are the arrangements?" she asked. "For the funeral, I mean?"

"No funeral," said Frannie. "Daddy was an organ donor. After they take what they can use"—here her voice almost broke—"he wanted to be cremated."

"But you'll have a memorial service, won't you, Mary?" asked Jean.

Mary nodded, her eyes filling up with tears.

"I just can't think what lowdown dirty skunk would sneak in here while y'all were at church yesterday and do this," rasped C.W.

So that was going to be the line for now, thought Amy. Put the blame on a nameless, faceless intruder.

"They found Jimson weed seeds in my jar of figs, too," Amy said.

It was as if the gorilla had smacked them with a tree branch.

"Huh?"

"No!"

"Oh, Amy!"

"They sure about that?"

"But how?"

"When?"

Amy looked down at her plate so she wouldn't have to meet anyone's eyes. Choosing her words carefully, she said, "One of Major Bryant's deputies found a couple of loose seeds on the floor under the edge of the counter next to the refrigerator. Agent Wilson thinks that whoever did it brought the seeds with them in a pocket. They're coming back tomorrow. They're going to ask you each to let them examine the clothes you were wearing."

There was stunned silence, then an outburst of dismay, anger, and fear. "They think one of us—?"

"Are they crazy?"

"None of us would—"

Amy's quiet voice cut through the hubbub. "It's amazing

what they can do in a lab these days. They said that even if the pockets were turned inside out and the clothes washed in bleach, if there were ever any crushed Jimson weed seeds in a pocket, microscopic bits would be caught in the fabric or in the seams."

She looked up then and saw Vera's thoughtful gaze on her.

"Is that true, Vera?" asked Ethylene, appealing to the most knowledgeable plant person at the table.

"We-ell," said her husband George, who was also a botanist.

"Yes," Vera said firmly. "Amy's right. If seeds were ever there, an electronic digital imaging sensor will show it."

Amy had no idea what an electronic digital imaging sensor was and doubted if anyone else here besides Jean or George did either, but it certainly sounded impressive.

And infallible.

Aunt Martha looked around the table in bewilderment. "I don't understand. Why would those officers want to take our clothes?"

"It'll clear us and make them start looking for the real killer."

"Clear us?"

"Vera and Amy are saying they suspect Curt was poisoned by one of us, Mama," said Pauline with a defiant toss of her tightly permed gray curls.

"No," said Vera. "It's what the police suspect. I showed them two patches of Jimson weeds this afternoon. One stand of it's behind those old tobacco barns on Aunt Frances's side of the line. Several of the seed pods had been twisted off. Whoever went in after them will also have *Bidens bipinnata* on their pantlegs."

"What's that?" asked Frannie's son, Mike.

"Spanish needles," Vera said. She looked down at the legs of her own white slacks where two or three still stuck to the cloth like tiny half-inch-long porcupine quills. "I was covered in them and thought I got them all off, but as you see—" She reached down, pulled one off, and passed it over to Mike.

"Oh, yeah!" he said with a grin. "Our dog's always—"

The kitchen door swung open and a determinedly cheerful woman poked her head in. "How y'all doing in here? Can I take anybody's plate? Who needs more tea?"

Amy pushed back from the table and handed the woman her plate. "I just remembered that I'm expecting a phone call," she said and hurried out to her car.

More cars were arriving with people who'd had time to get home from work, hear about their friend Curt while eating supper, and decide to come by for a few minutes. Would the person she suspected slip out under cover of so many people or simply wait till everyone went home?

Only one way to find out.

She couldn't believe that she, who had spent her life avoiding confrontations, was planning to confront a killer, but her determination didn't falter despite the increasing drumbeat of adrenaline that pounded out those old calming charms: *Think, Pink! Do, Blue!* Even though Maxie had grown to regret ever uttering them, her words were still a comforting mantra.

Amy eased her car through the farm's dark lanes, hid it in a thick stand of trees and bushes off the main lane, and walked the rest of the way by the light of a half-moon. With every nerve taut, she scanned the shadows. Nothing stirred. A big Breath of Spring bush grew beside the open car shelter, its curtain of leafy branches sweeping the ground. She pushed apart some of the branches and slipped inside. From here she could see without being seen. She wished, though, that she had remembered to bring bug spray and she wished that she hadn't suddenly thought of snakes.

Too late to risk a quick look around with her penlight, though, because another car was coming through the back lanes, its headlights flashing through the trees. This was way quicker than she had expected. She didn't know which scared her more: snakes or the person headed her way.

The car drove right up to the back door and the driver got

out and hurried inside. A few minutes later, the tall bulky shape emerged from the house holding a bundle of clothes. Amy watched as the clothes were dumped into the burn barrel that everyone on the farm still used for wastepaper and fallen twigs. A gas can was pulled from the shelter and sloshed over the barrel, then, before a match could be struck, Amy pushed aside the branches, and shone her light on the startled face.

"Couldn't you have just asked her for the money, Pat?"

Curt's sister-in-law took a step back, and to support herself clutched at a sturdy stick leaning against the barrel. "Amy? What are you doing here?"

"Watching you try to burn the clothes you had on last night when you tried to poison me. You killed Grandmother, you killed Curt—damn you, Pat, you even killed poor old King! In God's name, why?"

" 'Cause I was tired of his messes all over the house," she snapped. "He should've been put down two years ago, but she wouldn't hear of it and who had to clean up behind him? Me! With my knee killing me every time I bent down."

"And you killed Grandmother so you could pay for that knee operation. Why didn't you just ask her for the money, Pat?" she said again. "Or ask me?"

"Yeah, like you'd've come running down from New York waving your checkbook? And her! Tight as a tick. Curt tried to borrow money for a new tractor three years ago and you'd've thought he was asking for her to buy the moon. 'I never lend to relatives,' she says. 'That's just asking for trouble,' she says. I knew she had me down in her will for fifteen thousand if I was still working for her when she died, but I couldn't go on working with my knee hurting like it was and her doctor'd just told her she could live another ten years. Ten *years!* And I don't care what Miss Martha says. She won't never gonna sell. Dad won't never going to get in a nursing home. Mary and Curt couldn't help. Everything was going just fine and then you had to come and get Curt all stirred up, got him asking questions, asking Mary if I looked surprised when we found her. *You* did that!"

With a roar, the woman charged forward, and Amy had time only to register with horror that the stick Pat held was actually a sharp-tined pitchfork. She backpedaled desperately, banged into the shelter, tried to run, and went sprawling on her back.

Knee surgery might have slowed Pat down, but she covered the distance between them in three strides and raised the pitchfork high to slam down into Amy. At that instant, two bright flashlights blinded both women and a strong hand grabbed the pitchfork while it was still on its upward arc.

"I thought *I* was supposed to grab the pitchfork," said Dwight Bryant as he snapped on the handcuffs.

"Naw," said Terry Wilson. "You were supposed to grab Miz Steadman. I was supposed to get the pitchfork."

The yard was suddenly full of uniforms.

"We got to get our signals a little straighter next time," said Bryant, handing Pat Raynor over to Deputy Mayleen Richards.

Amy pushed herself into a sitting position, brushed the dirt from her shirt, and waited for them to finish sorting it all out.

CHAPTER
29

Amy followed Terry Wilson's car back to Curt and Mary's house and was there when he told the others how and why Pat had been arrested. Everyone seemed surprised and shocked, everyone except Mary, who retreated into a grief-stricken silence while the Barbour women around her chattered and exclaimed and turned the events inside out in nonstop verbal attempts to make sense of Pat's actions.

Amy listened as long as she could, then slipped from the room. Curt's sisters followed her out to the porch.

"Thanks, honey," Vera said.

Jean gave her a warm hug. "It would have gotten ugly if it'd dragged out for days, everybody looking at everybody else, wondering who picked those seeds. Things would have been said that might've split the family apart forever."

Amy turned back to Vera. "Just out of curiosity, what's an electronic digital imaging sensor?"

Vera laughed. "It was the only thing I could think of off the top of my head that sounded more sophisticated than a plain old microscope."

*　　　*　　　*

Now it was after midnight, but Amy Steadman was still too pumped to even consider bed.

Once more, Dwight Bryant and Terry Wilson sat at her kitchen table to share a bottle of wine. Except for the cheese and crackers she'd put out, it was a repeat of Wednesday night.

"That seems a lifetime ago," she said.

Leaning back in his chair, watching as she kept jumping up to fill their glasses, fetch napkins, urge them to try the cheddar or how about some of this brie?, Dwight realized that she was still on an adrenaline high. Civilians always had a little trouble coming down, and her small heart-shaped face sparkled with animation and excitement that occasionally darkened with sadness for her cousin and grandmother. He realized now that he'd read her wrong Wednesday night. The past few days might have changed her some, but a woman doesn't go from tentative diffidence to confident strength in five short days unless the foundation's already in place. She reminded him a little of his own mother, who'd been the fluttery helpless wife his dad had wanted her to be until his accidental death left her with four children to provide for, at which point Emily Bryant had slipped into the driver's seat and never once looked back in the rearview mirror.

He glanced over at Terry, who was sitting there with a bemused look on his face, as if he were watching a fuzzy little kitten turn into a golden lioness before his eyes. Dwight thought of the men who had ringed her so protectively at her grandmother's funeral: husband, father, brothers. He had a feeling they were in for a big surprise when they got her back.

If they got her back.

"—and when Vera came out with that electronic digital imaging sensor!" She broke off and looked at the two lawmen sheepishly. "I'm sorry. I'm just babbling, aren't I? You've been here, done this so many times, haven't you?"

"It never gets old," Terry assured her.

"Every time's different," Major Bryant agreed. "And you

were the one to realize that a little bit of money could be more important than a big chunk."

"Actually, that was my sister," Amy admitted. "She told me I didn't appreciate the real value of money to people who had none. Poor Pat. No money, no health insurance, and a leg that throbbed worse than my cut fingers every time she put her weight on it. Grandmother could have covered the cost of that operation out of petty cash without thinking twice about it."

Another one of those shadows flitted across her pretty face as she tucked a strand of blonde hair behind her small ear.

"Grandmother was always so good to me, I guess I didn't realize how self-absorbed she was." She stopped and corrected herself. "No, not self-absorbed. Self-absorbed is too mild. She was a selfish old woman or she would have had that poor arthritic dog put to sleep as soon as he became incontinent."

"I got most of why you suspected Pat when you called me this evening," said Terry, "how she was the last one to get to the party and how she probably got soaked going in and out at her sister's to poison the figs, but what was that bit about the note? She warned you not to eat the stuff. How was that suspicious?"

Amy pulled the cheese rake across the wedge of cheddar and popped the thin sliver in her mouth. "If she'd really wanted me to see that note, she'd have left it on the side door, not the back one. I never come in through the kitchen. Never. And she knew that."

"And the doctor's report?" asked Bryant.

"Now you're just being nice to me," Amy said with a smile. "You don't need me to spell that out."

"Well, no, I guess I don't," he said, smiling back. "Knowing Mrs. Barbour was in such good health was enough to tip Pat Raynor over the edge."

Amy nodded. "I really do think that was Grandmother's death warrant, because that's the only outright lie that Pat told me."

"What do you mean?"

"On Thursday when I was over there, she mentioned that Grandmother's doctor had given her a good report on her physical."

"So?"

"So she said she didn't know about it till after Grandmother's funeral. That Aunt Martha had mentioned it to Mary and Mary told her. It never happened that way. If Aunt Martha knew something, the whole farm would hear about it within fifteen minutes. Grandmother used to grumble that she couldn't set foot out of the house without everyone knowing. Once I started thinking about it, I realized that the only reason Pat would bring up something that minor and then lie about it was because it was majorly important in her own mind."

There was less than a half-inch of wine left in the bottle and the hall clock had chimed one-thirty before Amy finally came down to earth. When she yawned a second time, Bryant caught Terry's eye.

"Yeah, time we were going," he said. "We got a lot of paperwork to do in the morning. One thing, though."

"Yes?" said Amy.

"This sister of yours. Where is she?"

"I guess she decided to stay over in Raleigh tonight." Worry still gnawed at her, but Beth did have that money she'd earned and she was resourceful.

"You going to be all right here alone?"

Amy smiled down at the terrier, who'd been sleeping at her feet while they talked. "I'm not alone. I have him to guard me."

It might have been more convincing if Barkis hadn't yawned widely and promptly put his head back on his paws and closed his eyes again.

CHAPTER
30

Amy?"

The voice was so low and the touch on her bare shoulder so tentative that Amy would not have wakened except that Barkis bounded to his feet and happily danced across the bed.

Beth? Amy opened her eyes. "Beth!"

She sat upright and pulled her sister down on the bed so that she could hug her in exuberant relief. "I was so worried. Where were you? How did you get back?"

Beth's eyes filled up with tears and she looked like a scared and guilty child.

"What's wrong?"

"I begged you to let's go home!" she wailed as more tears spilled down her cheeks. "I knew it was going to be too late."

Amy took Beth's hands in hers. "What's wrong, honey? Why—?"

Her fingers touched metal and she looked down. There was a wide gold band on the ring finger of Beth's left hand.

"Beth?"

Her sister nodded and buried her face on Amy's shoulder.

"But how? Why?"

Sobs were her only answer at first. Then, "Mom's going to be so mad. She started planning my wedding the day after she finished with yours and Eric's."

"But who? Jacob Grayson?"

She felt Beth's nod on her shoulder. "Oh, Beth."

Dismayed, Amy knew this was her fault for blasting Beth on her faked pregnancy, for abandoning her and leaving Raleigh without her yesterday. "Listen, honey, it's okay. I'll call my lawyers. We can have this annulled and—"

"No!" She pulled away, shaking her head. Her eyes were red, her nose runny, but she seemed shocked by the suggestion.

"You want this?" asked Amy, equally shocked. "You love him?"

"I think so."

"*Think?* Beth, you only met the man two days ago."

"I know, I know." Despair and frustration mingled in her voice. "It's crazy. *He's* crazy. It's stupid. It means living in Raleigh. *Raleigh!* How dumb is that? I'm a New Yorker, for God's sake! He says he's going to keep me barefoot and pregnant. *Me!* There's no way in hell this fucking marriage can work."

Beth sounded so exasperated by the absurdity of the situation she'd landed in that Amy could only lie back on the pillow and laugh. "Where is this man? I want to talk to him."

"Downstairs. We came to get my car and pick up my things."

"Where are you going?"

"To his gallery. He's been camping in the back of the store while he restores the house. Wait'll you see it, Amy. It really is going to be beautiful. A lot of the stuff he's planned is wrong. He doesn't have a clue about color, but I was thinking that if you gave us some of the glass out of this house as a wedding present, we could use part of it around the front door and the rest in a folding screen in the bedroom. Pick up the colors from them. That cobalt blue, for instance."

"Wait, wait, wait!" Amy protested, picking up on the first part of her answer. "You're going to camp in his store?"

"It's only for a few weeks till we can finish off the bedroom enough to move in."

Abruptly, her own bedroom's brightness registered with Amy. "Oh, God! What time is it? I promised Eric I'd call before nine."

"Almost ten," said Beth. "What time did you get to bed? From those glasses and the empty wine bottle down there in the kitchen, it looks like you made a night of it."

Amy realized that Beth didn't know about Curt's death or any of the subsequent events.

"Let me get dressed and call Eric and I'll meet you downstairs and tell you about it," she said, throwing back the coverlet.

Once again she called Eric's voice mail. "I'm sorry, Eric. It's been crazy here. Call me when you get a chance, okay? I promise I'll be here."

Downstairs, she found Jacob Grayson making coffee. He wore cutoff jeans, those thick leather sandals, and a bright green T-shirt that advertised an Irish stout. A shaft of sunlight from an east-facing window lit up his red hair like a flame.

"Mr. Grayson?"

He turned with an easy smile. "Jacob. And you're Amy. We're family now."

She did not smile back. "This isn't going to work, you know."

"Sure it is." He poured three mugs of rich dark coffee. "Does Beth like it black or doctored?"

"See? You don't know a thing about her."

"I don't know how she likes her coffee, but I do know all the important things."

"Like what?"

"I know that she's been spoiled. That she has a dirty mouth. That she's impulsive and a spendthrift and I'm not the first man she's been with. She probably can't cook either. I also know that she's smart and funny and has a soft heart underneath all that

New York veneer. I know that she hasn't had a job yet that challenged her. Last and by no means least, I know that she's so beautiful every baby food company in America's gonna want to put our sons in their commercials."

"If you're together that long," Amy said dryly, taking the mug he held out to her. The coffee was deliciously fragrant. "This isn't something I bought."

"No, it's a blend I put together myself." He clinked his mug against hers as if toasting the future, and his bright blue eyes twinkled with laughter. "Look, I know it may not work out, but hell, a lot of marriages don't work. We could be engaged a year and it wouldn't make the odds any better."

"See?" said Beth, who came in as he was talking. "He makes it all sound so logical, and logic was never my strong point."

"Okay," said Amy, transferring last night's wineglasses to the dishwasher and putting the empty bottle on the counter. "Sit. I want to hear exactly what happened yesterday."

"Well, after you blew up at me—and I didn't lie to you, Amy, honest. I really did think I was pregnant when I drove down here Thursday night."

Amy glanced over at Jacob, who was loading the toaster with English muffins.

"It's okay. Jacob knows all about Hugo."

"I may have to kill him if we ever meet, but other than that . . ." Jacob's voice trailed off as he rummaged in the refrigerator.

"Anyhow," Beth continued. "I had Jacob's cell phone number and called him in Wilmington, then I waited in the library till he came, and the next thing I know, we're over at the courthouse. He's got a marriage license in one hand, his mother's wedding ring in the other, and we're standing in front of a magistrate. I say, 'Hello.' She says, 'I now pronounce you man and wife.'"

The toaster popped up nicely browned muffins and Jacob set a butter dish on the table. "Got any jam or honey?"

"No."

"Sure you do," said Beth. "Check the refrigerator, Jay. Her cousin brought over a jar of homemade fig preserves and—"

"No," said Amy, choking up in sudden memory of how she had picked figs only three mornings ago with her shy, gruff cousin and how he'd tried to warn her about asking too many questions: "You might not like all the answers you're gonna get."

"Amy? Sweetie? What's wrong?"

She swallowed the lump in her throat and gave them a condensed version of all that had happened since she left Beth the morning before.

"Holy shit!" said Beth, when Amy described how Pat had lunged at her with a pitchfork.

"You Voygt gals," said Jacob, shaking his head. "Y'all are something else, you know that?"

By the time they'd finished the breakfast Jacob had fixed, Amy was calm again and thinking clearly.

"Look," she said to him. "Realistically, how far are you from being able to move into your house?"

"Well, if the electrician and the plumber both keep their word and Beth turns out to be any good with a paintbrush, no more than two or three weeks at the most."

"Then why not stay here? I have till Labor Day and they probably won't raze the house before October. You can move into the guest wing for now. *And,*" she said, sweetening the offer, "it'll give us a chance to talk about your commission on selling off Grandmother's furniture for me."

"Okay," said Beth.

"Now wait a minute," Jacob said.

"Hot water," she told him. "Big claw-footed bathtubs. Besides, we can use the commission."

The phone rang sharply.

"That'll be Eric," said Amy. "Go fight it out somewhere else while I talk to him, okay?"

CHAPTER
31

For a while, it was almost like old times, listening to Eric talk about his weekend. Unless he was a better liar than she'd realized, he really had gone rock climbing with his new associates in Boston.

Could it be that Lisl was history now?

"Hank's the best rope man I've climbed with since college. He said it was only a five-point-six course, but it felt more like a five-nine. I'm really out of shape, though. I've got to start going back to the gym this winter."

He was excited about how the pilot was shaping up, but wanted to bounce some ideas off her the way they always had. "So do you think Max would react that way?" he asked after giving her a quick synopsis of a plot the writers had come up with.

"I don't know, Eric," she said, frowning in concentration. "It seems to me that makes Max too wimpy. Wouldn't he be more likely to—wait! What if we have him overhear Pink and Blue planning to play that trick on him and he only *pretends* to be scared—"

"Yes!" Eric exclaimed. "Because he knows it'll make them think they're braver and—"

"And really what he's done is reinforce his own character," Amy said, finishing the thought.

"Perfect!" Satisfaction hummed along the line between them, catching at her heart for the loss of all they'd once shared.

"So what's been happening down there?" he asked. "Michael tells me that Beth's with you. How's that working out? You almost finished?"

It took longer to tell him about Curt's death than it had Beth and Jacob because he'd barely met any of the relatives involved, although he remembered Pat because he'd enjoyed her biscuits the few times he'd come down to Carolina. She glossed over the part about the pitchfork and went directly to the fact that Beth had married an antiques dealer she'd known about twenty-four hours.

"Poor Claire," Eric said when he got over his first surprise. Amy was touched that Claire would be his immediate concern, but then, mother-in-law jokes aside, he'd always had a soft spot for her. "On the other hand, an antiques dealer sounds better than a hopped-up guitar player. And if we could tell Claire you like him—?"

"Actually, I do."

"Sam'll probably start a pool as soon as the word hits New Hampshire. I'm going to guess it'll last three weeks and seven hours. What do you want?"

"I don't know, Eric. I've never seen Beth like this. This marriage might actually work."

"So I'll tell Sam to put you down for two months?"

She laughed in spite of herself. "Idiot!"

"God, I miss you, sweetheart," he said huskily, and that husky intimate voice nearly undid her, told her that she was in danger of going the way of Maxie and Claire. There was no excuse for what he had done, but maybe part of it was her fault for never asserting herself and never confronting the issues when she disagreed with him. And yet their marriage had been so good in so many ways—the way they laughed at the same things, the way their talents meshed at work . . . and yes, the way their bodies fit together like two perfect halves to a whole. Lisl or no Lisl, her body ached for him. Her heart, too.

No more ducking issues, though. She took a deep breath. "Listen, Eric, we have to talk about—"

"Oh, wait, before I forget, Jordan says the woman from the symphony called and we're in line for those better seats if we go ahead and subscribe now. You still want them, don't you?"

"Absolutely." They had been waiting for those seats for two years now, and her response was automatic even though they might never use them the way this marriage was going. "Who's Jordan?"

"My new assistant."

"New assistant?" she asked blankly. "Where's Lisl?"

"Um, she heard about another job and, um, well, she's gone and now it's Jordan. Look, Amy. About Lisl . . ."

She heard his hesitations and sensed his embarrassment. "It's okay," she said quickly. "I know."

"You do? Who told you? Michael?"

"I'm not blind, Eric. You think I couldn't see what was going on?"

"Yeah, I was hoping you wouldn't. I'm really sorry, Amy."

"So am I," she said quietly.

"Anyhow, Jordan's my new assistant. Jordan Dondale."

"Is she pretty?"

Eric laughed. "Jordan's fat, forty, and going bald. I'm not having another female assistant till your father retires, sweetheart. I'm tired of watching him play the loving husband with Claire on the weekends when he's had someone on the couch in his office during the week. It makes me feel dirty."

"You mean, Dad and Lisl—?"

"I thought you said you knew."

"I knew he had someone," she lied hastily. "I just didn't know it was Lisl."

"Oh hell yes. That's why she came to Boston with us. One

more roll in the hay before he took off to the lake for two weeks. I talked to Michael and we agreed she had to go. She was starting to flaunt it at the office. I'm surprised you didn't realize."

"Me, too," she said as happiness and relief suddenly bubbled up inside and began to wash away some of the pain and misery of the last week.

"But I interrupted you before. You said we need to talk about something?"

"About the company," she improvised, thinking how wise Beth had been when she said that Eric always tried to smooth the ice in front of her.

In shielding her from the knowledge that Dad still cheated on Claire, Eric had nearly wrecked their marriage. Maybe it was his own nature, maybe it was love for her, or maybe it was something he'd picked up from the others by osmosis, an extension of the Protect-Amy-From-The-Truth policy that Dad and Grandmother had imposed on everyone since the day she shot Maxie. But whatever his reason, the need for it was over now and she intended to make that clear to all of them when she returned to the city.

Now was not the moment, though.

"We need to talk about Dad's retirement," she said instead. And even as she spoke, she realized that she had definite ideas of how that situation should play out.

"I know you want me to take over," he said, "but I don't have the mindset for it, sweetheart."

"Me either, but we can talk about it when I get home tomorrow."

"You're coming back? Now?"

Her heart lifted at the eagerness in his voice. "Beth can finish up here for me."

"Then don't come home. Come to Boston," he said and that husky note was back in his voice.

*   *   *

Upstairs, Beth and Jacob were moving the last of her things down to the guest wing. Beth's lips were puffy as if from much kissing, her hair was a mess, and at the moment she didn't seem to be wearing a bra under her yellow cropped top. Jacob Grayson looked at her as if he couldn't decide if she was his hope of salvation or his eternal damnation, and Amy realized that they were probably glad that she'd been so long on the phone.

"Everything okay up north?" asked Beth, her arms full of summer clothes.

"Yes," said Amy.

"You ready to roll?" Jacob asked Beth.

"In a minute. Why don't you come with us, Amy? I'll show you the pumpkin shell Peter here thinks he's going to keep me in."

"Not now," she said. "I've got to pack. I'm flying to Boston tomorrow."

"That must have been one hell of a phone call," Beth said. "You look like the cat that just cleaned out a cage of canaries."

Amy laughed and gave an exaggerated brush of her lips. "Damn feathers," she said happily.

"Don't cook," said Jacob. "It'll probably be after dark, but we'll bring supper."

"I won't cook," Amy promised, amused that he would assume she otherwise would. Her cooking skills weren't much better than Beth's and she wondered how much variety Raleigh offered in the way of take-out. If Beth stuck with this marriage, she'd certainly put the town to the test.

As they were leaving, a FedEx truck delivered a packet of mailing labels from Dr. Basil Mills, and Amy spent the next hour attaching them to the boxes of personal papers she was shipping out to the university. By midafternoon, she was fairly sure that none of the boxes left in the attic contained any of her grandparents' papers.

The doorbell rang a little after four.

"I guess I should have called first," Terry Wilson said.

"No. I was hoping you'd come."

She saw that he was carrying the paper bag that held her cowgirl costume and the old heaviness settled on her chest again.

"It was my mother's blood, wasn't it?"

"Well, it was A-positive anyhow, only now we've got us another little problem."

"What do you mean?"

"The lab analyzed the splatter and drip patterns. Here, let me show you."

The top of the little skirt was pinned to the vest, which he'd hung on a wire coat hanger.

"These," he said, touching the splatters on the back of the vest, "were from when she was first shot and her blood spurted over you. The stains here on the front of the skirt are smears where you either wiped your hands or brushed against someone bloody."

Puzzled, Amy asked, "How could I have shot her if my back was turned?"

"You couldn't have," he said gently.

"She killed herself with me standing right there?"

He picked up the little hat and pointed to a dark spot on the right edge of the crown. "See that? It's gunpowder. And from the direction of the blow pattern, the shot came at fairly close range from a gun that was aiming upward."

He held the coat hanger out in front of himself at the height of a small three-year-old and set the hat on his hand.

"It missed your hat and hit her."

"I don't understand."

"I think it's time we both had a talk with your Aunt Martha," he said.

Aunt Martha was alone when they got there.

"They're so short-handed at the hospital, Paulie felt like she had to go work her shift. Y'all come in. Can I get you something to drink?"

"No, thank you, Aunt Martha."

"Well, let's go on into the den," she said, threading a path through packing cartons.

The den had a stripped-down air to it. All the framed photographs had been removed, the shelves were empty of books and knickknacks, and the curtains had been taken down so that the orange afternoon sun slanted though the western windows and gave the room a reddish gold haze. Aunt Martha gestured to the couch and she herself sat in a Queen Anne–type armchair with padded seat and back and wooden arms and legs.

"You're that SBI man, aren't you?" she asked Terry.

"Yes, ma'am."

"So, so sad about Curt. And Mary's about to go crazy. Her husband dead, her sister in jail, and Herbert can't get it through his head that Pat's not coming back any time soon."

"Aunt Martha," said Amy.

"Yes, honey?"

"Yesterday, you told me that when Maxie was shot, that Grandmother was going to say I did it, but that you stood up to her and told her no."

"Honey, ought we to be talking about this right now?" She smiled nervously at Terry, who tried to look innocuous.

"He knows about it, Aunt Martha. And it's time to set the record straight."

"But it was so long ago, Amy. What's the good of it?"

"You and Grandmother covered up what happened back then. You let me think all my life that Maxie killed herself. It isn't fair to her to keep saying it. Please, Aunt Martha. Tell me what happened that day."

"But you said you knew."

"I want to hear it from you. Please?"

The old woman sighed and her shoulders slumped.

"It was such an awful time. Bailey wasn't too bad after his first stroke, but that second one? He had good days and not-so-good days. It broke my heart to know he was never going to be himself again. Frances wouldn't believe it, though. She was sure that with enough therapy, enough nursing, he could come all the way back. He could get in and out of bed with his walker and he could get around all right in his wheelchair, but he hated being an invalid and it seemed to turn him bitter. You know that he went to New York to write poetry?"

Amy nodded. "I never read any of his poems, though."

"That's because he burned them all."

"Why?"

"He said he'd turned his back on poetry, so poetry turned its back on him. After Maxine was born, it was like he couldn't write anymore. He and Frances—you know there are some people who should just never have children. He used to write all day while she was working and then at night they'd go out for drinks or go to concerts and lectures. But Frances had to go back to work after Maxine was born and he had to stay there and wash the diapers and sterilize the bottles and she was colicky and cried the first three months. Mama went up to help whenever she could, but the apartment was so little, he couldn't get away from the crying."

She looked at Amy anxiously. "I know that sounds like he didn't love Maxine, but he might have been a famous poet if she hadn't come along and you can't blame him for wanting that, can you? As she got older, she tried to be quiet, but he still couldn't concentrate when she was around. Then when he thought about writing down the cute things she said to her little stuffed animals? I mean, it made him and Frances a lot of money and Maxine never wanted for a thing, but he was never really happy writing those books. In fact, I think he was always a little ashamed about it, like he'd sold his birthright for a mess of pottage, but the money got a-hold of him and . . ."

Her voice trailed off and she sat lost in memory.

"The day Maxie died, Aunt Martha?" Amy said.

Aunt Martha sighed. "It was one of his black days. He and Maxine never did get along too good since she grew up. Frances told me they had a nasty fight that day. You were running around in your little western outfit, pretending to shoot everything in sight, and for some reason that seemed to set him off. He said you were as noisy as she used to be and if she hadn't been born he could have done something really important. She said he was a hack who never had an original thought in his life, that his poetry was third-rate, and he even had to steal his first ideas about Pink and Blue from her.

"Frances said he almost had another stroke right then and she was furious with Maxine for getting him all upset. She thought she'd gotten him calmed down, but as soon as she went downstairs to get him some juice, he rolled himself into their bedroom and came out with his old pistol and he aimed it straight at you."

"At *me?*" Amy asked, startled.

"Frances was coming up the stairs and she saw that he had the gun. She yelled at him to put it down. Maxine came running, saw what was happening, and she had just snatched you up when the gun went off."

Tears were streaming down Aunt Martha's cheeks. "He said he didn't know what came over him, honey. It was like you were Maxine and he had to kill you so he could be free to write what he was meant to write. He would never have hurt you if he hadn't been so mad at Maxine that he wasn't thinking straight."

"But if Grandfather shot her, why did all of you say Maxie killed herself?"

"We were so afraid that they'd take him away, say that he was criminally insane, and lock him up in a mental hospital for the rest of his life. You don't understand how much we loved him. It would have killed Frances not to be with him. And the newspapers would have made such a fuss. Frances said it could even hurt the Pink and Blue books, too. That parents wouldn't buy books written by someone who'd shot his own daughter, even if it really wasn't on purpose. She called me to come over and help her. The Hahnemanns were too scared to help. We had to get

Bailey back in bed and make him take enough pills to knock him out before the police came."

"She wanted to tell the police it was me?"

"She said no one would do anything to a little girl, that it would just go down as a terrible accident. I told her no, I couldn't let her do that. To have you grow up thinking you'd killed your own mother? That would be horrible. And besides, you were a smart little thing. You knew Bailey was the one with the gun, and I was afraid you'd tell the police the truth if they asked you how it happened, so we put the gun in Maxine's hand and I brought you back here and we said you'd been here the whole afternoon."

The sun was heading for the horizon and shadows had grown long in the room. Aunt Martha got up and switched on a nearby floor lamp.

"Poor Bailey." Aunt Martha sighed. "He was so smart, so handsome, so *sweet*. I wish you could have known him before his strokes. You do understand why we couldn't tell anyone, don't you, honey?"

"Did Dad know?"

"Jeffrey? Oh, no. We never told anybody. And Frances got rid of the Hahnemanns the very next day."

Amy was silent on the drive back to the house.

Terry Wilson pulled around to the side door and looked over at her. "Are you sorry you asked her?"

"My mother saved my life, didn't she?"

"Probably."

"I didn't kill her and she didn't kill herself."

"Nope."

"But Grandmother was willing to say either of those things to protect Grandfather."

"Love makes you do strange things, they say."

"Sacrifice your daughter to it? Your granddaughter? Is that love or selfishness?"

He didn't answer.

They sat in comfortable silence for a few minutes as the sun sank over fields that would soon be turned into parking lots.

"When are you going back to New York?" he asked.

"What makes you think I'm going back?"

"Let me ask you this: You like sushi? Ballet? Riding on a subway?"

"What about you?" she countered, smiling back at this big decent man who had not taken advantage of her when her muddled emotions had left her so vulnerable. "You like fried pork chops? Country music? Hunting? Fishing?"

He laughed, then leaned over and kissed her very gently on the cheek. "Take care of yourself, Miz Steadman."

"You, too, Agent Wilson."

C H A P T E R

32

(November)

Subj: Thanksgiving
Date: 11/7/2002 4:12:43 PM Eastern Standard Time
From: EVGrayson@NCAntiques.net
To: Amy.Steadman@PBMEnterprises.com

Es from Mom and Michael this morning. Sounds like Dad's adjusting to retirement almost as well as Michael's adjusting to
being the new pres. of PBM. Michael and Jane want us to come
up for T'giving and for some ungodly reason, Jay wants to see
the Macy's parade in the flesh, but can I say that you and Eric
asked us first? Only you've got to tell Eric to quit trying to get
Jay into rock climbing. I'm too freaking young to be a widow.

Bulldozers are due tomorrow. We got the last of that molding
this morning and I'm going to scrape and stain it for our dining
room. Oh and guess what? Tarzan must have finally stuck it to
Jane because I found an enormous egg case up at the edge of
the awning where that web used to be. I've moved it to our yard

here and I had to put it up high —Barkis thinks anything round is a ball. Spiders still creep me out, but I know you got off on this one.

And speaking of eggs, my stomach's gotten so big I've had to quit wearing my navel ring. I'm scheduled for a sonogram next week. What about you? Wouldn't it be a hoot if both our babies were girls?

Talk to you soon,
Beth